RENAISSANCE

THE JACK RANDALL THRILLERS
BOOK 9

RANDALL WOOD

TENSION BOOKWORKS

For information contact:

Tension Bookworks

248 Nokomis Ave. Venice, FL 34285

www.tensionbookworks.com

Tension Bookworks and the portrayal of the screw are registered trademarks of Tension Bookworks.

Jacket and Cover design by Derek Murphy

Book design by Matty Dalrymple

Cataloging-in-Publication Data is on file at the Library of Congress

Wood, Randall, 1968-

Renaissance / Randall Wood – 1st ed.

ISBN-13: 978-1-938825-68-2 (Ebook)

ISBN-13: 978-1-938825-54-5 (Paperback)

ISBN-13: 978-1-938825-55-2 (Large Print)

ISBN-13: 978-1-938825-56-9 (Hardcover)

ISBN-13: 978-1-938825-57-6 (Audio)

2024122701

WARNING!

This book ends in a cliffhanger!

The story of The Twelve Shepherds was originally released as a serial novel and was published in several separate episodes. Due to the readers' requests, it has now been re-published in novel form. The resulting manuscript was too large to fit into one novel and as a result the Shepherds saga will now encompass six novels.

This book, *RENAISSANCE*, is part five of The Twelve Shepherds saga, and also book nine of the Jack Randall series.

The author and the publisher apologize for any confusion.

1

> *"Let us remember we are all part of one American family. We are united in common values, and that includes belief in equality under the law, basic respect for public order, and the right of peaceful protest."*
>
> —Barack Obama

The cab let them out in front of the building, and Jack grumbled a little when

Sydney grabbed his arm as he got out. The stitches over his eye and the splint on his arm, combined with the bruising, made him a bit of a sight. A few passing agents eyeballed him curiously as they made their way inside. Jack and Sydney crossed the lobby and walked over the seal on the floor to the front desk. Karen looked up and her mouth fell open.

"My god, Jack. Are you okay?"

"I'm fine, Karen. Had a little run in with some bad guys down in Florida."

"We heard. But I ... Are you sure you don't need a few days off?"

Jack gave her his best disarming smile. Karen had been at the front desk of the building for many years and couldn't help regarding the agents as her own children.

"No, it looks worse than it is; the doc says I'm fine," he lied. "And duty calls."

"Okay. I'd maybe get a second opinion if I were you. How are you, Sydney?"

"A little beat up, but Jack got the worst of it. Is Deacon in his office?"

"Yes, and I was told to inform him of your arrival. Are you heading straight up?"

"Yes."

"Okay. Good luck."

They passed through the security gate and headed for the elevators, both of them still exhausted from their ordeal in Florida. Sydney reluctantly punched the button for the top floor and then let herself fall back against the wall with a sigh.

"A massage, at an all-day spa. Someplace with no phones."

"I said all right the first dozen times," Jack replied.

"Someplace with wine."

"Okay." Jack had promised her a day off at a spa after she'd pointed out repeatedly that their injuries were all his fault for choosing to drive through a hurricane. Jack had quickly given in just to placate her. He was hurting himself, but he knew there was not going to be any time for a spa day. They had come straight from the airport to the Hoover building to report in. Luckily, Debra had gone to the beach house to batten down the hatches in case Hurricane Nancy decided to work its way up the coast. He'd called her on the way into town, and she was already on her way. He'd have that do deal with after they met with Deacon.

It was going to be an ass chewing. Like a disobedient teenager, Jack had refused to come home when told to and instead gone off to Florida to pursue the latest Twelve Shepherds' target. The encounter with the drug traffickers could not have been predicted, but he doubted that was going to lessen their boss's wrath any. Maybe his injuries would help a little? Either way, they would soon find out.

He turned his head to check on his partner. She was leaning against the wall with her eyes closed, grabbing whatever rest she could before the doors opened. He didn't blame her. They had been through two days of hell in Homeland, and the flight from Jacksonville to DC had been too short and bumpy to get any real rest. The hurricane was out to sea now, but its reach was still sufficient to make their flight a miserable one. The hours of inactivity had done nothing but allow their battered muscles to cramp and stiffen, and they both now made noises when they sat or got up. It was like they had each aged twenty years.

"You okay?"

Sydney opened her eyes. "Yeah, a little stiff, but—"

"No, I mean ... are you okay?"

She turned and looked at him. It wasn't just a casual question. In the last few days she had survived getting shot at, beaten up, held hostage, and then almost drown in a sinking car. It was a lot for anyone, even a seasoned agent, to take.

"I ... I'll know in a couple of days if I'm not, I guess." She shrugged.

"Where's Lenny?" Jack asked. Sydney's current boyfriend was an Interpol agent based in France. The two of them had been trying hard to make a long-distance relationship work.

"I sent him a text. He's flying in on Sunday."

"Good."

Before any more could be said, the doors opened.

"Let's get this over with." Jack said as he led her off the elevator and down the hall. A passing secretary glanced at Jack's face and then smiled a nervous apology before quickly moving off on her way.

"Is my face really that bad?" he asked Sydney.

"Compared to what?"

Before Jack could answer they arrived at the office and were met by Margaret's shocked face.

"Jack, my god. You look worse than Greg! What the hell is going on down there?"

"I ... you know, Margaret. I'm fine, really, and also a little tired of explaining that. Can you be a dear and just accept that, so we can move on to the next thing? I'll be happy to tell everyone the whole story later."

He got a sour look for that, but she quickly nodded. "He's inside. They're expecting you."

"Thanks." Jack moved past her, and Margaret used the moment to shoot Sydney a questioning look. She gave her a nod of reassurance and another when Margaret pointed at her. They would catch up later, her look said.

Jack walked in to find Deacon standing behind his desk with Larry and Greg sat in the corner. Greg had a bandage on his head, and another on his neck, but other than that, he was dressed in a clean suit and sporting a fresh haircut. Larry looked his usual disheveled self, and he stood at the sight of the two of them entering.

"Jack, you two okay?"

Jack waved to Sydney. "Your turn."

"We're fine, guys. Jack got in a fight, and I almost drown, but other than that, it's just come cuts and bruises. We'll live. How're you doing, Greg?"

"I still gotta headache, but I'm good."

"Laurie?"

"At home with her ankle up. You two just can't stay out of trouble, can you?"

"It wasn't anything we planned; the guys opened up on a cop right in front of us. It became a running shoot-out and then just got worse from there. I'm sorry for the delay, sir, but it just couldn't be helped."

Deacon rounded the desk and walked over until he was standing in front of them both. He'd read the hasty one-page report Jack had sent from the plane, as well as the report filed by the local police, and now looked them both over from head to toe. Seeing now that Jack had sugar-coated their injuries, he couldn't help but shake his head as he addressed them.

"I had a royal ass-chewing all prepared and ready to let fly, but Margaret tells me this room has heard enough cursing in the last twenty-four hours to last a year. You two okay? Seriously?"

"Yes, sir."

"How's that local sheriff doing?"

Sydney answered that one. "He's stable. He coded on us once, after we got him closed up, but we got him back. Tyler deteriorated on the ride to Jacksonville. They're both still in critical condition, but the doctor there was optimistic."

"Good. Some things happened while you were gone."

Deacon pointed to the TV in the corner. It was on mute, but that didn't stop them from seeing that Jack and Sydney were the top story of the day.

Scenes from the streets of Homeland traded spots with footage of Jack and Sydney leaving the hospital. Pictures of them in New York and again in Niagara Falls soon followed.

"You're getting a lot of airtime. Fortunately, it may be just the thing you need right now."

Jack traded a questioning look with Sydney and then another with Larry, who frowned. Whatever his boss's remark meant, it was something Jack wasn't going to like.

"You have any clean clothes here?" Deacon asked.

"Uh ... yeah. I have a spare suit in my office. Syd?"

"I have some downstairs. Are we going somewhere?"

Deacon turned back toward his desk and answered the question on the way.

"The White House. Go get dressed and meet me downstairs. The president wants to see you."

"I ... " Jack glanced at Greg, who waved his question off. Don't question, just go, his gesture said.

"Okay. Ten minutes?"

"Make it less. The man's waiting."

He and Sydney turned to leave.

"I'll walk you." Larry said, jumping up to follow.

The three of them walked in silence until they were back on the elevator. Once again, Sydney pushed the button and then collapsed against the wall as the doors closed.

"Okay, what's going on?" Jack asked.

"Remember that whole 'face of the investigation' thing you said I wouldn't have to do?"

"Yeah?"

"You were right."

CARTER WOKE when the rocking of the railcar diminished. The train was slowing down. He gazed out the window to see them entering the edge of the city, and then examined the GPS's tiny screen to confirm it was indeed Denver. They had passed through Pueblo and Colorado Springs without stopping, and both he and Tye had relaxed after, confident that their car was going to make it all the way. Tye's enjoyment of the modern car and its luxurious leather interior was short-lived, as the mild rocking and warm seat soon had him nodding off. It had given Carter time to think.

There was a Shepherd's cache in Denver. One that any of them could access if needed. It was small and held no vehicles; just the necessities to assist one of them if they were on the run. It was monitored by William, just like all the others, so if used, he would immediately know. Carter had been thinking about the cache and weighing the risks of visiting it for the entire trip up from El Paso. If Dayton's intent had been to take him out, he could be waiting for him there, but Carter doubted it. The things happening in the paper had him wondering about the General and the mission. Was it time? Had Rubicon been activated? He didn't know. He needed information, and for that there was only one place to go.

The flashing lights and ringing bells of a major road crossing flashed through the interior and across Tye's face. It was enough to make him stir.

"Where we at?"

"Denver. Should we be thinking about getting ready to get off?"

Tye rubbed his eyes and took a good look at the passing scenery before replying.

"Got about ... fifteen minutes, I'd say. Thas if they goin' to the yard they did last time. I was on a box then, so not sure."

Carter slid down in the seat as they passed another busy intersection. It wouldn't do good to be seen riding in the car right now. Someone could call it in and have the cops waiting when the train stopped. There was really nothing to see but the lights of city's suburbs passing by anyway. He watched their progress on the tiny map instead. He had dimmed its brightness to its lowest setting hours ago.

"So, we get off in the yard," Carter said. "Then what?"

"Food would be good. There's a kitchen not too far from there. Be open in a few hours."

"After that?"

"Hell, I dunno. I take it one problem at a time, ya know?" Tye laughed.

Carter rubbed his growing beard. It was still in the itchy phase, and he was dealing with it. He thought about how he might separate himself from Tye—at least long enough for him to visit the cache.

"Is there somewhere you hang out around here?"

"Stayed a few times at a mission when the snow was bad and the trains weren't running. It wasn't a bad place, just not my thing. Likes to keep moving, but the snow don't care about that, I guess. Why?"

"I got an old friend, here. He may have a few spare dollars. Thought I might stop by."

"Hmmm. You sure? In my experience, it's a good way to lose the friend."

"Old Marine Corps buddy."

"Oh, well, thas different. At least for a few visits. I s'pose I could hang around a bit."

Carter turned to the GPS and played with the buttons. Tye watched for a minute before losing interest and taking in the passing buildings. Carter found the yard they were travelling to and then explored the area around it. Like in most cities, it was a mixture of things. The railroad had been built early, and the town had grown around it. The yard was now surrounded by three major highways in what would now be called an industrial section. He saw a lumber yard and distribution complex for the Coors Brewing Company nearby. Several warehouses. After that, it was a short walk to the suburbs in one direction, and downtown in the other.

"You see that Pepsi place, you know we getting close." Tye said.

Carter saw the Pepsi Center on the map and nodded. "Got ya."

He kept scanning the downtown area until he found it. It was another ten blocks or so, but that was nothing to Carter. Just south of the park, he found the library. Moving the map around, he memorized the route and the major landmarks before moving on and locating the storage facility. It would be another schlep from there and even farther back to the yard after. Could he do all that in one afternoon? Was it best to keep traveling with Tye? He'd have options after the cache. Maybe best to think about them once he was in and out safely.

"Where this mission at?" Carter was adopting Tye's poor English without realizing it.

"Oh, about a half mile towards town. Just past the stadium and then south a few blocks."

On the way, Carter thought. *Good.* He'd drop Tye off there and then continue on. He checked the clock in the corner of the dashboard. Three hours until sunrise. He wanted to be through the city and waiting when the place opened. If the distances were easy to navigate, he should have no problem.

"There she is." Tye pointed.

Carter looked up in time to see the stadium appear on their right, its rust-colored façade lit up by several lights even at this early morning hour. It faded away behind them as the train slowed and then passed under a major road.

"We best be gittin' out," Tye said.

"Right."

They both popped the doors and slipped out onto the railcar itself. The cold night air found its way inside their clothes, and they both shivered as they hunkered down behind the Lexus. Carter reached up and returned the keys to their previous hiding place, before huddling on the steel next to Tye.

"Gonna have to remember that key trick; this'a been a bad ride without 'em," Tye remarked.

"Yeah, I guess so. Didn't think it'd be this cold."

"We been going uphill for the past four hours," Tye said.

"You can tell."

They sat in silence as the train slowed further and finally stopped. Tye hopped off with a practiced motion and immediately set off in the direction of the downtown high rises. Carter followed with only one look back toward the engine. Nobody emerged to challenge them, so he kept walking. Soon they were across the yard and through a convenient hole in the fence. It seemed like the buildings were right in front of them.

"I'll meet up with you at the mission."

"Okay." Tye shrugged.

Carter left his friend at the first street corner

they came to and broke away to the south. Once he was out of sight, he quickened his pace to the mile-eating stride of the infantry soldier. He kept to the shadows and moved with purpose, following the map in his head until he came upon his destination.

The Denver Public Library. He walked its perimeter and finally decided on a dark corner belonging to the art museum next door to wait in. He checked his watch before settling back. A few hours. He made sure the rising sun wouldn't reveal his location too soon and then looked for any company which might find him interesting. He ruled out both, before closing his eyes and letting himself relax a bit.

He was about to take a major risk, one that could end in disaster—or something else. Something he wasn't sure of yet.

2

____

"There may be times when we are powerless to prevent injustice, but there must never be a time when we fail to protest."

—*Elie Wiesel*

J ack left Sydney on the elevator to go to her office in the basement while he and Larry walked off in the direction of his. They both

kept their mouths shut until they got to it, and Jack quickly opened the door before motioning Larry inside.

"Okay, what's going on?" Larry said.

Larry walked to Jack's desk and planted his butt on its edge. Jack noticed a pile of mail on its surface and forced himself to look away. It was not unusual. If the box on the wall outside his door got too full, the night security team would move it inside. As much as he wanted to paw through it right now, he had to wait. For a moment, he considered telling Larry about the message but discarded the idea quickly. He didn't know enough yet.

"You mean with your meeting?"

"Yes, with the meeting. It's more than just to brief them on what happened, isn't it? Why's Deacon being cagey?"

"I'm guessing he made you the same deal he made me, and now he has to go back on it."

Jack walked to the closet while stripping off his shirt. Inside, he found two still in the plastic from the dry cleaner and breathed a sigh of relief. He couldn't remember if he had restocked the closet or not. Maybe Margaret had conspired with Debra? It wouldn't be the first time.

"It's become a popularity contest—at least that's what they think. They've decided that

Deacon is too much of an official face. With the Director in the hospital and unlikely to return, he's no longer the face of the investigation. I mean, the people expect him to be in charge. Nobody is surprised or ... intrigued, I guess, when they see him on TV giving a briefing. That, and, well, you know."

"What?"

"He looks too ... bureaucratic. Another old white guy in a suit. One that looks like he should be behind a desk. They want someone less, I don't know, rigid? Is that the word I'm looking for?"

Jack worked on getting the suit on over his fractured ribs and sore muscles. He grimaced while he pulled a new shirt on and crunched this new information. He tugged too hard and a button popped off. Cursing himself, he stripped off the shirt and reached for the second.

"What you're telling me is that I'm the new face of the investigation?"

"Pretty much. Like Sydney said, you're already famous."

Jack slipped a tie over his head and snugged it down.

"How's my hair?"

Larry gave him a grin. "You're asking me for hair advice?"

Jack eyeballed Larry's head and his perpetually mussed mop of hair. "Good point."

"If you really want to know, I think the style goes well with the bandages and sutures. It's a defined look."

Jack finished with the tie and put on the jacket before standing in front of the mirror on the inside of the closet door. He tried to smooth the hair into place, but the bandages only allowed him so much. A few strands still stuck up no matter how hard he tried. The bruises on his jaw, combined with the sutures and bandage over his eye, seemed to nullify the hair anyway. Screw it. He gave up.

"Why Sydney?"

"What do you mean?"

"Deacon said both of us. Why her?"

Larry shrugged. "She's famous, too. Maybe not at your level, but they want her standing next to you just the same, I imagine."

"Show the public we're taking it seriously, that kind of thing?"

"I imagine you'll get all this from Deacon on the ride in."

"Yeah ... all right. Let's you and I have another drink real soon. Okay?"

"Sure."

With that, Jack filled his pockets with his keys,

his wallet, and a small notebook, before they both filed out of the room. Jack's gaze landed on the pile of mail sitting on the desk as he pulled the door shut. He'd be back here soon to examine it.

Larry waked him to the elevator. The doors quickly parted, and Jack hopped on.

"Any advice?" Jack said.

"Keep your mouth as shut as possible. Write everything down the minute you leave."

The doors started to close.

"Will do."

3

"To sin by silence, when we should protest, Makes cowards out of men."

—Ella Wheeler Wilcox

The clang of the trashcan lid hitting the sidewalk woke him, and he flinched before seeing the man attending to it. The sun was up, and a sliver of it stabbed its way between the two buildings and warmed his feet. He shook the cobwebs from his mind and scanned his surroundings. It was still quiet, Carter noticed, and he wondered why. This was still the downtown area, and it should have been busy with people on their way to work. Odd. He got to his feet and checked the watch.

Saturday. He had lost track. 8:12 am. The place should be open. He looked up to see the man finish with his trash duties. He nodded a polite greeting in Carter's direction, before climbing the steps and disappearing inside. Carter moved to follow.

Inside, he found an open lobby with several signs and an empty desk surrounded by a low wall. As he gazed about, a middle-aged woman appeared with a stack of books piled high. She attempted to get through the narrow opening to the desk and the books fell. Carter leaped forward in time to save most of them, but some made it all the way to the ground. The woman stepped back on seeing his size and attire, but Carter ignored her look and offered the books with a friendly smile.

"Here you go."

"I ... Thank you." She took the books and stepped back. She smiled nervously as she rounded the desk, and Carter wondered how bad he looked.

"Ma'am, I was just hoping to check my email, real quick?" he told her. "Just that, and I'll be on my way."

The woman relaxed a bit at his politeness and pleasant tone. She pointed to a room off to the left.

"You can use one of the computers in there. The password and rules are on the wall."

"Okay, thanks. I won't be long."

She just smiled and nodded before glancing across the lobby. Carter turned and saw the trash man watching from the hallway. He gave him a nod and smile, before moving off to the computers' room. He chose a seat from which he could look out through a window at the lobby and through the front door. The woman returned to her stack of books, and the man began sweeping the lobby after a few words with her. Nobody reached for a phone.

Good.

After a few tries, he managed to get online and input the password. The message was waiting, just as he expected. He read it twice before sitting back and giving it some thought.

The message urged him to make contact. It also gave updates on the FBI and their pursuit of him. Nothing about the rail lines was mentioned. Jack Randall was being called back to DC. Were they removing him from the case? Carter rubbed his knuckles, still sore from when he had knocked the man out back at his storage area and thought about the agent who had interrogated him in the jail cell. The man was smart, Carter had to give him that, and he had treated Carter with respect, despite the fact that he was his prisoner. In the end, Carter had had no choice but to respect the man. He was a formidable enemy; of that, he had no doubt.

But what of the Shepherds? Were they his enemy, too, now? Carter's days with them were over. His face was known, and like an undercover cop who had been exposed, he was no longer any good for missions. So why were they calling him in? Did Dayton merely wish to keep him out of the hands of the FBI? Or was it to permanently remove him, as he was now too great a risk? Or did they have other jobs he would be good for? Could he still contribute to the mission? Perhaps. How, he wasn't sure, but it was a possibility.

What were his alternatives? A life on the run? Where would he go? Africa came to mind first, for the simple fact that he would be able to blend in easier. Maybe find an ex-pat community to join while he learned the local language? South Africa, maybe. Or Namibia.

He shook his head at the thoughts. There was no way he was going to Africa, and he knew it. It just ... wasn't in his nature. Besides, he wanted answers, on his own terms, and there was only one way to get them.

He left the email site behind and punched up a map of the pacific northwest. After dragging and zooming around for ten minutes, he finally turned on the satellite view. He explored the area for several minutes, writing down names and landmarks on a piece of copy paper. He then expanded the search, looking for railway lines. The closest yard was a town called West Glacier. He wrote it down and underlined it. It was his new destination.

A couple of students walked in and gave him a look before settling in behind a pair of monitors across the room. Carter kept an eye in that direction and tried to get caught up on the news. Protests were happening. A lot of them. What that meant, he couldn't be sure. Was it Rubicon? Had the Shepherds launched it? Or were they just spontaneous gatherings prompted by the issues the Shepherds were uncovering? He had no way of knowing.

He caught the first student looking his way

again, and determined it was time to go. He pocketed the paper and logged off, before rising and
heading for the nearest exit. He caught the man, in
the reflection of the glass, aiming a phone his way.
Or was he just holding it? Carter couldn't tell. He
kept his back turned and walked out, past the now
empty desk and on out the door into the morning
sun.

He would find Tye. But only after he made a
run to the storage unit. He rounded the building
and moved in the opposite direction of his destination for a few blocks, before circling back and
changing course. Nobody followed him, but he
found the students in the computer room a bit
worrisome. Had he been recognized? There was
no way to be sure. He increased his pace just the
same.

A block later, he heard a siren. He stopped and
listened closer before determining that it was
headed his way.

"Shit."

DEACON'S DRIVER stood next to the running limo
with the door to the rear open. Inside, Deacon was
sat in the back with a file in his hand. Sydney

waited in the seat opposite him with a nervous look on her face. Jack wasted no time and slide in next to him.

"What's on the agenda?" Jack asked his boss.

"Larry filled you in, did he?"

"A little."

Deacon flipped the file shut and tossed it on the seat next to him in disgust.

"They're reneging on the deal. Evidently, now that I'm the acting Director, I'm no longer pretty enough to be in charge of the investigation. At least the public side of it. They want you. I wouldn't be surprised if they have you booked on the morning shows, come Sunday."

"Larry suspected."

"This was not my idea, Jack; they came up with this all on their own. It stinks of Parker, but it could have been Cook, too."

The car pulled out onto the streets of DC and began weaving through traffic. Protestors soon appeared, and they all examined them as they walked the streets in groups of two and three, silently holding their signs as they circled the area. A few shouted at their car as it zipped by. The driver was good, keeping the car away from the curb and out of range of any attack. They hardly felt the application of the brakes as he weaved through the traffic.

After two turns, they were almost at their destination. Jack forced his attention back inside the car.

"What's the difference?"

"I'm … not sure. But something is off. Parker is a political animal through and through. Cook is … something else. Let's be very careful in there, Jack. I'm not sure what their real motivation is here. We, or you, may be getting set up to take the fall. If so, I'm not going to just roll over and take it."

Jack thought about it as he exchanged a look with Sydney. It was what she had predicted back in California.

Deacon spoke rapidly as they pulled up to the gate. "If they suggest anything that's out of bounds —anything at all—I'm ready to hand over my resignation. Just so you know. You'll have to make your own decision; I'm just letting you know where I stand."

"Yes, sir."

"Yes, sir." Sydney echoed.

"Okay. Let's go see the man."

HE QUICKLY SCANNED THE AREA, but the options were few. Between a pair of dumpsters, an ally led off a short distance away, and he ducked there. Gazing up at the building, he saw that the windows had all been bricked in some time ago. Encouraged by that, he ducked down behind the dumpster and opened his backpack.

Colors. He was switching every one he could. The black coat was wadded up and replaced by the fat man's blue shirt. The red ball cap landed on his head, and he tucked the shirt in and smoothed the wrinkles best he could. The backpack was moved from his back to his hand. Color of clothes were the first thing cops and people describing others used.

He waited.

Less than a minute later, the police unit roared past the mouth of the ally. Carter immediately picked up the backpack and walked to the ally entrance. The car had disappeared around the corner leading to the library, and Carter moved out quickly, walking with purpose while still being as casual as he could. He caught up to a threesome of young males with backpacks of their own heading in the same direction, and he got as close as he could to them without rousing their suspicion. They were all dividing their time between the phones in their hands and the sidewalk in front of them, and Carter used that to help him blend in.

Another police car came down the street. Carter closed ranks on the three men in front of him and tried not to look in the officers' direction. He saw the officers gaze pass over the group and held his breath when he left his line of sight. After a half block, he couldn't stand it any longer and glanced behind him, only to see that the cop had continued on without slowing.

"E and E," he mumbled. At the next intersection, he stood with the group at the light and then crossed with them before breaking away and heading north.

The storage unit was several blocks away. If he could make it there, he would have a number of options. He was contemplating them, when the police car appeared at the next intersection in front of him.

The cop was looking right at him.

4

"Against eternal injustice, man must assert justice, and to protest against the universe of grief, he must create happiness."

—*Albert Camus*

When they entered the room, Jack was not surprised to see the usual suspects. He was, however, surprised at the greeting they got. The president stood from behind the Resolute desk and crossed the room to meet them halfway, shaking Jack's hand and then Sydney's, before motioning them to sit. Jack chose a chair across from the president, and Sydney sat with Deacon on the couch. James Cook joined them, and Parker left his usual place against the wall, to stand behind him.

The president gestured toward the desk which held an open file. "I was just reading the report on what happened in Florida. Are you two all right?"

"A little beat up, sir, but otherwise we're both fine."

"Good. I talked to the head of the DEA this morning; he says they have several leads on where all those drugs were headed. You may have opened the door into several organizations they've been targeting for some time."

"That's good to hear, sir."

"They shot a man right in front of you?"

"Yes, sir. We were lucky to be where we were when it happened."

"Indeed. The storm did a number on the town, but I've requested daily updates. Janet's trying to get me to fly down there and look it all over, but since I can't go anywhere without a hundred people going with me, I said no. I'd just be getting in the way. Maybe in a week, when it's all gotten a bit more stable."

"Yes, sir."

The president looked to his chief of staff, who promptly segued to the real reason for the visit.

"Did you find anything useful while you were down there?"

Jack thought quickly. If there was a reprimand for not returning to DC quickly, it was not coming. They were playing nice. He'd go along until they didn't.

"Not yet, sir. The local office is still investigating. They're looking at camera footage from the area and trying to find the car which was seen leaving the area. Other than that, they're still processing the scene itself." Jack left out that most of the cameras' footage they had so far was defeated by the rain. Even the hooded cameras at the traffic points were clouded and foggy or just blurred by motion and put off their center of focus by the wind. They had nothing, and Jack didn't expect that to change.

"I see. What's your next move?"

Jack took a deep breath and glanced at Deacon who charged in.

"We intend to continue the manhunt for the escaped prisoner. I've dispatched more agents to the LA office to augment the force there. The state and local offices are all on board, and the man's face will be on the TV for a second showing very soon."

"No one has come forward with an ID?"

"The opposite, actually, sir. We've had so many reports that we're already backlogged. I have someone assigned to sorting them as they come in, and the more viable the ID is, the higher priority its assigned. But we'll never have enough people to keep up with the tips people are calling in. It's the nature of the beast; everyone wants to feel they are in on the hunt for the bad guy. Sometimes it works against us."

"This is going to sound racist," Parker interjected. "But I thought the man looked, well, ordinary?"

Sydney answered that one. "The software agrees. The facial recognition program puts his facial signature in the high potential category."

"I'm sorry. In English?" the president asked with a smile.

"His lack of distinguishing features is going to result in a high number of false positives, sir. His face is, as Mr. Parker said, ordinary. He's been gone long enough to grow some hair on his head and face too, and that makes it even harder for the software to see him."

"I see. What about the other killings? Do you have any leads there?"

"I'm afraid not, sir," Jack answered. "They've proven to be very good at hiding their tracks."

"The ambush?" Cook asked. "Surely we can get something from all the items they left behind?"

"Usually, we can, but so far, it's been nothing but dead ends. We're assuming now that they operate from several pre-stocked locations, similar to the one left behind by our escaped prisoner. If so, they have the ability to react to targets anywhere they are staged and to do so in a sterile manner."

"Premeditated." Parker voiced.

Jack had to agree with the term he was assigning. "Yes."

The president shared a look and the slightest of nods with Cook before the man spoke up.

"We feel the public deserves to know what's really going on here. The press has been painting these ... Shepherds as Robin Hood like characters, and unfortunately, the public are buying into it. The evidence is right outside the fence there as I'm sure you saw on the way in. Evidently, it's going to be up to us to remind them that these people are criminals. Someone needs to get through to the public that vigilantism is not the way we do things here in this country. Nobody elected the Shepherds. Their brand of justice needs to be countered. Jack, we've decided that you're the best man for the job."

"I'm not sure—"

The president cut him off and leaned in, adopting the grandfatherly tone he was famous for using. "Jack, the public knows you already. They trust you. New York. The terrorist leader in Sudan. The incident at Niagara Falls. Your record with the Bureau and Homeland Security. All these things, they get people to listen, to hear you out, and that's half the battle these days. The people are reacting with their emotions—that's understandable. We need them to listen to reason, though, to understand what's really going on here, and what it is they're supporting. For that, I need you."

"Will I still be involved in the investigation, or will I just be the face of it?"

Parker broke in, "We're not telling you how to run your case." Parker made sure to look at Deacon too when he said this. "We're just asking you to address the public while you do so. Let them know that you're out there, and who it is you're pursuing, and why. Sort of ... educating the public, if you would."

"How do I—"

"We've taken the liberty of booking you on a few shows for this coming Sunday," Cook answered. We'll also do a press conference with the president tomorrow. My staff has written up a few statements—more of a guideline, really—on what kind of message we need to get out there."

"I'll be making a statement later today," the president added, "pledging my full support for the three of you."

Jack traded looks with Deacon and Sydney. Did they have a choice?

"Sir, I ... Okay."

"Excellent. My staff will be in touch. If you need anything, just ask. I know the public side of this was not what you signed up for, but the circumstances necessitate it, I'm afraid. Mr. Deacon, if you get any pushback from other departments or agencies, my people can always find me."

"Yes, sir."

"Excellent. Mr. Parker will give you all the details. I knew you were the man for this."

The president rose, signaling that the meeting was over. Unable to change that, the three visitors rose, as well. The required handshakes were ex-changed and dutifully recorded by the White House photographer, who had snuck in unannounced. The president made sure to smile broadly and pose with each of them this time and it didn't go unno-ticed. They were led out by the president's secretary.

As soon as the door closed behind them, the president dropped his smile and returned to his seat.

"Well?"

"They're playing along, but not liking it," Cook voiced.

"Randall hates the politics; says so many times in his file."

"Doesn't mean he doesn't know the game."

"True. Will he play along?" the president asked.

Parker considered it before replying, "Yes, right up until he thinks he's getting screwed."

"And then?"

"He'll either fight back or walk away."

"Hmmph."

"What's next?"

"We release the hounds," Parker replied. "Get the media writing more puff pieces on him and, what's her name, Ms. Lewis, before the Sunday shows. Then make sure he has good things to say for the cameras on Sunday. They'll repeat that for a cycle, and by then we'll have some more to feed them. I'll call in a few congressional favors and have some key people make some nice statements supporting him. Either way, we make Jack Randall the government's and the people's hero. The man facing down the Shepherds."

"So, he's our Superman now? Is that it?"

"I was thinking more like Captain America, sir."

The man frowned at Parker's attempt at humor. "Whichever works. Just get it done. And soon."

CARTER DIDN'T BREAK STRIDE, nor did he change his facial expression as the cop exited the car and stepped toward him. The officer was alone, Carter could see nothing but an empty interior behind him. The cop had Carter locked in his gaze. He was young, no doubt new to the force.

"Excuse me, sir. Could you stop right there for me?" he called and held out a hand indicating Carter was to halt. It was a mistake he would soon learn from. Carter smiled as he took one more step; it was all he needed.

His arms shot out and grabbed the man's wrist. He yanked hard, and the young officer was immediately off balance and locked in Carter's grip. Carter used the brief period to manipulate the man's arm around, forcing the man's body further off balance and causing him to pull his opposing hand away from his firearm and flail it in the air in an attempt to stay on his feet.

But it was not to be. His feet soon left the ground, and he impacted the concrete hard enough to force the air from his lungs. While the officer struggled for air, Carter quickly stripped him of his firearm and tossed it aside, before doing the same with the man's cuffs and radio. The deputy had barely regained his breath when he found himself cuffed, hoisted into the air, and dumped in the back seat of his own cruiser. The door was slammed shut, and Carter reached in the front to remove the ignition keys, before doing the same with the driver's door.

"Hey!" the cop yelled. But his breath was not fully back yet, and the shout had no volume. Carter ignored him and moved off down the sidewalk, looking in all directions for other officers. But it was still early, and the area was still coming awake. The sidewalks were bare.

Except for one. An elderly man in homeless

attire sat on a park bench on the opposite side of the street. He was doubled over in laughter and slapping his knee as he struggled to breath. Carter tipped his hat in the man's direction and quickly moved on. The man returned the gesture with a mock salute and laughed louder. It was the last thing Carter heard when he rounded the next corner.

A delivery truck was idling in front of a store a half a block down the street. The driver climbed aboard just as Carter reached it, and he hopped aboard the tailgate, unseen, as it pulled away from the curb.

Distance. He needed some distance. Keeping an eye out for more police, he stayed aboard for several blocks, before hopping back off at a red light and heading off toward another ally.

The cop would be found quickly. He may even be able to get himself out of the cuffs. But without the keys to the cruiser, he'd be trapped in the back seat until a fellow officer could set him free. That would buy Carter some time and distance. He compared the street sign with the map in his head and decided he had about ten blocks to go. Tossing the keys down a sewer grate, he hurried off.

5

―――――――

"You can't just sit around and make protest albums all your life; eventually it comes to the point where you have to do something."

—Paul Kantner

The ride back to the Hoover building was a quiet one. As they had expected, it had been a well-planned ambush, but when executed by the president, they had no choice but to walk right into it. Envelopes had been pressed into their hands by the president's press secretary on the way out, and they were going through the reams of paper as they glided through the late afternoon traffic. "Talking points," they were labeled. A nice way of describing the words they were putting in both Jack's and Sydney's mouths.

They parted ways on the way upstairs after agreeing to meet again in the morning as Jack and Sydney were exhausted and they all needed some time to think. Jack headed straight for his office. The hallways were empty now, as most of his coworkers had left for home already. He had to hurry; Debra was on her way home as well and was expecting him to be there when she arrived.

Jack opened the door and flicked on the lights. The two piles of mail were still on the desk and had not been touched. The faint odor of glass cleaner was in the air, and the trash can was now empty. The cleaning crew had come through accompanied by the security people while he was gone. His tell was still in place, and the clothes he had worn on the plane were still piled on the chair.

He ignored it all and shut the door behind him before moving to the pile of mail. Picking it up in handfuls, he quickly sorted through it. In less than a minute he found it.

A simple white envelope with nothing but a number for a return address:848262

The same as in the phone message.

He held it up to the light with his fingertips but saw only the shadow of a folded piece of paper. If it had held anything suspicious it would have been flagged and held by the security team. Since it had made it as far as his inbox, he felt sure that it contained nothing but paper. He set it back down and then hunted in a drawer for a pair of gloves. A knife parted the seal, and he shook the letter out onto the blotter before prying it open.

He read the message twice before sitting back in his chair and peeling off the gloves.

Options. Try to trace it? He doubted that would get far. It was a piece of copy paper. Even if they identified the brand and source, it was still one of millions out there. The message was printed in block letters with what looked like ordinary pencil. The PO box code indicated a town in Tennessee. One that had two major highways passing through it, if Jack's memory served. Even if they traced the three items to the same area, it was still a long shot at best.

Jack cleaned a fingernail with the knife before

making his decision. The knife went back in the drawer, and the letter went back into its envelope and then into the pocket of his coat.

He had a sudden urge to leave. But there was one more thing to do.

Walking across the room, he opened a closet. In a drawer, under some more spare clothes, he found a small lockbox with a digital lock. He punched in the code and the lid silently popped open to reveal a Glock 9mm pistol. He worked the action twice, before loading a magazine and working the action a third time. He then ejected the magazine, loaded another round, returned it to the butt of the weapon and slammed it home. Two more magazines found their way into his pockets, before the gun was safely tucked into his belt at the small of his back. He eyeballed the smaller pistol at the bottom of the case for a moment, before picking it up and checking to see if it was still loaded. He added it to his pocket as well. He had holsters for each at home, but until then he'd have to rough it.

He'd just stood up when his cell phone vibrated. After glancing at the screen, he answered the call.

"Deb, I'm on my way home."

THE GATE CODE WORKED, and Carter walked past the closed office to the second row and peered around the corner. It was clear. He'd navigated his way around the facility for two blocks in all directions before approaching the entrance. The usual cameras and fence were seen but nothing beyond that. It looked ... normal. There was no way to know if the unit next door held a squad of SWAT team members, or if he were standing in the crosshairs of Dayton's scope, but there was only one way to find out.

He left the corner and walked straight to the unit. The lock was a combination one, and he quickly spun the dial and snapped it open. With a deep breath, he raised the door.

Inside, he found several lockers against the wall, a small bench, and a few cardboard boxes. That was all. He pulled the door shut behind him and threw the latch.

The lockers first. He opened them one-by-one and inventoried their contents. One carried a variety of handguns, and he swapped the one he had with a newer model which had several magazines to go with it. In another box, he found cash—several thousands of dollars— and he stuffed a few stacks in his pocket. The backpack was emptied onto the floor, and he exchanged some items and discarded others. A disguise kit was found, and he used the trimmer, disposable blades, and other toiletries to make himself more presentable, before packing away what was left.

Clothes. There was a whole closet full of them, and he pawed through them until his entire wardrobe was replaced with warmer attire. He selected a few which would fit Tye as well and packed them into a larger pack he found in one of the cardboard boxes.

A phone. He searched until he found a new one still in its plastic from the store and pocketed it without turning it on.

Tools. He found a pic set, one that would work on both doors and cars and shoved that in a pocket along with a multitool. There were knives, but he decided to keep the K-bar he had lifted from the campsite. The baseball hat would stay until he was out of town again, but he added a wool hat for when that happened, and he no longer needed to cover his eyes. On a shelf, he found a few maps and selected two that covered the direction he was going.

In the last cabinet, he found some food. Canned goods and some jerky which had not expired. A case of Coke. He popped the top of one and helped himself to some jerky before searching on.

At the bottom of the cabinet were several jugs of water. He eyeballed them and then the drain in the center of the floor.

"Please, tell me there's some soap."

He found a bottle of shower gel in a box and wasted no time carrying it all to the drain and stripping off his clothes. Despite the cold, it was the best shower he had ever had, and he grinned broadly as he stood naked and shivering while he waited for the air to dry him. He'd been dirtier for longer periods in the Marine Corp, but there was always the knowledge that he could get clean when the mission was over. Being filthy and having no option to change that drove the point home repeatedly.

He couldn't help but grin as he donned the clean clothes and left the others in a pile in the corner. He was a new man. Lacing up his boots, he planned his next move while he brushed his teeth with the remaining water.

The cops would be looking for him and would be doing so in two possible ways. Either they knew who he was—and if that was the case, the guns would be out—or they thought he was just a homeless man who had resisted arrest. Either way, it would not be a time to run into one of them. He scrapped the idea of meeting Tye at the mission and decided to head straight for the railyard once the sun was down instead. He'd wait for him there.

THE GENERAL SAT QUIETLY in his chair while the three men read. He had spent the night crafting the letter, going through several drafts and revisions. Charlie had checked on him three times before the General had finally shooed him to bed. He'd woken the General an hour later than normal, and the first thing he had done was indicate the red burn bag on the floor next to the bed. The shredded drafts had immediately found their way into the basement incinerator.

Meetings over breakfast were one of the man's favorite rituals, and they had all cleaned their plates before receiving copies of the draft. There were two. One to the members of the Twelve Shepherds and the leaders of the various Occupy branches across the country. The other was to the American people. Each would be released on a carefully planned timeline, triggering an operation that had been prepared over the last two years. One that would take weeks to execute and culminate on a cold day in January.

Dayton flipped his copy shut and placed it carefully on the table before looking out the window. The General examined his face. It was still what most would consider a young man's face, until you looked in his eyes. His eyes revealed a life of great labor, both physical and mental. They were the eyes of an old man, one who had seen too much in too short a time. There was also a great sadness to them, a hint of a burden that was carried involuntarily. Perhaps when this mission was over, that burden would lessen. The General could only hope so.

Charlie finished next. He set the two letters down and nodded once to the General, before sipping his coffee and waiting for William. He and the General had talked before the others had arrived, and Charlie was still a bit uneasy about the operation. Contemplating treason was not a casual conversation, but then they had all seen governments change hands in other countries. It was never pretty. Whatever he had to say, he kept it inside.

William's lips moved as he read. An annoying habit for those watching or sitting close by—for obvious reasons it was something he'd been forced to stop doing at his former NSA job. Since coming to work for the General, the habit had returned, and they were all forced to tolerate it. Dayton watched for a moment before sharing a look with the other two. William was not using his speed-reading skills; he was going slow and soaking up every word. Fortunately, their wait wasn't long.

"The codes are correct, sir."

"Excellent. Are the timelines feasible?"

"I believe so," Dayton replied. We want to use commercial travel, so there's no telling what delays the airlines might cause, but I feel we can have everyone in place well before the required time. Many of them are already in place. Two of the targets have moved, but the new locations have already been dealt with. I think the operational side is a go."

"All right. Are we ready on the communications end?"

"The addresses have all been verified, and for the most part, the people are in place."

"For the most part?" Dayton asked.

"We lost a couple in New York to a car accident last month, and a woman in DC is hospitalized with cancer. Other than that, the cells are intact."

"And the competition?"

William smiled at the General's use of his pet

name for them before answering, "Nothing at the NSA or FBI. Our friend Mr. Randall had himself a little adventure down in Florida but managed to emerge victorious and only slightly scratched. He returned to DC only yesterday."

"The storm. I'd forgotten about it. Will it hit the eastern seaboard?"

"No, it's currently dying a natural death in the mid-Atlantic."

"All right. Back to the FBI, you see them getting any closer?"

"The files I've been able to access tell me no. Since we've stopped operations, they have nothing new to go on. The focus seems to be split between the manhunt for Mr. Carter and the forensic evidence they recovered from the storage unit."

"Wouldn't the fire have taken care of that?"

"Not everything. If Mr. Carter followed procedure, we should be safe. But the van he had was new to him, and he may not have had time to properly sterilize it. And then there's always the serial numbers that were missed. A receipt in the trash that somehow survived the flames. The possibilities are many. His residences are still untouched, so I'm hopeful."

"Speaking of Mr. Carter. You sent the message?"

"Yes. No replies as of this morning. Wherever he is, he has not accessed the account."

"Leads as to his location?" Dayton asked.

"They get several hundred a day. Most are easily dismissed. Nothing that I would deem worthy of follow-up. I think Mr. Carter will make contact when he is ready. Until then, we wait."

They all frowned at the statement. They needed number six. Without him, they were down a man. That, and they still had one that was not fully on board yet.

"Who's going to take his place?" Charlie asked.

"Hugh reports that two members of the Trust are planning to be on the boat that night. He'll handle both."

"And number twelve?"

Dayton sighed. "We usually wait until a Shepherd has a few missions under their belt before they are informed of Rubicon. She's only performed one, and it was resent."

"She handled herself well in California," William said.

"True," Dayton stalled.

"If she's not needed to take Mr. Carter's place ... then perhaps she can assist you?"

"Without informing her of the real mission? I won't do that."

"Then perhaps you feel she should sit this one out?"

They sat in silence for a moment. The mystery of Number Twelve and what to do with her was a heavy question. Finally, the General spoke.

"You know her best, Dayton. I will leave it up to you whether to bring her into the fold or not. But please, decide quickly; time is our enemy."

"Yes, sir."

"Then once again, it comes to a vote. Is the letter I crafted approved?"

He got a round of yeses in reply.

"Very well. Rubicon will commence, starting today. William, you'll see to the letters getting to the proper people?"

"Yes, sir."

6

"Nothing exasperates the spirit in man more than power which seems unconquerable and which makes impotent all protest."

—George William Russell

Laced up and suited up, he placed the backpack on his shoulders and listened at the door. Hearing nothing, he was quickly out and on his way. He kept to the side streets and moved toward the sound of the interstate to the west, using it as a rough guide back to the railyard.

He hoped Tye was there. If not, he'd have to figure out which train would get him north. And quickly.

Carter entered the yard the same way he and Tye had left it and paused to take in the area.

"You're a tramp," he told himself. "Where would the tramps go?"

He spotted an area off to one side, which held some steeper terrain covered by thick vegetation. The dirt in front of him was hard packed from foot traffic, but it led in that direction. With no other options in sight, he followed it.

A train entering the yard prompted him to speed up, and he reached the edge of the trees just as it passed. Footprints led him on, and he soon came to a path into the scrub brush.

"Welcome," a voice called.

Carter froze.

"Hello?"

"Over here."

Carter followed the voice and soon found a man sitting just inside the bushes.

"Hey."

The man looked him over. "Never seen you before."

"My first time. Up from El Paso, heading north."

The man nodded and then pointed out to the yard. "That one there on track three looks north-bound to me. Maybe the one behind it. Got any chow?"

Carter remembered the rules: share if you have it; ask if you don't. He pulled the remainder of the package of jerky from his pocket and handed it over.

"All you got?" the man asked. It wasn't a rude question; it was to measure how much he would take.

"I had a good meal in town; you go ahead."

"Much obliged." The man helped himself to half and handed the rest back. Carter added a Coke without being asked to.

"This the place to wait?"

"Yup. A few more of us up the hill a piece. Yard boss don't bother us long as we stay in the trees. No fires or they come down and run us off. Heading north, you say?"

Carter was a bit confused by the man's short memory; hadn't he just said that? "Uh ... yeah. No place in particular. Running counter."

"I think one of 'em said the same. You'll have to ask around." He jerked a thumb over his shoulder, and Carter took it as a signal to move on. Evidently, the man had appointed himself as the gatekeeper of this particular jungle. Since Carter had paid the toll with jerky, he was being allowed to pass. He took it before the man asked for something else.

Climbing into the trees, he encountered the usual trash and abandoned camping gear he had seen in the other yards. He picked his way through the empty liquor and wine bottles and made his way up the hill. A man's shape appeared off to one side, and hearing the accompanying snore, he stole past him. Judging by the number of Coors beer cans around him, it was going to be a long nap. Carter remembered the distribution center adjacent to the yard and wondered if the man had raided it. He dismissed the thought, when the orange glow of a cigarette revealed another man's presence. Carter approached slowly.

"Heh. There he is. Knew you'd find your way here sooner or later."

Carter dropped his pack and took a seat next to Tye.

"Sorry I'm late."

IT WAS SMALL INDUSTRIAL PARK. One that had a few medium-size box buildings selling or manufacturing items in low volume. Like most industrial parks, it sent out a large quantity of mail, and the delivery services had installed a row of large steel drop-off boxes to handle it all. The high volume and traffic would help him blend in.

Charlie pulled up to the car at the box and watched as the woman struggled to load a large quantity of envelopes into the narrow chute. She finally put her phone down and used both hands to both hold it open and feed in the maximum number of letters the box would take. She noticed him waiting behind her and offered a wave of apology before driving off. The phone was back to her ear before she reached the next intersection.

Charlie let the car roll forward until he was even with the box. There, he paused.

He'd been in the office when the General had summoned him, and he found William waiting with him on arrival. William had silently passed Charlie a large envelope, and without a word to either of them, departed, leaving him and the General alone.

"We need you to run that into town and get it sent off."

Charlie fingered the envelope and weighed it. It was lite, less than half a pound of paper. Yet, it had immense power. This was the pebble that, once nudged, would start an avalanche. It seemed so fragile a thing.

"What it holds will affect your generation much more than it will mine," the General had said. "I thought it fit that you deliver it."

"Yes, sir."

The drive down the mountain and into town had given Charlie plenty of time to think. Things were moving fast now, and while he was sure he knew the overall mission, there were still sections of it which were secrets to him. Each Shepherd would get the message and move to their targets as individual missions. It was better that way. It gave each man a small measure of deniability.

But what about after? Charlie had tried to avoid the subject, but it kept coming back. If everything went as planned, they could stay and, hopefully, aid in the coming change. If the outcome were different, they would be fugitives, ones that even the General's money couldn't hide.

Was he prepared to do that? Live a life of secrecy? It would be hard. Between the General's condition and his famous face, he doubted there was anywhere on earth he could go and not be recognized. Charlie's own face was even more memorable. Was he ready to live like that?

He picked up the envelope and weighed it again in both gloved hands. Inside were two dozen smaller envelopes, half of them addressed to the Shepherds. This large one would travel to a person he did not know in a place he had never been. Whomever they were, they had been entrusted by the General to mail the smaller envelopes on. He or she would travel to a mailbox much like the one he was currently at, open the envelope, dump the contents inside without handling them or even reading their destinations, and then burn the original envelope, thereby severing the link to their original origin. A simple process, but one that was very important.

Was Charlie ready to do this? The simple act of sending the envelope on its way amounted to treason by several definitions. But that was what it all hinged on: definitions. One man's traitor was another man's freedom fighter. Which one was he?

Charlie knew. With a flip of the metal lid, the envelope dropped into the steel box. An hour later a truck would arrive, and the letter would be scanned and sent overnight to its destination.

There, the process would repeat itself, again and again, until an army was raised.

He rolled the window up and then gripped the wheel tight with his gloved hands. What was the word? Rubicon. A small river that had somehow become synonymous with the point of no return.

Charlie, and the Twelve Shepherds, had just crossed it.

THE SCREAM of the passing jet woke Archie, and he jerked at the sound. F-15, his brain instantly labeled it, and he held his breath waiting for the bombs to hit. They did, eventually, but the impacts were several miles away. Close—and getting closer. Was it the main body in retreat, or had a small group gotten caught out in the open? He had no way to tell.

He lifted his head and looked across the small tent. It had been his home now for several weeks, and the smell had long since grown invisible to his nose. The dandruff and the growing beard, combined with the layers of dirt, served to help him remember how long it had been since his arrival. He did the math in his head every morning and was fully aware that he was about to enter triple digits. How he had remained alive was a miracle.

No, not a miracle. A man. The one now cowering on the dirty floor across from him and gazing out the door at the sky. This man. He was the reason he was alive. Archie had no problem admitting it.

"Not at us," he told him.

The man relaxed only slightly. The attacks had been getting more frequent. Archie's ability to identify the planes by sound alone was something the doctor marveled at. Only once had he gotten concerned. Russian planes. His American patient had called one a Frogfoot. The doctor had never heard the term. The planes had skimmed the ground heading south, only to return thirty minutes later at a higher altitude. Archie had spotted them outside the tent flaps and named them by shape. A combination of fighters and close ground support aircraft, they had no doubt been on a mission to shore up the army of Assad.

"They are closer?"

Archie raised himself up on his elbows and shuffled his body to the open door of the tent. The leg had healed somewhat; the scare of the infection had passed. The leg was still very tender, but he could now move himself around enough to lessen the workload on his friend and caregiver. They had both celebrated the day he wiped his own ass. It was a small victory for both of them.

But now he had a new problem. The cough had started as a minor annoyance, only to progress to a constant hack. In the mornings, he would expel a modest quantity of sputum, the color of which the doctor would frown at. The boy was now kept away from him, and the doctor would spend his time outside the tent rather than inside. Archie didn't blame him. He would sometimes cough until he couldn't breathe. A dry hacking torture which left him gasping for air and doubled over in pain. It was pneumonia. The type of which they didn't know. The antibiotics the doctor had given him did not seem to be having any effect.

"No. I don't think they are closer."

The Doctor nodded and asked nothing further. Any attempt at speech would produce a coughing fit, and he wished to save his patient that anguish. Archie lay back and scanned the sky for the millionth time, hoping to see the first sign of a helicopter swooping in to retrieve him, or at least a drone whose camera he would smile for. But the sky remained blue and clear, save for the contrails of passing planes. He took a few deep breaths prior to speaking; he'd found that it held the coughing off when he did so.

"The Rebel?"

The doctor rose and made a show of checking his leg. It looked the same as the day before. The bruising was fading, and the puckered skin was solidifying into a ragged scar. Archie thought it looked great. Far better than one of a man who'd arrived here the way he did should look like. A few days ago, he had finally dared to accept that he would keep his leg. Now, if he could only keep his life as well.

"I have not seen him. There was no talk of him this morning at the well."

Archie nodded so as not to speak. They had taken to calling the mystery ISIS fighter "The Rebel" after their talk of *Star Wars*. He had not returned, but they both felt he was nearby. Neither of them could say why, it was like they sensed his presence.

"You think he is waiting?"

Archie nodded again. The man was close, he knew it.

"Then he must feel they are coming for you?"

"Yes."

The doctor's smile was the opposite of Archie's frown. The doctor saw Archie as the only way they might leave this place. To return him to the world outside this warzone and let him start the search for his family. His patient, however, saw it as risking the lives of his fellow soldiers in an effort to rescue him, an effort he was sure The Rebel was counting on them to do.

"Would you not come for them?"

Archie refused to look at his friend. They both knew the answer to that. Of course, he would come; they all would, without hesitation. It didn't change the fact that he was bait, that men like him were walking into a trap. A trap he had given them. If he had maybe flown in the opposite direction, or stayed lower on the bomb run, or not gotten so cocky with the AA gun. It was his fault, and now others were going to have to pay for it.

"We have to warn them."

"Warn them? Of what? A trap we only fear is here?" the Doctor protested. "We know nothing. The Rebel may be kilometers away from here."

Archie shook his head. The man was letting emotion drive his decision. He suspected the man was close. Why else had he taken the beacon, if not to draw a recuing force into a trap? There were facts and there were feelings. Lt. Archie Bunker operated on facts.

"The crates."

The doctor was confused. What about them?

"New message." Archie coughed and fought to control it.

"What do you ... no. No, they would not come."

"We have to ... warn them." He fell into a coughing fit and the doctor sat him up to combat it.

"Be still. I ... will see what I can do."

7

---

*"The Adequate Protest demands far more than protests.
It calls for Great and Daring Leaps of Integrity and
Courage to See."*

—Mary Daly

J ack was in his office. Again. While it was considered spacious by the government's standards, it was still an office, and he had never been able to tolerate one for long. He'd had several; the one he'd inherited at his father's company would fit several of his current one inside, with room to spare. Jack had lasted about two weeks in it, before moving out to something that didn't have its own echo. It had clearly been his father's office, one designed to bolster his ego and project power over those that entered it. Jack had found it uncomfortable. His move had prompted some jokes from the board members, but his stock with the employees had risen overnight. He'd ended up hiring two more secretaries and giving them all the space. He traded the floor to ceiling windows, and the fancy marble floors for a small corner office with blinds that shut out the world. His output had doubled soon after. Amazing what a small change in work environment could do.

Like now. He had two sheets of paper on his desk. One was the most recent update on the Shepherds case, the other a list of talking points sent over from the White House to go with his next TV appearance. He wanted to focus on the first and circle-file the second but was forced to do the opposite. Not that it mattered much; the update consisted of less than ten pages of bureaucratic speech that basically amounted to two words: nothing new.

A scan of the talking points revealed them to be more of the same. Some assistant to the press secretary was wearing out their *Thesaurus*. How many ways were they going to find to say nothing? It was getting ridiculous, but the AG was close to the president. With the Director of the FBI out for the next six months, possibly forever, that made Deacon the Acting Director. They had to toe the line. Somehow, that translated into Jack on TV. He'd searched for days for a way out, but nothing had presented. Not even a hot lead he could use for an excuse.

"Paper bullshit!" he swore to the empty room before tossing the papers down on the desk.

As if the room had heard his thoughts, there was a knock on the door.

"Come!"

Larry stuck his head in and scanned the room.

"Is there somebody here?"

"No, just me bitching out loud. What's on your mind?"

Larry entered and dropped his bulk into a chair, before tossing a file across the desk. Jack picked it up. It was thin. He set it back down.

"Am I going to like this?"

"A lead. I think it's worth following up."

"Oh? Gimme the highlights."

"It's out of Denver. Seems a man fitting the description of our fugitive came into the public library early Saturday morning. The woman running the show that day described him as a homeless man, a big guy that she had never seen before. He was polite and asked to use a computer to check his email. Not an unusual thing I'm told, so she steered him to the computer room and saw him get online through the glass. No issues, so she went back to work. A bit later, a few students came in and noticed the guy. That got him a bit nervous, and he left, but not before one of them got a good look and a picture."

Jack pointed silently to the file and Larry nodded. He flipped it open to see a somewhat blurry shot of a large black man in a heavy black coat. A beard darkened his face, and from the profile shot, only the nose and eyes were partly visible. Was it the man he had spoken with in the jail cell in LA? Maybe. It was not enough, and Jack's face showed it.

"Look in the glass."

Jack did and saw a reflection of the man's full face. It too was blurry, but it was full on from the front. With the beard and the hat, he couldn't be sure. For the lab, though, it might be something they could work with.

"The lab?"

"They're working their magic on it. If it's enough to run through the facial recognition software, we might get a match. Should know in an hour or two, they say."

Jack closed the file and placed it on his desk, before pointing to the second one still in Larry's hand.

"An eyewitness statement is thin. What else you have?"

"An unconfirmed second incident. The librarian called the sighting in after the student talked to her. They pulled up the old newspaper article with his picture and then phoned the police."

"What makes you trust these two over all the other calls we're getting?"

"The librarian is a cops' wife, and the student is in the academy."

"Ahh, I see. Go on."

"They call it in, and since it's a slow morning, they send two units. One goes to the library, while the other checks out the area. Unit two, a rookie, spots a guy who fits the description and approaches him."

"Oh, no."

"Yup. Long-story-short: rookie ends up cuffed and stuffed in the back of his own cruiser. They find him about thirty minutes later, after he doesn't answer his radio. No witnesses of the actual event. Plenty of bystanders for the rescue, though. Anyway, the cops report is in there. They swept the area after the cop was found, but the man was gone."

"The cop's on the internet already?"

"Oh, yeah."

Jack opened the file and scanned it. It took him only a few minutes to see that the descriptions fit, and that the takedown of the cop had been performed with skill. He sympathized with the man he was about to become famous.

"Welcome to the club," Jack muttered.

"What?"

"Nothing. So, our guy, if it is our guy, made it all the way to Denver and is posing as a homeless man. Any theories as to why?"

"Given the time that's elapsed, I would have thought that the Shepherds would have taken him in and hidden him by now. This whole thing raises a bunch of questions."

"Why is he not back in their group?"

"Why is he still in the country?" Larry countered.

"Why the homeless act?"

"Where is he going?"

"Why is he going there?"

Jack sighed and closed the second file. He placed it directly on top of the first and squared the corners. Larry watched and waited.

"How long to confirm the ID?" Jack said.

"Two hours."

"Once its confirmed, I want you on a plane to Denver. Go over everything in person with the Denver office and the locals. Try to get some forensic confirmation as well. On your way, try to answer some of those questions."

"Thought you might say that. I guess our roles are getting reversed. They have you on the Sunday shows again?"

"Yeah."

"Sorry, Jack."

"It is what it is. You find something good out there ... "

"Yeah?"

"Tell me first and keep a lid on it."

"What ... never mind." Larry saw where Jack was going. If he had an excuse, he'd go first and then ask permission. UNODIR, it was affectionally known as. It stood for Unless Otherwise Directed. If done right, it gave you the escape you needed while covering your boss's ass at the same time.

"Okay," Larry said. "Anything else?"

"Take Sydney with you. See if she can work her magic."

"Okay. We're on it."

Jack watched Larry heave himself to his feet and walk out, every fiber of Jack's being wanting to go with him. The door shut behind him, and Jack cursed it before picking up the talking points again.

A minute later, the words were a blur, and he threw the pages down in disgust. He knew of only two ways to rid himself of the frustration. One was in the bottom desk of the drawer, and the other was in the basement of the building.

Ignoring option one, he stripped off the suit and changed into a set of gym clothes. The weight pile had not seen his presence in some time, and it was time to change that. He'd work off the anger there.

THE BROWN TRUCK had a distinctive sound and prompted him to leave his writing and roll the chair to the door. He opened it before the man could knock.

"Morning, Andy."

"Hey, Steve. I got a hot one for you—needs a signature." He held out the clipboard and pen. Steve took it and scrawled something illegible on its electronic surface.

"Abraham ... Lincoln."

It was their running joke. Steve came up with a new president for every package. Andy didn't care as long as it was signed for. The man gave him a mock salute, before hurrying back to his truck. Andy was a busy man.

Steve shut the door and rolled himself back inside. It was a package from the General—he could tell by the coded return address. He ignored the desk and the book he was working on and instead made his way to the garage. With the envelope in his lap, he rolled himself up the ramp and locked himself in place behind the wheel. A minute later, he was on the road and heading away from the brown truck.

It took him less than an hour to distribute the letters that were inside. He dropped them in various overnight mailboxes around the city and used at least three different services. When he was done, he stopped at his favorite drive-through for a bucket of chicken and then hurried home to work on his new book.

As usual, the drive had given him an idea. He had to get home and get it down on paper before he forgot it.

He wondered for a brief moment what actions the letters would start—he had never mailed so many before—but he put the thought aside. He'd watch the TV a little closer over the next few days, and the answer to his question would no doubt find its way there.

Until then, he would trust in the General and work on his new novel.

IT WAS A HIGH SCHOOL GAME. One of the last of the season, and the promise of snow was in the air. The players' breath could be seen as they stood on the sidelines with their hands tucked inside their jerseys. The coach screamed instructions at his quarterback, and the crowd watched his every move as the ball was slapped into his hands by the center. The boy scrambled left with surprising speed and dodged a tackle before launching the ball down the left field sideline. It brushed the fingertips of the intended receiver, before hitting the ground and bouncing out of bounds. *Too bad*, Jack thought; *it would have been a touchdown for sure.*

Ignoring the crowd, he examined the bleachers. Above the huddled families sharing blankets and the younger siblings of the players, there was a large crowd of students using the game for a social meeting. Off to one side sat a lone figure wearing a hoodie. His hands were thrust deep in his pockets, and the new haircut was hidden from view. A motorcycle helmet sat on the cold aluminum bench-seat next to him. The cold breeze at the top of the bleachers assured them of privacy, and Jack gave a silent nod of approval as he ascended the stairs. He used the newspaper in his hands as a cushion and took a seat next to the man.

Eric examined Jack's face from inside the hoodie and frowned.

"Damn, boss. You look like shit."

"Thanks, Eric. You look like a pedophile."

"I do?"

"Hoodie. Sitting alone. Stop checking out the girls. Try to be a little less ... NSA-ish next time."

Jack leaned back against the cold steel rail of the bleachers and watched the quarterback launching another one down the sideline. This time he connected, and the home team picked up thirty yards before he was knocked out of bounds thirty yards short of the goal line. The crowd stood and cheered, and Jack joined them. Eric quickly mimicked his old boss.

"There you go. Anybody keeping tabs on you?" They both sat back, and Eric doffed his hood.

"I saw the usual guy questioning the neighbors a couple weeks ago—that's routine. I think I'm good until next month. But nobody followed me here, if that's what you're asking."

"Good."

"What's this about?"

"I need some help, and I can't go through the FBI's people, or even normal NSA ones."

"Must be pretty bad."

"Short version: I got a letter from someone—and a phone call."

"Both should be easy to trace back, especially the phone call. What's the issue?"

"A lot of little things. But this phone call was from a woman. She claimed she was being re-cruited by the Twelve Shepherds. She sounded scared, but said she was going along with it and would be in touch. She left me a six-digit number to serve as verification. I got a letter from her while I was out west, and it had the same number on it for a return address."

"You have it traced?"

"No. Not the phone call, or the letter. It's in my pocket."

Eric squirmed on the cold bench seat and stuffed his hands back in his pockets. What Jack had just told him he had done was against procedure, which meant what he was going to ask him to do was most likely that way as well.

"You want me to trace it, and to do so outside channels? Why?"

"I'm convinced the Shepherds have a way inside."

"The FBI?"

"No, the NSA. Maybe both."

"Inside the NSA? Seriously?"

"You don't think it can happen? I seem to recall a kid from Vegas getting in a few years ago."

"True, but I got caught. I also showed them how I did it. Those holes have been patched, and we have a team of people that do nothing but look for new holes all day, every day. If someone was making repeated access from outside Fort Mead, I think we'd have seen it."

"Either way, I think they are. We get headed off too easily. I kept the communication around that prison transfer tight, yet they still knew well ahead of time where and at what time we were going with him. It took a few hours to set that ambush up, and the equipment wasn't just laying around either; they had it ahead of time or they acquired it pretty fast. You know about the truck?"

"The one they used in the ambush? A little."

"There was paperwork filed. The computer had the truck signed out to one of the mechanics. The keys and a fake work order were in the front seat. The person who swiped it just walked up and drove it away. Nobody even noticed it was gone. Whoever got into the counties motor pool computer did so without leaving a trail. Whomever they are, they're good."

"The mechanic checked out?"

"He was out in the ocean fishing with a half-dozen friends at the time."

Eric suspected this already, but didn't have an answer for Jack. He began tapping his foot, something Jack had learned was a sign of heavy thought. He turned back to the game and watched the next play to give Eric time to think about it.

"How long have the Shepherds been in operation?"

"About ... two years. Maybe six months or so after Sam died."

"They're very prepared."

"An understatement," Jack echoed. "What are you thinking?"

"I'm not sure yet. You have a copy of this letter for me?"

Jack pulled the newspaper from under his ass and handed it over. Inside was the letter and the phone message. Jack had copied it on an old machine which had been stowed away in his basement. Eric gave it a quick look and then the attached note.

"This the time and date and number of the call?"

"Yeah."

"I'll see what I can find as to where your letter originated, but I don't want you to get your hopes up. It's harder than it looks. You know the PO address just tells you where it was processed from, right? And the phone call? Other than having a voice print—and that's if she spoke long enough to even get one—it's probably from a burner phone."

"I know. But I have to try, and I'd rather it not get to them that this woman is trying to speak with me. It could end badly for her if it does."

"Okay, I'll think about this inside man you mentioned, too. I have an idea."

"Do I—"

"No. You definitely don't want to know."

"Then I guess that's it. I left a phone number where you can get me. Just me."

Eric nodded. A burner phone. Jack had thought ahead.

"My ass is freezing. Anything else?"

"Nope."

"Okay, I'll call when I have something for you. I'm going home before it snows."

Eric had gone only three steps down when he stopped and turned.

"This woman who called ... didn't you say there was a woman at the ambush site?"

"Yes."

Eric just nodded before turning and descending the stairs. He joined the crowd at the bottom and was soon lost from Jack's view. He heard a motorcycle fire up in the parking lot a minute after.

Jack checked the scoreboard. The game was tied, with only a few minutes remaining. He decided to stay and see who would come out on top.

8

"The opposite of corporate greed is personal generosity. Government policies that enable the former and prevent the latter are both worthy of protest."

—*Cynthia Dill*

When asked, he told people he was a writer and online marketer. A freelancer. One who used a pen name for himself and ghosted for others. Anything beyond that, he would politely decline to answer and blame it on the contract he'd signed. It was enough to let him come and go as he pleased without raising any suspicion from the neighbors. It also explained the mass-mailings he would both send and receive at the local UPS store. He had a girlfriend who was studying political science, and a few friends who would visit on occasion. Other than that, he kept to himself and was what most would consider a good neighbor.

None of his neighbors suspected for a minute that he was involved with the Occupy movement, and if they ever did, they would have double the trouble picturing him as its leader.

Today was cold. Winter had come early in New York, and after a summer of record high temps most New Yorkers were welcoming the colder weather. While no snow had fallen yet, the leaves had changed color rapidly and begun to fall in great numbers in Central Park. He brushed a few from his coat as he entered the lobby of the building.

The building was like many in New York, a once spacious warehouse converted into condos. His was on the fourth floor and fell somewhere in the area of industrial sheik, as far as décor went.

While the exposed brick, steel columns, and high ceilings crisscrossed with plumbing and ventilation were coveted by many, he didn't really care; it was the location that mattered most to him. He smiled a greeting to one of his neighbors and made his way to the mailboxes.

Among the junk mail, he saw a letter that made his breath catch. He tucked it away in an inside pocket before pushing his bike to the elevator. It was all he could do to leave the envelope in his coat until he arrived upstairs and entered his apartment. The bike was hung on a convenient hook, and the coat was quickly doffed, stripped of the letter, and tossed aside.

He opened the envelope quickly but read the letter slowly and carefully, decoding its message as he went. To most, it would appear as a simple form letter. A fundraising campaign, one in support of a Shakespearean club currently touring the country. The real message was in the third paragraph.

One word. Rubicon.

He walked to his desk and sank into the seat. It creaked slightly as he leaned back. With a start, he realized his heart was beating rapidly in his chest, and he took a few deep breaths to calm himself down.

It was time.

He read the letter again, this time counting words and applying them to a formula memorized years ago. He came up with a date. It sounded familiar.

Turning to his computer he pulled up his personal calendar. He had a notation made on that date. A reminder. He clicked it.

"The State of the Union address. That should work nicely."

Armed with this information, he began writing a letter of his own, one he had conceived long ago and committed to memory for when the time would come. The words poured forth and landed on the page with precision. A space here. A hyphen there. The first word of each sentence carefully chosen. It was done within thirty minutes and carefully read several times before landing on the copy machine. Thirty copies were produced and carefully folded into plain white envelopes. Forever stamps purchased while on a vacation trip were already attached, and the addresses were added from memory as well.

Thirty from one. That thirty would repeat the process and become nine hundred. And that nine hundred would become twenty-seven thousand. Until the number was too large to comprehend.

Force multiplication they called it. It was how armies were built.

Emboldened by the contents of the message, he retrieved the coat and stuffed the letters in the inside pocket where he could access them easily. This time he added a hat to his head, one that would hide his features from the many overhead cameras in the city. Checking his pockets, he made sure he had his back-up wallet, with its expertly crafted false identification, and a few hundred dollars in cash. He made sure the phone was left behind before leaving the condo for the stairs. He would duck out the service entrance this time so as not to be seen by the neighbors. The subway was only two blocks away.

For the next three hours he roamed the city, dropping letters into multiple USPS mailboxes at random. The last was mailed in Chinatown, and he decided to enjoy a walk across the bridge to have dinner in Brooklyn, before taking a cab home. Halfway across, he turned and took in the sight of lower Manhattan. Despite the protests happening, it looked peaceful tonight, with the sun setting behind the new Freedom Tower. He spotted a red tour bus rolling along the FDR, its occupants gazing up at the tall buildings of Wall

Street and beyond. A normal night in the Big Apple. Soon that would change.

For the good or the bad was yet to be seen. With one last look, he turned east, toward tomorrow.

WILLIAM HEAVED himself upright and grabbed his cane. It was time for another walk. The screens showed the bots hard at work, scouring the Internet, banking systems, and several government agencies' networks for information. Like most days, this one had been spent filtering the information, discarding that which was not supported with evidence and steering the bots to find more when the information demanded it. The files continued to grow.

Leaving them to work, he headed for the server rooms. He checked them several times a day now, as the General's stroke had prompted him to move around more often. This time he angled for the farthest room. It was the first of its kind and, by far, the most important he had constructed.

After the coded access key and palm reader were satisfied he was who he said he was, the doors slid open, the rush of cold air sending a chill down his back. The cane clicked on the hard tile floor, as he shuffled inside and wandered the spaces.

The servers sat as tall as a man and stretched for over fifty yards, all of them humming and blinking as he wandered past. He stopped at the environmental controls to check the latest diagnostic, and after finding it within the set parameters, he moved on. The overhead pipes converged a few yards later and exited the room through the stone walls to the fire suppression system. Oxygen masks adorned the wall every few yards in the event of an accidental discharge. If that were to occur, the halon gas flooding the room would quickly choke off the air to any fire, smothering it within seconds. Unfortunately, it would do the same to any person who happened to be inside as well. The poor soul would have to ride out the event with a mask on or rapidly develop the skill of digging through several meters of solid rock before running out of breath. It was not something William preferred to dwell on.

The halon system informed him of its readiness after a self-check, and William moved on, working his leg as his eyes scanned the equipment. Inside these servers were the accumulation of ten years work. Several hours daily of time at his computers, sifting and processing and watching as the country was slowly eaten from within. It was all carefully gathered and preserved here, before the perpetrators could hide, erase, or conceal it. Every day, the files grew in both size and number. When they needed a name, he had dubbed them Pitchforks. The General had approved.

Someday, the files would be released to the world, but the time was not right yet. But it was coming.

Reaching the entrance, he paused for a moment to look back. The servers winked and blinked at him, humming as they worked. Tireless little soldiers. If they were sentient, what would they think? He shuddered at the thought.

He left the room and re-entered the common area. His cane clicked on the stone floor as he passed another door. This one heavy steel with a locking mechanism to match. No sign labeled its contents or destination and never would. The door was for William; no one else needed to know.

He made his way back to his desk to find the bots still hard at work. The leg protested as he sat back down, and he downed a couple of pills while reading a few files that had been flagged while he was gone.

"Interesting," he mumbled. "How will our friend the senator react to that?"

He typed some instructions into the program and sent it on its way. Leaning back in his chair, he glanced at the room he had just left. The servers still blinked back behind the thick wall of glass, as if telling him they were ready.

"Soon," he answered. "Very soon."

THE POLITE DING of the email account announced another addition to her inbox, and she reluctantly glanced away from her homework to see if it was worth viewing. The subject line contained the codeword, and her eyes widened when she saw it. She promptly forgot about the PowerPoint presentation in front of her and quickly saved it to get it off her screen.

"Honey?"

"Yeah?" her husband answered from two rooms away. He was no doubt on his own machine, working on his own degree while watching a football game at the same time. It was something she could never do; she needed a room with a door to get anything done.

"Did you get the mail today?"

Silence.

"Honey?"

"No. Forgot. You need it right now?"

She listened closer and heard the muffled cheers of the crowd through the door. It was a playoff game, and normally she would wait, but not tonight.

"Yes. It's important."

She got a mumbled reply followed by the door opening and closing. He was back a moment later, and the door was closed and locked before he walked past the big screen without looking.

"You got an email?" he asked on entering the room.

"Yes. What was in the box?"

He handed her the letter and she glanced at it before opening it. No Post Office mark. It had been addressed by hand, with no return address, and then dropped off by someone personally. She opened the one-page document, and he read over her shoulder.

"Tuesdays. I'll have to make a few adjustments, but that shouldn't be a problem. You?"

"I'll have Mrs. Johnson watch Jeremy for us."

That said, he walked to the closet and opened it. Unzipping an opaque garment bag, he revealed a pair of long winter coats, both a size too big.

Hanging behind them were two sets of body armor. Dragon skin. It had been close to a year since they had obtained them from a pawn shop two states away with cash. The pockets were already stocked with wire-impregnated zip-ties, face masks, gloves, and a pair of small airhorns. He laid everything out on the bed before returning to the closet for a box on the top shelf. From inside, he pulled a pair of hand-held tasers and a number of pre-paid cell phones.

"I'll charge all the batteries. You'll handle the signs?"

"They just need to be attached to the new poles," she answered. "They're under the bed."

Her husband reached under the bed and pulled the two signs free. They were old ones, but still effective. Their statements bold enough to get noticed by the press and appear on the TVs of millions when they had carried them in Justice Park. That was a few years ago. They had at first kept the signs as reminders, but now they kept them for future use.

Tomorrow she would fix them to new poles. Metal ones which broke down and were easier to carry. The coded letter listed three buildings, and on Tuesdays they would rotate from one to the next on a set schedule, never standing still long enough to be accused of loitering or blocking traffic or any other reason the police might use to arrest them or drive them off. The original Occupy movement had made those mistakes, but they had learned from them, and this time things would be different. It was even more important now.

Small footfalls brought them the reason for their planned actions. Jeremy had woken up.

"Mommy? I'm thirsty."

"Okay, baby. Mommy's coming. You go back to bed, and I'll bring you a drink, all right?"

"O ... kay."

"Should we send him to your mom's, until it's over?" he whispered.

"Maybe. I'll call her tomorrow."

He just nodded and plugged in the chargers. Soon, the little lights of the tasers and the phones were blinking as they gathered electrons from the power strip. They both watched them in silence.

Across the country, other letters were received and similar actions taken, and in that calm a storm grew.

Eric sat down and logged in before leaning back and checking the overhead screens. There were several here at his NSA job, and he examined them for any information he might need. One of them held a word that was highlighted. He scooted his chair back until he could address his neighbor.

"Hey, Kim?"

"Yeah."

"What's with the word list?"

Kim stopped her typing and looked up at the same screen Eric had noticed. The word list was just that: a list of words that the computers had flagged as showing an uptick in use. The monitoring software scanned millions of emails, phone calls, and internet searches an hour and flagged words which appeared in large numbers or at accelerated rates. The ones which climbed faster got different color designators. She saw now that one of them was red, the highest designation they had.

"Rubicon? I have no idea. Some river in Italy, isn't it?"

"Yeah. Kind of an odd word to make the list. Anybody checking it?"

"Not me. They got me watching Nazis in Idaho."

"Anything in the daily?"

"Not that I saw. May have changed since I came in. Why? Does it mean something to you?"

"No, just wondering."

"Nazis can't spell for shit," Kim informed him. Her keyboard clicked louder.

Realizing he had lost her attention, he went back to his own keyboard. He had work to do himself. But before he started, he wrote the word #Rubicon# on a post-it and stuck it on his monitor. He would explore the word later.

He clicked his mouse and checked his assignments.

"Russians, again?"

9

"In a world filled with hate, prejudice, and protest, I find that I too am filled with hate, prejudice, and protest."

—Bob Gibson

Stan Johnson was going over the sales receipts of the last month and liking what he was seeing. While his store had opened as a pawn shop a few years ago, it had rapidly become less about pawning goods and more about selling guns. It was now his main focus, and if things kept going the way they were going, it was sure to stay that way.

The bell announced another customer, and the owner looked up to see a pair of middle-aged woman standing in the door. Looking around for his employees, he saw them all busy with other customers. He couldn't complain; business had been slowly picking up the last few weeks. They had talked about it briefly and decided it was just early Christmas traffic. Whatever it was his little gun shop was doing very well. He shut the leger and stowed it under the counter before standing up and addressing the new arrivals.

"Can I help you, ladies?"

The woman stopped gazing around and walked over to him. The younger one sized him up, while the older one gazed at the row of handguns in the case between them.

"Do you have any tasers?"

Another one, he thought. For some reason tasers were flying off the shelf lately. He'd sold out of them last month and had increased his order for more just in time. The man on the phone had told him they were having a hard time keeping up with the increased demand. So, it wasn't only him that was selling out. He'd briefly wondered why but then realized that he didn't really care. With the media and the current administration jacking up the fear factor every night on the news, everyone was getting paranoid. And fear was good for business. As a result, he had limited the inventory he kept in the case and raised the prices by ten percent. Sales hadn't slowed down. He was considering jacking up the price further.

"I still have a couple left in the case, here. Do you have a certain kind in mind?"

"What kinds are there?"

"Well, basically, two: you have the design that shoots a pair of darts which implant into the targets skin and then initiate the shock; and you have the contact type, which requires you to be close enough to place the weapon against them to deliver the shock."

"And ... it'll stop somebody, without killing them?"

"Won't kill them; it works by shutting down the signals from the brain to the muscles. I know a few people who have had to use them, and most of them say that just pulling the thing out and giving the attacker a demonstration is enough."

"A demonstration?" the older one asked.

"Like this." Stan unlocked the case and retrieved a taser from the top row. He clicked it on, held it out and pressed the trigger. At the top of the device, a bright arch of electricity began to jump between the two metal probes. The loud crackle of arching electricity cut through the many conversations going on, and the whole store turned to see what was going on. The two women flinched and stepped back.

"Oh! That's ... convincing."

"Yes, it is. This is a popular model. Small enough to fit in your purse or pocket and easy to use—just turn it on and pull the trigger. If you'd like, we have other models that double as flashlights—a little bigger, but they have the same amount of power."

Stan glanced across the room to see one of his people smiling in his direction. They all enjoyed scaring the naive customers from time to time. It was cruel, but it also usually resulted in a sale.

"Can I?" The woman held out her hand.

"Sure. Just hold it here, and the trigger is this button on the side."

The young woman held out the device and pressed the button, the crackle of the electricity again filled the room.

"Wow. It doesn't jump or anything. You want to try?"

Her friend gingerly took the device and repeated her moves. The noise was now a bit irritating, and a few of the other customers paused their questions while they waited for them to stop.

"Okay, that's enough for me." The woman handed the device back with a nervous laugh before turning to her friend. "What do you want to do?"

"I think it's what I want."

"No pepper spray? Not a gun?"

"No. Carol had her pepper spray go off in her purse while she was driving. She almost drove into a semi, and she had Jimmy in the backseat! She couldn't even see to get him out of it. They both had to go to the emergency room. And a gun is too much. Maybe when Roy has time to teach me, but not now."

"Okay. I guess I'll get one, too, then."

"Two, then?" Stan asked.

"Three, actually. I want to get one for my daughter, for Christmas. She's away at school."

"Okay, I only have three left, but one of them is pink. Is that okay?"

"Pink? Seriously?"

"They come in black or pink, yes."

The two women shared a look and then some quick laughter. "I guess Sherri can have the pink one; she'd like that."

"Okay. Two black and one pink."

Stan smiled and pulled the boxes from the shelves below the case. A few minutes of sales-talk later, and he'd added spare batteries and charges to the pile. The items were bagged up. The woman both paid in cash. Something that was rare in most places, but not uncommon in his shop. Soon, they were on their way. Stan watched them walk across the street and get into a grey minivan, just like the suburban moms he had labeled them as. He'd wait until they were gone before replacing the inventory in the display.

The two women dropped the bag in the backseat among three others, before consulting a list. The naïve suburban mom façade was quickly dropped.

"That brings us to six total. We need at least two more."

"What else?"

"Body armor. You see any in that store?"

"No, but the next one has it, I think. What about the airhorns?"

"Next time. We don't want to buy too much in one day. Two more tasers today, and that's it. In three or four days, we'll go out after burner phones. Somebody else will get the air horns."

"Okay. Where to?"

"The next shop is on the south side. Can we make it before they close?"

"I think so."

STEPHEN MOPPED the sweat from his forehead and then shielded his eyes from the African sun in an attempt to see the well a few hundred yards to the south. The heat rising off the sunbaked earth distorted his view, but he was able to see the vanes of the windmill turning in the slight breeze.

A pair of women left the group around the pump and walked toward him, heavy plastic bottles of water balanced on their heads. The water was clear and clean, and smiles adorned their faces. It was the result of several months of work. Before, the water had come from a nearby river, one polluted by herbicide runoff and raw sewage. The people had no choice in the dry season but to drink and bath in the same water. The new well had been driven deep, and the wind-driven pump had made it much easier to draw the clean water to the surface. The only issue now was that the water attracted the nearby wildlife, some of which had no problem regarding the people as food.

He checked the African sky, but it remained as cloudless as it had for several weeks. The summers were getting longer and hotter every year. The rains should have been here already. Once they arrived, the area would bloom overnight with the dusty earth turning dark and then green. But life would be hard for everyone, even the animals, until that day arrived.

"Pumps working okay?"

Stephen turned to see his partner Tom walking up, his floppy camouflage hat keeping his bald head from getting sunburned. His muscular frame off-set Stephen's slim one, but they were otherwise very much alike. They had been together since the army. Both of them medically discharged after being seen together at an off-base club. The rules had changed since then, but they had already left that life behind.

Returning home, they had both been outcast by their conservative families and chose to settle among friends in San Francisco. When two of those friends had been killed on a trip to Idaho simply for being gay, they had used the skills the army had taught them to extract justice. Shortly after, a tall man had met them while on a rural hike. Striking up a conversation, they quickly learned that the encounter was no accident.

A month later they had the titles of Shepherd Number Seven and Eight. Thinking it safer to spend as much time out of the country as possible, the two now worked for various overseas charities. Usually in places their former country ignored. The land here in this African nation held neither oil, nor gold—just people trying to eke out an existence under the constant threat of starvation, disease, and tribal warfare. The new well was a big part of that.

"So far, it's doing better than I expected. I'm glad we were able to put in the beefier model, hopefully it lasts for a decade or so."

"Either way, it should knock down the cholera problem."

"Let's hope so. How's your treatment plant coming along?"

"It's slow-going, but we're making progress. I mean, you can only dig so fast with a few shovels."

"Maybe the General can arrange for a backhoe to be air-dropped in?"

Tom laughed at that. "Not sure where he'd find one within a hundred miles, but it never hurts to ask. You checked in yet today?"

Stephen glanced at his wrist. He'd broken his

watch while working on the tower the previous day, and Tom had given him his.

"It's time right now, actually. Be right back."

Tom mopped sweat from under his hat, while Stephen moved off to their tent. Draped across its roof were a pair of solar panels. The cables led inside to the battery chargers for the satellite phone and the laptop. They checked in every day at noon, and again at six pm, before shutting down for the night and reading whatever William sent them about what was going on back home. They had returned to the States a few times, to escort supplies back to the village and to perform the occasional mission, so Tom wasn't surprised when Stephen emerged a few minutes later with a frown on his face.

"We're being called in."

"Okay. Both of us, you mean?"

"All of us. It's Rubicon."

Tom took the news silently, watching the smiling woman and their jugs full of clean water get closer. The woman chattered and laughed as they traveled, and Tom wished he could hear what they were saying. The people would be sad to see the two of them go, and they would be just as sad for leaving them, but the mission had been waiting for the right time.

Evidently, that time had come.

"Okay."

MILT EXAMINED the stacks of paper on his desk. Where had he seen it? The one on the right, he decided. He shuffled through it for ten minutes before the document found its way into his hand.

He'd used the pink highlighter that day, and it drew his eyes to the Vehicle Identification Number. The van in the storage unit had been consumed by the fire. That hadn't stopped the FBI forensics team from taking it apart and examining every inch, including the engine. A part number had been stamped into the upper manifold, and with it, and some pressure from the FBI on the manufacturer, they had been able to trace down the make and the model. Combined with the charred mechanical options, they had narrowed it further until Milt had been sent the vehicles VIN.

Seventeen characters long, a combination of letters and numbers that allowed someone with the know-how and available database to track a vehicle all the way back to its factory origin. The number and its corresponding dates told him the van had rolled off the assembly line in Claycomo,

Missouri, in early 2013, and was shipped to a dealership in LA, sold to a plumber in Encino, and then traded in on a new one two years later. The van had then sat on the used lot for five months, before being bought by the missing member of The Twelve Shepherds.

But how had the transaction happened? That was his job.

A dummy corporation. That was no surprise. This one had used the address of a Pac-N-Mail in a strip-mall outside Pasadena to hide its tracks. An agent had paid the place a visit and discovered that the account was attached to a PO Box which had been allowed to expire after the first six-month payment. The payment had been in cash, and the employee currently behind the desk was a new one. A dead end.

Or was it? Remembering the vacant lot, he began examining the area around the strip-mall. It was the usual suspects. A Dollar Store. A pool supply company. A furniture store. A hair salon. A sandwich shop. A dry cleaner. He checked each one and found nothing.

He then checked the owner of the mall. A development company with a long history of such businesses. One hundred and four of them, to be exact. Mostly in southern California and Florida.

Milt was ready to give up, when a notation caught his eye.

The strip-mall was new. Less than eight months old. It had gone from a vacant lot with a condemned building in one corner, to a slab of concrete and multiple stores in a matter of months. Who had owned it before that? Milt began digging.

An hour later, he had the sales history for the property. A list of standard commercial development companies, many of them subsidiaries of subsidiaries. But Milt was in his element and soon had then all sorted and labeled and grouped, until he found it.

The real owner of the land was General Developments. A real estate company with worldwide holdings. Only one of which was a commercial retail property.

Its owner name was listed as General Nils Marr.

Milt took the paper and walked it to the wall in his office. He'd removed all manner of photos, diplomas, and other decoration in favor of using the drywall as a giant bulletin board. The paper went up at the end of a long line of similar ones that had started with the van. It was now the second trail leading to the man. Coincidence?

Maybe. After all, the man's company was huge. Billions in assets sprinkled all over the world. The odds of it happening were not outside the realm of probable. Maybe even less than that.

Still.

He stared at it for another few minutes before rounding his desk and snatching up the phone. It rang before he could remember to check the time. He often lost track and would call people at odd hours because of it. The clock read 5 P.M. Hopefully Jack was still at the office.

The line went to voicemail, and he hung up without leaving one. He hated voicemail.

Tapping a pen on the desk, he decided to switch gears. He typed out a quick email telling Jack what he had found and sent it out. He then compiled the information into one file and uploaded it to the Shepherds case file. That way, Jack, and anyone else with access, could see it and make a decision on what to do with it.

10

"We must build a confrontational movement to reclaim our democracy, a movement committed to active and sustained protest against the present order."

—Mark Lloyd

Senator Lamar re-crossed his legs and stared at the one-page his secretary had handed him on the way out. He wasn't reading it; it was to appear busy and keep the prying eyes from thinking it would be a good time to disturb him. The eyes of Teddy Roosevelt seemed to follow him when he had entered the room, and he'd declined the offered coffee from the president's body man, before finding a seat at the end of the table.

Through the glass doors, he could see that the West Wing was busy. Staffers flowed by in both directions, many of them glancing in to see the number three man in the line of ascension. Despite his position and length of time in the Senate it wasn't often he came to the White House—especially alone. But he and the president had known each other a long time, so when the request for a one-on-one had come, it had been reluctantly granted.

The curved door across the hall opened, and he saw the head of Charlie Parker emerge. He looked through the glass to see the senator waiting, before leaving the room and shutting the door behind him. He took two steps across the hall and repeated the process to join the senator.

"Senator Lamar. Sorry to keep you waiting; he's on a call with the Mayor of New York and the Ambassador to the UN. Should be just a minute or two."

"Parking tickets?"

"I'm sorry?"

"The diplomats think they can park wherever they want. The mayor eventually gets enough complaints and starts towing cars. The diplomats complain to the ambassador, and the ambassador foolishly thinks it's something the president can smooth over. Happens in every administration."

"Really? I didn't—"

"I only need five minutes."

"About that, is there something I can—"

"Nope."

Parker waited for the man to say more, but the senator silently returned to his briefing paper and ignored him. He was on a fishing expedition and the senator knew it. It wasn't going to work. The two waited in silence until the president's body man appeared in the doorway.

"The President will see you now, sir."

"Thanks." Lamar got to his feet, his six-two frame towering over Parker.

"Mr. Parker. I'll see you on my next visit, I'm sure." Don't follow me was the interpretation. They shook hands, and the senator followed the body man across the hall. The door shut behind them.

"Yes, sir," Parker said to it. He waited for a

count of twenty before heading straight to Cook's office.

———

INSIDE THE OVAL, Lamar was treated to the president rounding the desk, as the door on the opposite side closed behind the body man.

"Remy! Good to see you. How's the family?"

"Good, sir. Rita is back to work, and Tessa just started at Stanford."

"Her heart?"

"The new drugs are working well—no rejection issues. She wants to play tennis, but the docs say not yet."

"Amazing what they can do, these days. Your child is a miracle."

"Yes, she is."

"Have a seat and tell me what's on your mind."

Lamar gave the door leading to the chief of staff's office a long look, and the president took the cue and shut it, before finding his normal spot on the armchair. Lamar planted himself directly across from him, on the edge of the couch.

"The pilot."

The president sighed. "Look, Rem. I know the man is the son of a friend of yours, but they tell me a rescue could be more dangerous than waiting right now."

Lamar said nothing at first; he just gave the man his full gaze.

"With all due respect, Walt. That's the public line. Why are you really waiting?"

The president's face fell. The two men knew each other too well. They had attended college together, and then both risen through the political ranks. Despite a few disagreements along the way, there was a deep respect. The fact that he got away with using the president's first name was a testimony to that. The president squirmed in the chair and tapped the armrest a few times before replying.

"It would be best for the region if the Kurds were to rescue him. If we go in, it makes ISIS look weak, and we need the public to think the opposite. If the Kurds make progress, we can arm them more without the public backlash."

"Balance of power. Is that what this is about? We arm all the parties involved in the region equally, in the hope that they think twice about going to war with each other when ISIS is gone?"

"In as few words, yes."

Lamar leaned back and contemplated his friend.

"Bullshit."

He spat the word out and it sounded unusually loud and vulgar in the room they were in. It caused the president's lips to tighten.

"Did you just call me a liar, Senator?"

Lamar softened his tone, but he didn't let up on the man. "Don't give me this crap, Walt. I've been in this town too long, and we're both too old to be bullshitting each other. You've never done this before with me, so why now? What's going on?"

The president looked away and out the windows behind the desk. He could just make out the signs of the protesters on the other side of the fence. They had become a fixture.

"It's complicated, Rem."

"Too complicated for an old friend?"

The president turned and met his gaze.

"I don't want to include you."

Lamar nodded. He saw it now; it was as he had suspected. He turned away before speaking toward the wall.

"I don't need to know what they want, but if it calls for the sacrifice of one of our pilots ... what the hell happened to you, Walt? How is this even a debate?"

"There are thousands of men, just like him, to consider."

"No, no, there are not. And you know it."

The president suddenly felt the need to pace. He did two laps before pointing at his friend.

"And if ten die going in after him?"

"That's the job. But it's never a question of numbers. It's a question of faith. It's a promise we make to them when we send them off to war. They don't become political pawns for someone's agenda. You know that!"

"But there are political ramifications! What if—"

"Only after," Lamar cut him off. "Never before."

The president placed his hands on the desk and cursed. The room was a prison in many ways. Truman had called it the nicest cell in the federal system. Bush had said the room was oval so there were no corners to hide in. He agreed with them both.

"Never before, Walt," Lamar repeated quietly. "Go get the boy. We'll fight the fallout together. I'll help you."

The president deflated and walked around the desk, before lowering himself into it with a heavy sigh. He shared a look with his old friend, and they both grimaced at the position they were in.

"This job sucks."

Lamar nodded. "Sometimes."

"It should be you sitting here. I told them that four years ago."

"They picked you."

"Still."

"Maybe when you're done with it." Lamar brushed the thought aside.

The president snorted. They both fell silent for a minute.

Lamar rose to leave and waved his friend back down. He'd said what he needed to say. It was time to go and let the man make his own decision. He'd know soon enough what that decision was going to be.

"I know the way out." He made it as far as the door.

"Hey, Rem?"

"Yes, Mr. President?"

"Thanks."

"Anytime, sir."

The senator opened the door and let himself out, greeting the man's secretary and staff on the way. The body man appeared in the doorway.

"You have a phone call waiting with the Secretary of Energy, sir. And a meeting with the Joint Chiefs, in thirty minutes."

The president waved the young man in and motioned for him to shut the door. He did so and approached the desk.

"Sir?"

The president nodded to himself, as if he'd made an important decision. When he spoke, his voice was strong.

"Push the phone call with the Secretary to later this afternoon and move the meeting with the Chiefs to the Situation room. But before that, I need you to get me something."

"More shopping, sir? Your wife's birthday isn't until next month."

"It's not that; I need something else. And I need you to be quiet about it."

He explained what he needed in less than a minute, and the boy's eyes widened at the request.

"I need it right now."

"Yes, sir."

MARCUS SAT AT HIS DESK, half-listening to the homeless woman in front of him explain her latest issue with the Social Security office. The phone on his desk had hold-music playing, the kind that he was sure had been picked with the intention of making people hang up. Fortunately for his client, he had grown immune to it after the first few months of his job here at the legal clinic. He glanced through her file while they waited, trying not to look at the computer screen, but the message screamed for his attention. From the heading, he knew it was from William, and the subject line was one he had not heard of in some time.

His client stopped for a beat, and Marcus waited to see if he had missed a question. He hadn't, and the woman picked up where she had left off after a cleansing breath. Her story was like many he heard on a regular basis. Her name was Emma, and she was a member of a growing sub-category which they called "the revolving home-less." Emma had a minimum wage job, so there was no hope of private housing anywhere in her future. She was long past the point of even dreaming about it.

Since the minimum wage had not kept up with the rising cost of housing, she got further and further behind every month. Despite the Department of Housing and Urban Development saying that she should only spend a third of her income on a roof over her head, seventy percent of her earnings went toward keeping her and her two children in a small one-bedroom hotel room.

She was enrolled in two government assistance programs, but the last two administrations had saw fit to cut their budgets, so less money was available to help keep her off the streets. Every six to eight months she would miss a rent payment, and since it was a hotel, and not subject to eviction laws, she would quickly find herself homeless. It took very little to trigger such an event. A missed paycheck. A trip to the emergency room. A theft. Any one of them resulted in them losing the shelter she had labored hard to maintain.

When it happened, Emma did what most did and turned to friends and relatives. Unfortunately, most were in the same boat as she was. The majority of them also lived in hotels with occupancy rules, or subsidized housing that had the same. Wishing to avoid the shelters at all costs, they would shuffle from one temporary home to another, sometimes dividing her kids among a few different places, until she could find a new place, or the social workers got wind of the situation and took the kids. All this under the constant temptation of drugs and alcohol that permeated the homeless community.

Today, the kids were with a sister, one whose

address she was unable to recall. Marcus hadn't pushed the issue. Emma had found new housing, but the landlord at her last address was withholding her mail from her until she paid the rent he was owed. Something that was illegal as hell, but not unheard of. Marcus had already solved that issue by making a phone call and adopting his pissed-off lawyer voice. Emma had listened with wide-eyed shock as Marcus tore into the man, not letting him speak more than three words, before cutting him off and threatening all kinds of legal action.

The landlord had quickly caved, and Marcus had used the opportunity to convince Emma that she should make the office, here, her new mailing address, explaining that she could move around as much as she needed too now without losing her check. The landlord had agreed to send the mail to him. Now it was only a matter of letting the Social Security office know of her new mailing address. That was a simple task that would require about an hour of hold music and two minutes of conversation to accomplish. In the meantime, he stewed.

The music finally ended, and Marcus quickly held up a finger to silence the woman, before addressing the person on the other end. He compared her name to a list on the wall and determined they had spoken a few times before. He used the notes on her to make the call personal, and soon the woman cut through the red tape, and he had his chore accomplished. His client sat in awe as she had when he had berated the landlord a few minutes ago. The call quickly ended, and he walked her to the door, the relief putting a smile on her face as she shuffled off down the sidewalk.

Marcus locked the door and returned to his office. Before he even sat down, he grabbed the mouse and clicked to open the message. Reading it twice, his eyes widened when seeing the code word. The date was a shock as well. He made a few notes in his own personal shorthand, and then stuffed the note in a pocket, before writing a longer one explaining his sudden absence to the two street lawyers he worked with. A family emergency, the details of which he was vague about. He apologized and would return as soon as possible. He made a similar note for the kitchen and asked his partner to deliver it for him. After that, he scrubbed all evidence of the email from the computer, and after one long look at the shabby furniture and dusty file cabinets, left the office.

There was nothing he needed at his small

apartment, so he headed straight for the storage facility twenty miles away. Once there, he switched vehicles, hiding a few items from the shelves inside the plain white panel van, before pulling it outside and locking the door behind him.

The drive to West Palm Beach would only take a few hours. He planned to do it without stopping. Another storage unit awaited him there, one he had purchased and stocked over a year ago. One that was only a few minutes driving time from his target. He reviewed the file on the man in his head, as he made his way to I-75.

PARKER IGNORED the man's secretary and knocked as he entered. Cook looked up with a phone to his ear, and Parker gave him the universal signal for "wrap it up."

"Yeah, okay, Matt. I'll get back to you. I've gotta go; the man's calling for me." He hung up without waiting for a reply.

"What?"

"He changed the meeting."

"I'm going to need a little more than that."

"The meeting with the Joint Chiefs. He moved it to the Situation Room. Did you know?"

"That's in twenty minutes. How did you—"

"He did it after meeting with Senator Lamar. Nancy told me right after he left."

Cook sank back into this chair, while Parker chose to pace the room.

"It has to be the pilot."

"We don't know that," Cook countered.

"What else can it be? There was nothing in the Early Bird, no threats on the horizon at the CIA briefing this morning. Did you hear anything new?"

"No," Cook reluctantly admitted.

"So, what do we do?"

"You do nothing. I'll attend the briefing, and we'll see what's on his mind."

"But—"

"Go back to your office, before someone starts wondering and making speculations."

Parker nodded twice and moved toward the door. Cook stopped him for a second with his parting comment.

"Try not to make any yourself."

11

"To make democracy work, we must be a nation of participants, not simply observers."

—Louis L'Amour

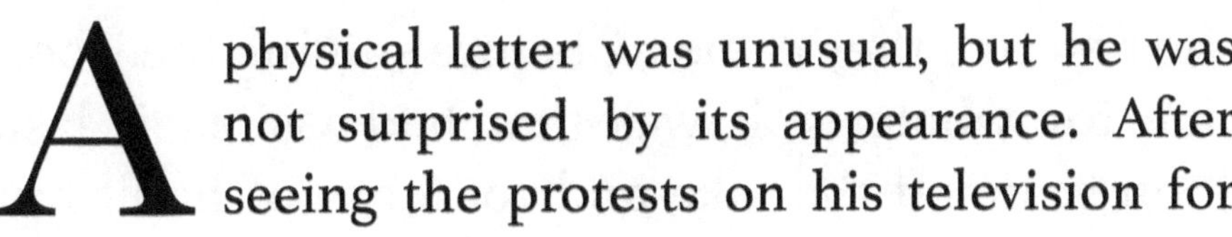

A physical letter was unusual, but he was not surprised by its appearance. After seeing the protests on his television for the past few nights only grow in number, he'd almost been expecting its arrival. He read it twice before sinking into his chair.

Rubicon. He wasn't sure if the time would ever come, yet here it was.

It was a good thing, he decided.

Irving chose that moment to rise from his new favorite spot up against the back door and padded over to nuzzle his hand. John obliged by scratching him behind the ears.

"A new job, Irving," he told the dog. "Perhaps, the last one, even,"

Irving nudged him harder and then walked toward the door, where he looked back to see if John had followed.

"Kinda late."

Irving scratched the door and yipped in reply.

"A sunset stroll? Okay, then."

John rose and fetched the leash. He'd never need it, but you never knew when you might encounter another dog walker, one whose dog wasn't as well behaved as Irving.

They left the quiet house, and Irving peed on the first tree they came to, before sniffing the wood line for whatever it was that had visited it last. John scanned the lake and road out of habit but saw nothing beyond the usual fireflies and other evening creatures. The deer would be out foraging soon, and he hoped to see some before they returned. He clicked his tongue for Irving to follow and set off down the road.

They each had a target. One assigned based on each member's location and individual skills. Many of the Shepherds were in close contact with theirs, according to Dayton. John did not have that luxury, but he'd established a way in several months ago and exercised it twice to establish himself. It would require a drive to Houston, and a bit of a disguise and some acting, but it was nothing he had not done before.

Irving suddenly bounced through the tall grass after something he had scared up. Most likely a rabbit or raccoon. He never caught anything, and for that John was glad. It wouldn't be eaten, and Irving would most likely come away with an injury. A coon could really tear a dog up if he had no choice but to fight. Despite his current job, John was against senseless killing.

Were his planned actions in that category? He'd thought about it long and hard. for some time. The man he was assigned to had a long list of offences, most of them committed to benefit only himself and the other members of the Trust. Many had suffered, both inside the country and outside, so establishment of guilt was not the issue. It was the question of change. Would John's actions result in the change the General had envisioned? He truly hoped so. His contribution certainly would not, but perhaps the combined effort ...

He dismissed the thought. He had no idea of the man's full plan, but only of his small part and that of his fellow Shepherds. It would take many more than them to accomplish the goal. Millions. All of them speaking as one. Nameless, faceless soldiers. Revolutionaries. All of them working together, fighting side-by-side for a common goal, without knowing the man or woman they fought next to. It was a bold undertaking. One for which the outcome was a dangerous unknown. They could emerge on the other side with nothing but opportunity, or they could find themselves all doomed by their own efforts. Still, they had no choice but to try. John believed that most of all.

They reached the small rise in the road, and John took the opportunity to watch the sun kiss the horizon and then slowly sink out of sight. The bats were working the field, and he enjoyed the way their broken-wing flight took them in and out of the setting disc of amber. It had just disappeared, leaving a pale sky of pink and orange behind when Irving joined him. He was panting hard from his half-hearted chase and covered in seeds from the tall grass.

"What a sight, huh, boy?"

Irving sat on the cooling asphalt and watched as well as the sky darkened. John finally turned away and mumbled for the dog to follow. The temperature was now dropping rapidly. Winter was coming to Texas.

"A few more weeks, and we might see some snow. Getting later every year."

Irving said nothing; he merrily padded alongside as they made their way home, now too tired to do any further exploration. On arrival, he'd get a quick brushing to remove the seeds before a drink, and then a return to his new favorite spot for the evening. His wants were few.

John, however, was lost in thought. His mind was now going over the plan and its countless contingencies. There would be no room for error. He had kept the mission as simple as possible in an effort to cut down on surprises. It was a good plan, but he would examine it from every angle until there was no more time to do so.

He didn't think about what would happen

after—there were too many unknowns for that. He'd have to just wait and see.

"THINK IT WILL GO ANYWHERE?"

They were watching the protest on the multiple TVs in Ed's office. The last few news cycles had been full ones. First the Shepherds escape, then the editorial published by them on the same day they took out a child molester. The protest that story sparked had made the front page for the next two days. This was followed by the Hurricane in Florida, and then the story of Jack Randall being caught in a small town with armed drug traffickers while it raged. The hurricane was out over the Atlantic now, but the storm of protestors was still going strong.

"There's a new one outside the state capitol, in Tallahassee." Ed muted one screen and turned the sound on of another. The two reporters struggled to match the sound with the proper screen.

"No surprise there," Danny quipped. "The guy is not well-liked."

"An understatement," Steve echoed. "Your old paper didn't give him enough flak."

"True. But they didn't have an owner with deep

pockets like we have here. They had to toe the line. Nobody liked the guy there, though, believe me. You know what they called him?"

"No?"

"Voldemort."

"What?"

"The bad guy, from *Harry Potter*?"

"Never read it."

"Seriously? You need to expand your horizons. Anyway, the description fits, both physically and character-wise."

"I'll add it to my list. What is it about the Governor of Florida they're protesting?"

Ed had been taking notes. "The same. Corruption mostly. He passed a law requiring anyone getting welfare to take a drug test, then gave the testing contract to a company owned by his wife. His Attorney General is under investigation for taking bribes in return for dropping state investigations into some fake online university that a Palm Beach billionaire started up. It's since gone class action. The list goes on and on. Florida seems to be a popular place for these types."

"The original Sam Shepherd took out a target, there," Danny said, "and the Shepherds themselves have killed three around the state since they started. It gives Florida the lead."

"Something to be proud of," Steve added.

They watched in silence for a few more minutes until a commercial came on. Steve spun his chair around.

"You didn't answer my question."

"What was it again?"

"Will this—" he waved his hand at the multiple screens and the protests on each one "—go anywhere?"

Ed tossed the remote down and tapped his foot on the leg of his desk. The wood was gradually being chipped away, and someday the desk would collapse, but until that day came, he would continue to do so. It helped him think.

"If they keep it up, and their numbers continue to grow, maybe. I'm sure we'll see some lip service given and a few bills passed to placate the people as usual, but beyond that, not much. As soon as the crowds start getting smaller, the pols will declare victory and go back to business as usual."

Steve nodded at the answer, and Danny took that as a sign of agreement. He quickly countered.

"I'm not so sure. When have we ever seen nationwide protests like this before? They're in almost every state now, and they seem ... different, to me, anyway."

"Different how?"

"I don't know. I can't put my finger on it yet, but they seem ... organized? No, that's not the word. Disciplined, maybe? Nobody is screaming or provoking the police. I haven't heard of one arrest yet, have you?"

"No."

"Maybe they've learned is all. They know what they can and can't get away with now from the whole Occupy campaign."

"Still ... " Danny let the subject drop, but it had triggered his curiosity. He suddenly had an urge to join the protestors. He searched the screens until he found the local station. It looked like a crowd was forming around the White House again. It was only a couple of blocks. He jumped up and headed for the door.

"Where you off to?"

"I'm gonna hit the streets for a bit," he managed to yell before the door shut. Ed watched him race off toward the elevators.

"Think the kid's right, Ed?"

"Dunno. If he is, though ... "

"Yeah."

"IF WE SEE any more activity at the launch site, we'll have to notify the South Koreans and the Japanese."

The president nodded from the end of the table. The briefer was a Colonel with the Strategic Air Command, the man responsible for ballistic missile defense. The North Koreans were still playing with missiles while their country starved. It was a necessary but unsurprising briefing.

"We have assets in the area to counter in the event of a launch?"

"Yes, sir."

"Very well. Thank you, Colonel."

"Thank you, Mr. President."

It was the last item on the agenda, and the men and women around the table gathered their papers and made ready to leave when the chairman of the joint chiefs of staff noticed that the president hadn't yet moved. He cleared his throat, and the others took the cue. A glance at Cook got him only a shrug.

"Sir? Was there something else you wanted to—"

"The pilot. What's his status?"

"Its ... unchanged, sir. He's still in the tent and only moves within it. There's been a few trucks and some other traffic moving through, but the man is still in place."

And the operation to retrieve him?"

"Valkyrie One, sir. It remains on stand-by."

The room fell silent as the man tapped a thumb on the metal table. The chairman exchanged inquiring looks with his fellow joint chiefs, but they all looked as surprised as he was. Cook squirmed in the silence until he could no longer stand it.

"Sir, I don't think it's a good—"

The president cut him off, "Chances of a successful rescue?"

The Chairman gestured to his army liaison and the man spoke from memory, "Eighty percent, sir. Slightly less if the weather is not optimal."

"Sir, the Kurds are getting closer every day. If they can—"

The president cut his chief of staff off again, "How soon can you launch?"

The Colonel exchanged a look with his counterpart in the Air Force. He consulted a paper from a folder in his stack and held up five fingers.

"We'd need about two hours to prep, and another five to get on sight."

"The weather?"

"It'll clear tonight, with forty percent cloud

cover at high altitude. Not the most optimal, but within parameters."

Cook wisely held his tongue, while the president tapped the table some more.

"Who's got a cigarette?"

An aid leaped forward and shook one out of the pack in his pocket. The president accepted it with a nod, and the chairman lit it himself with his silver Zippo. The man drew hard and then blew a cloud over their heads before examining the map that had been brought up on the large screen. The assets for operation Valkyrie One were in place and labeled. The man followed the lines to the tiny green dot in central Syria. He took another drag and then rose to his feet. The men and woman all stood with him.

"Navy Lieutenant Andrew Bunker," he spoke.

"Yes, sir," the Chairman confirmed. Was it a question?

"Go get him."

The cigarette went into the glass of water in front of him with a hiss before he turned and stalked out of the room.

The Chairman shared a look with Cook before the Chief of Staff moved to follow. He then turned to find the people all staring after him.

The Chairman snapped his fingers, and the

man standing against the wall lifted the phone and brought it to him. He had already dialed.

"Lieutenant Parker? This is the Chairman. I have a go-order for operation Valkyrie One. Repeat, operation Valkyrie One is a go. Acknowledge."

The man listened for a moment before replying.

"Good luck, Lieutenant."

"*Anywhere, anytime ordinary people are given the chance to choose, the choice is the same: freedom, not tyranny; democracy, not dictatorship; the rule of law, not the rule of the secret police.*"

—*Tony Blair*

"How is it?"

Waqas smiled as he changed the

dressing over the incision. The soldiers had brought the pilot to him slung in a blanket soon after his plane had crashed, and he had set the man's leg blindly on a large kitchen table covered in plastic with the light of several flashlights. His few surgical instruments had been sterilized in boiling water, and the rest were what you might find in the average man's toolbox. He'd used every suture he'd had and irrigated the wound as much as possible as he'd sewn in an effort to fight off the coming infection.

He could not imagine a more primitive setting. It had been a fool's errand from the beginning, one that had little hope for success, but the prodding gun barrels and loud demands of the ISIS leader had compelled him to put forth his best effort. The fact that the man had not bled to death on the table was a miracle in itself. That he had survived the infection doubly so. Perhaps the pilot had someone watching over him? Whatever the reason, the leg was no longer the biggest threat to his life. The antibiotics had worked, and the wound was healing, covering the jagged wound with a thick layer of scar tissue. The color was returning to normal. If left alone, he would be walking again in a few more months. If they both lived that long.

"It's healing nicely now."

"It is. How is your cough?"

"Better. Thanks to you."

"I did what I could." He shrugged. "We are ... how do you say? Out of the pan?"

"Out of the frying pan and into the fire?"

"Yes, that is it. Is the traction comfortable? We can start to lessen it now."

"That would be great."

Waqas worked the rope and repositioned the padded end of the board in Archie's crotch. Without access to a modern traction splint, it was the best he could do. Archie had adjusted it once himself and accidently pulled the thing loose. The pain of that mistake was still fresh in his mind, so he let the doctor work the rope and knots to ease the pressure a bit.

As he watched him work, he thought about the doctor's words. There was another idiom. One that was distinctly American. 'Out of the frying pan and into the fire' was not something the man would have heard in his home country, nor in England.

"Who taught you?"

"I am sorry?"

"English."

"I learned in school. In Pakistan, they start the children on languages in the first few years. A holdover from European influence I believe." He tightened the last knot. "Better?"

"Yes."

Waqas inspected his work and then glanced at his patient's face. What he saw there gave him pause.

"What is it? Is there pain?"

"Out of the frying pan. You didn't learn that in school, nor in England."

Waqas sat back on his heels and let out a breath.

"No. No, I did not."

"Am I the first American you've treated?"

Waqas glanced outside and then at the boy. With the jerk of his head, he ordered him out. The boy left without a word. Waqas watched him go and then checked the area outside, before returning to sit close to Archie. His voice fell until it was barely audible.

"There was a woman. An American. She was ambushed and captured while working for the American government. She fought them, and they broke her arm. I treated her for some time before they moved her again. I overheard the men talking. The vehicles were attacked by Russian aircraft. And then the Syrian army came for what was left. Some children saw them. One of them said

they took the woman away. I do not know her condition—only that she was alive when they took
her."

"And she was American, you're sure?"

"She spoke like one, as you can tell from my
own speech. Her teeth had western fillings. I think
she was married, but she never spoke of it. Nor
would she say what she was doing here. I stopped
asking."

"You think she was married?"

"Her finger. It had a pale ring around it. I
would catch her rubbing it, as if something was
missing."

"I see. How long did ISIS have her?"

"I'm not sure. They would take her away for
hours, sometimes days at a time. She would come
back to me beaten. I cared for her as best I could. I
tried to win her trust, but she was very wary of
speaking to me. I think she thought I was one of
them. I did the best I could to ease her pain, but
they would not let her rest."

"The leader?"

"The one you killed, yes. An evil man. Too ...
radical. Not a thinker like the rebel we met. I'm not
sure which to fear more. Or if it even matters."

"You have any idea where she is now?"

"In the hands of Assad. I'm not sure if that is

better or worse. I prefer not to think about it. She was a lovely woman. Intelligent and strong. But I fear that may only prolong her suffering. But since you asked, it was her who taught me the American sayings."

They both fell silent for some time, and the wind chose to fill the quiet with its grip on the tent flap. Waqas crawled over and secured the opening before sitting back with a sigh.

"There are no good deaths under Assad. But I do hope hers was quick."

"What was her name?"

"Valerie."

***

JACK BRUSHED his hair back out of habit and winced when his wedding ring bumped his eye. His face was still bruised and swollen, and it had prompted a variety of facial expressions from passing coworkers when he walked the halls of the Hoover building. He didn't really care right now; he had something else on his mind, and it wasn't the subject of the meeting he was currently in.

Public perception. That's what the man was yapping about. As if the FBI were marketing themselves. They were their own worst enemy in that department anyway. Much like the CIA, the public only heard about their mistakes. When something went not according to plan, it automatically attracted press coverage. The Twelve Shepherds case was very press-heavy, they made sure of it. But countering that was not his job, and he was starting to resent even being here. But he had to placate the politicians, so he had agreed to meet their people. How much more of this he could take, he wasn't sure.

His phone vibrated on the table in front of him, and he jabbed the screen. Danny.

He exchanged a look with Sydney across the table and got a subtle eye roll for an answer. She tapped her watch without breaking eye contact and raised an eyebrow. He checked his own and nodded a "yes" to her unspoken question, before standing up. The man who had been speaking stopped mid-sentence.

"I'm afraid that's all the time I can give you," Jack said. "I have another meeting to attend. Just put all this in a memo, please, and forward it to me ... wherever I may be. Okay?"

Without waiting for an answer, he gathered his files and made for the door. Sydney and Larry did the same, and they were out in the hall before the man could protest.

"We got time?"

"Plenty," she answered. "Robert's waiting outside."

"Danny's just answered my text."

"Let's go."

SAMUEL JACKSON WAS LOSING WEIGHT, for a variety of reasons. With the hurricane gone, the Florida heat had returned with a vengeance, and with the power still out in the club, he was sweating off some pounds. He was also pacing it off. Wearing a path in the tile floor as he walked back and forth, waiting for his cell phone to ring. His crew was overdue. Four men and fifty keys of product were in the wind. Had they been stopped by the storm? Was the satellite phone not working? Had they decided to make a go of it on their own? Wallace wouldn't do that, neither would the kid. The other two hated each other, but still. Fifty keys was a lot, and enemies had come together over much less in the past. Worst case scenario was that the cops had them, but he was sure he would have heard something by now if that was the case. Since the cell phone had started working, he'd been on it constantly, first calling in extra crew, and then putting out feelers for the missing crew. So far, he had come up with a big fat zero.

"You okay, Daddy? You need another drink?"

Jackson frowned at the girl. One of the dancers had somehow made her way there and was now hanging around, for no reason other than she needed a fix and had lost her neighborhood supplier to the storm. She was even dressed for work —or undressed, depending on your point of view. Jackson had put her to work emptying the refrigerators before making her tend bar.

With a warble, his cell phone rang. Jackson snatched it up.

"Wallace?"

"Do I sound like Wallace, Sammy?" the voice spoke back with a thick New England accent.

"Liam? What the hell you want?"

"I got product due in a few days, and I hear you're having problems."

Jackson thought fast and decided it was a good time to tell the truth. "Storm knocked out my usual routes. I had to move it ... another way. Slower, but it's coming."

"You sure?"

A knock on the front door distracted him for a moment, and he waved the girl toward it. She tottered off on her high heels to answer it, her lack of dress not entering her mind.

"Yeah, I'm sure. Couple stops on the way, but you'll have yours soon."

"I don't like what I'm hearing, J. This delay is gonna set me back. I think we need to talk about this when—"

A scream from the front door made Jackson spin in place, and he saw black-clad men wielding shotguns and wearing armor pushing their way in the door and running toward him. He dropped the phone and turned to the stage.

"Police! Nobody move!"

His gun was ten feet away.

He made it halfway there before two men took him to the ground. He knew better than to fight back and silently endured the boots, and knees, and twisted arms, until he was cuffed. He had barely caught his breath when they flipped him over and he was able to eyeball the group. Ten of them. All of them wearing black SWAT gear and armed to the teeth. The letters DEA stood out in thick white letters across their backs. A German Shepherd growled at him from the end of a short leash.

The phone on the floor spoke.

"J? You there? J? What the hell?"

Another cop appeared and pushed his way to the front to squat down in front of Jackson. He picked up the device.

"He'll call you back," he said into it. The line stayed open for a moment and then died.

The man smiled at the number on the screen before setting the phone back down.

"Boston's going to be disappointed."

Jackson said nothing.

"Samuel Jackson, I'm Lyle Smith of the Drug Enforcement Agency. You and I are going to be spending a lot of time together."

He jerked his head, and the agents yanked Jackson to his feet. Smith watched as they walked him and the girl outside and parked them in separate cars. An evidence team walked in to fill the void.

"Tear it apart," Smith told them.

As the team descended on the room, Smith walked outside and pulled his cell phone from his pocket. He used a recently added speed-dial number. It was answered on the first ring.

"We got him."

"THANKS."

Jack pocketed the phone and smiled at his companions.

"They got him."

He got smiles in return. It helped a little. Jack rolled down the partition of the limo and called to the driver.

"Robert? I need you to swing by the *Washington Post*, first, please. Just pull up to the curb outside."

"You got it, Jack," the driver answered.

"Should I ask?" Larry inquired.

"No, probably not."

A few blocks later, they pulled up to the curb in front of the building. A rumpled looking man with a shock of curly red hair was waiting on the curb. On Jack's instruction, Robert pulled up to him, and Jack rolled down the window.

"Danny! Over here."

Danny Drake bent down to look inside the car.

"A Bureau limo, Jack? Am I worthy?"

"Today, you are. Shut up and get in."

Jack slid over, and Danny took his vacated spot on the bench seat. He silently greeted each of them.

"A sour bunch. Want to tell me where we're going?"

"You'll see."

"Okay." Danny folded his hands in his lap and joined the silence.

The car looped around the mall and crossed the Potomac before heading into Arlington. The curves of the road were handled by Robert's expert hands and feet until they arrived at the gate of Arlington National Cemetery and were waved through.

Danny shot a look at Jack. *What is this?* it said.

"I want you to meet a few people, Jack said, "one of which needs his story told."

The limo pulled up to a line of cars. Most were of the cheap rental car variety. A small group were taking their seats.

Sydney led them off, while Jack hung back with Danny.

"We're getting together tonight for some drinks. If you come along, you'll get a story about a great guy. One who deserves a little recognition."

"What kind of story?"

"Drugs. Major trafficking in five cities. The raids and arrests are happening as we speak, all up and down the east coast, including some people right here in DC. Some of them have political connections."

Danny's eyes popped at the statement. "And the guy under the flag?"

"He made it all possible."

Danny stalled. "You buying?"

"Yeah, I'm buying."

Danny gave himself a few paces to think about it before replying. This was unusual, but Jack had never wasted his time before. Could have warned him about the dress code, at least.

"Why me, Jack? Don't get me wrong here—I'm thankful for the head start. I just ... What gives?"

"Two reasons. One, I owe you one; and two, because you're a pretty good guy."

"Okay."

They moved forward to join the crowd at the gravesite. The coffin was draped in the American flag and an honor guard stood at attention nearby.

"Am I ever going to get a chance to ask about the Shepherds case?"

"Not today, Danny. I need some time. When I'm ready, you're my guy."

"Okay."

Jack left Danny standing in the back and joined Sydney. His eyes gathered in the people present. Sheriff Connor Clancy, in full uniform. Jerri Neilson sat with Aaron on one side, and Frank Warner on the other, his arm in a sling with the other holding the hand of the man sat next to him. Aaron fidgeted a bit and rubbed his hand where the two scratches were healing. Jack wondered if Jerri knew how they had gotten there.

On the other side sat Kyle Warner, wearing a heavy coat over hospital scrubs and perched in a wheelchair. He wore a look of painful determination on his face. A uniformed flight medic was close at hand, and an attractive young woman in a Navy uniform—who very much resembled Jerri—sat next to him. She whispered something to him, and he smiled for the briefest of moments.

In the front row sat a small family from Detroit, one that Jack had never met and had only recently spoken with on the phone.

It was a small but fitting group. All of them gathered together to both honor and say a final goodbye to DEA Agent Tyler Turner.

CARL CHALKED his hands one last time before slipping one and then the other back into the crack of the cliff. He shook his head to seat his helmet back and then gazed upward to find his next set of holds. His right ankle was starting to complain from the odd angle he was supporting his body with, so he set his safety line off to the left and pulled himself up. Left leg. Left hand. Chalk. Right hand. Repeat.

He could now see the top of the cliff. Three more moves and he was there. A fellow climber gave him a thumbs up as he pulled himself over the edge. He returned the gesture as he turned and dangled his legs over the chasm. A look down brought a smile to his face, and he clapped his hands together in celebration, releasing a cloud of chalk to the wind. Not his fastest time, but certainly one of his best climbs.

He pulled his line up and stowed it before sitting back and pulling out his sports bottle. The liquid was warm, but it went down easily, as he adjusted the climbing harness out of his crotch while he drank.

"Good timing," his neighbor said, pointing to the horizon off to their right.

Carl turned and saw the storm clouds advancing from the west. The weatherman had given a fifty-percent chance of rain that morning. Carl had muttered a "might rain-might-not," before making his decision and loading up his gear. The weather would turn cold soon, and there weren't many good climbing days left. He could already feel the chill of the evening air approaching. His neighbor got up and started packing in his gear.

The trail down would take over an hour. Half that, if he chose to run it. Carl was a runner.

He decided to allow the fellow climber a few minutes of head start and pulled his phone out to see if he'd missed anything. It had buzzed several times on the way up, and he was not surprised to see the icons stacked across the top of the screen. Massaging the scared muscle of his left leg while he thumbed through his messages was a habit of many years, and he did so without thinking. The deformity of the muscle often brought odd looks, but never when he was on the wall. If anything, they added a level of respect. He wiped the chalk off his hands as best he could before swiping the tiny screen.

An email caught his eye. He glanced around first to ensure himself that the other climber had left, and ignoring the approaching thunder, opened the message.

"Yes, sir," he voiced to the wind. The General was making his move. Rubicon was in play.

Energized by the message, he placed the pack back on his back, swapped his climbing shoes for a set of Teva's, and quickly coiled the rope. Slinging it over his head, he set off down the path. He forwent the run in favor of a walk, so he could think about the mission. The rain arrived before he was halfway to his Nissan Xterra. The roof racks on top and the bike rack hanging off the side spoke of a man who lived outdoors.

He tossed his gear on the backseat and climbed up behind the steering wheel. He toweled his head off, before starting the car and thumbing the seat warmers on to chase the chill from his skin. He forced himself to concentrate on the task, before releasing the brake and driving down off the angled rock he had parked on. The Xterra's multiple headlamps came on and helped him navigate the backroad through the now heavy rain. Before he got to the road, it had become dark, but navigation occupied only a fraction of his brain, as the rest was already planning an equipment list for the mission in Las Vegas.

"Glass cliffs," he said aloud. The idea had come to him on his second recon of the target. Others had presented, but this plan was the one he had always come back to. It was something he was good at.

He rubbed the leg some more as he traveled— the rain always made it ache. Soon, that pain would be redirected.

"Milt? It's Jack. You found something?"

"Hey, Jack. Sorry for the vague email; I hate leaving voicemails."

"No problem. What did you find?"

Milt noted the eagerness in Jack's voice and immediately felt bad. The information was paper-thin. If Jack was hoping for something concrete, he was going to be very disappointed.

"I don't want to get your hopes up, Jack. What I have is little more than what could be called a co-incidence. But I've seen cases move forward on less, so I thought I'd kick it up the chain, ya know?"

"At this point, I'm ready to entertain Internet conspiracy theories."

"That bad?"

"The Shepherds have gone quiet. No new com-munications, and no new victims. They haven't contacted us or the press for over seven weeks now. That's the longest they've gone. We're at a loss as to why."

"I see. Sorry, I tend to get bogged down in the details and miss what's going on. It's kind of the nature of my job, really."

"I imagine. So, what are the details telling you?"

"Another purchase traced back. The van from

the storage unit. We were able to put enough part numbers together to figure out the VIN number. From that, we traced the purchase back to the origin, and as expected, it was the usual mess. I'll spare you the long and short of it, but whoever paid for it used a PO Box at one of those strip mall mailing places for the address. The box was cancelled for non-payment six months after it was opened, and the payment was in cash."

"A dead end," Jack said.

"I thought so. But I remembered the vacant lot from the last trace I ran, so I did some poking around. The strip mall is one of about 140 or so owned by a developer, who does primarily that. Mostly in California and Florida. They all have the same basic footprint. Grocery store, hair salon, Chinese takeout, dry cleaner, you get the picture."

"I don't see the connection."

"Stick with me for a minute here; I'm almost there. The mall was fairly new when the box was used, so I looked into the ownership. The store itself is owned by a retired cop and his wife from Chicago. Clean record. Just a couple who retired and got bored, I think. They run it with a couple part-time employees. No flags there either. Other than the couple taking a crazy number of cruises and trips to Disney, there's nothing there. But I kept looking."

"And?"

"The owner of the strip mall didn't own the land until one month before they broke ground on the mall. They bought it from an outfit called General Developments. A real estate company with worldwide holdings. Only one of which was commercial retail property."

"Is this going where I think it is?"

"The owner of General Developments is our old friend General Nils Marr."

Jack let out a sigh at the news, and Milt waited for more.

"Jack?"

"Yeah, I'm here. What are the odds that this is a coincidence?"

"A little more than plausible, I'd say; it's a big company with a lot of holdings. But ... "

"Yeah, me too."

"What do you want me to do?"

"What can you do?"

"Well, if you have another thread to track down, I can see where it leads. Other than that? I'm not sure."

"If we can find another connection ... " Jack let the thought trail off. Then what? Confront the man? They'd need something solid to even get a grand jury into consideration.

"I'll talk to Syd; maybe she has an idea. Did you update the file?"

"Yeah, right before I emailed you."

"Okay. I'll give it a read. Thanks, Milt. Nice work."

"You got it, Jack."

Jack severed the call and punched up the Shepherds file. It only took a few seconds to find, and Jack saw the information. It was only a few pages. He chose to print it off to read later.

"Not like I have much else to do," he groused.

He picked the phone back up to call Sydney.

COOK TRAILED behind the president as far as the top of the stairs. He'd opened his mouth twice to speak, but the man's pace was a clear indicator that he didn't wish to do so, so Cook had bit his tongue instead. This was uncharted territory. The man had always been pliable. Subject to suggestion from him and a few select others. The occasional outburst or other show of frustration was rare, but not unheard of. This president had a tight rein on his emotions, the result of which gave the outbursts that much more of an impact. Cook now sensed one boiling just beneath the surface, so he silently followed along a pace behind until they reached the oval office.

"Sir?"

"Tell them I want updates every thirty minutes after they launch."

"Yes, sir. I'll be in my office if—"

"All right."

The man stormed past his secretary and into the oval office, slamming the door behind him. His secretary raised an eyebrow in the chief of staff's direction, but he gave her nothing by way of an explanation. Cook retreated toward his own office, only to meet his own secretary in the hallway and the president's body man coming out of his door. He shot a questioning frown at both of them.

"The numbers on the infrastructure bill," the bodyman explained, "I left them on your desk,"

"Thank you." The young man hurried on, and he turned to his secretary.

"Bathroom."

"Okay. Just make sure you shut my door if you leave."

"Sorry, boss."

Cook mumbled something the woman

couldn't make out and stalked into the room. She followed as far as the door.

"Did you want lunch at your desk again?"

"Uh ... sure."

"Anything in particular?"

Cook waved her away. "I ... don't care. Surprise me. And shut the door, please."

The woman did as he asked, well-familiar with her boss's quirks. She knew the signs. Whatever had happened in the situation room, it was going to occupy his mind for the next few hours. That meant the door would stay shut, and the phone calls would be limited. It was not the first time. She'd order a sandwich for him, but the chances of him eating it would be slim. She frowned at him sitting behind the desk, his eyes focused on nothing, as she pulled the door shut.

Cook stewed in the leather chair. How was he going to handle this one? The president obviously didn't want his council on this matter anymore. He'd followed his chief of staff's suggestions for the last several weeks, but that was obviously over. The pilot was political dynamite—millions of dollars of campaign funding rested in the balance. Not to mention the interests of the Trust. To go against them ... it was something Cook didn't wish to think about. There was no good scenario he could picture.

Right now, the military was pushing buttons and pulling levers to get the mission underway. It would take a few hours for that to happen, and then the planes would take off. In under thirty minutes, the number of people involved would reach the thousands. He would have to get the word out now, though, stressing the importance of waiting to take any action that tipped their hand. But something had to be done.

The keys were in his pocket and never anywhere else. He soon had the bottom drawer unlocked, and in the back of it he found the phone.

"Yes?"

"We have a problem."

"What kind of problem?"

"With the Syria plan. The President just gave the order to rescue the pilot."

"Dammit! I thought you said you had handled that?"

"Charles, I told you and your brother that he was going along with the operation, but you can't expect everything to stay that way. The man is not an employee—I can't just order him to do things."

"What changed?"

"I'm not sure, but he did meet with Senator

Lamar this morning, that may have had something to do with it."

"He didn't discuss it with you before he made the decision?"

"No. He gave the order at the end of the morning briefing. But he had to have made up his mind beforehand. He's the one who moved the meeting to the Sit-Room."

There was silence on the other end while the head of the Trust thought this new information over.

"Lamar. We may have to find a way to nullify him. But not today. You've informed Haney?"

"No, I called you first."

"How long?"

"The order just went out fifteen minutes ago. I'd wait at least an hour or longer before revealing that you know anything."

"I need to discuss this with my brother. No moves until you hear from us. I'll call Haney and explore our options. Can you get away?"

"I better stay close."

"Yes, that's probably a good idea. I want to know immediately if there are any changes."

"You will."

The man hung up without warning, and Cook checked the phone to see if it had malfunctioned before deciding it was the man who had ended the call. He replaced the burner in the drawer and locked it, before triggering the intercom.

"I need Mr. Parker."

"I think he's on the Hill, at the moment, sir."

"Then get him here—now."

"Yes, sir."

———

THE PRESIDENT SANK into the leather chair and let it fall back. It was custom-made to fit his frame. The leather seemed to envelop him in a warm embrace the first time he had done so. It had Kevlar layers hidden beneath layers of foam and hide. It was symbolic in a way, a constant reminder of the pleasures and dangers of the job. He rocked a bit, and the mechanism creaked ever so slightly. A flaw. There was always one—no matter how finely something had been crafted, there was always a weak spot.

A knock on the door preceded the head of his body man. The president waved him in and then checked the intercom to assure himself it was off.

"It's in place?"

"Yes, sir."

"Very good. Thank you."

The man left without further comment.

His eyes followed the young man out and he closed the door behind him. The room had four entrances. One to the outer office, where his secretary and body man sat. Another to the hallway across from the Roosevelt room. A third to the portico leading back to the residence. And a fourth, which led to his private study and bathroom, and then on to the office of his chief of staff. He contemplated it now, trying to picture what was happening beyond the thick wood. What was being said? Who was it being said to?

He had an idea.

"Dig a hole," he whispered.

"*Democracy is a device that insures we shall be governed no better than we deserve.*"

—*George Bernard Shaw*

Hugh read the message twice before removing it from his screen. Unlike many of the other Shepherds, he was already in place. Something Dayton had frowned at hard, until Hugh explained that it was just too good of an opportunity to pass up. After seeing the purchase by the target and knowing he had the skills for the job, he had arranged to have William help him get the position. Yacht Captain. It was something he had done growing up, delivering boats to their buyers for a manufacturer in Florida. After a few interviews, he had landed the job. He now not only saw his target on a regular basis, but the man paid him for being there. Hugh loved the irony of the situation.

Yacht Captain. The title sounded good, and he had used it on occasion with the ladies of the city. In the rich man's circle of friends, a few of the younger daughters had shown some interest in him. They found the battle scars and rugged frame he had acquired in the military to be interesting. But he had always managed to keep the temptations at arm's length. He was here for a different reason. One he certainly wasn't going to share with them.

The boat was a trophy, much like everything else in the man's world. Fifty feet of polished wood and fiberglass. It had every bell and whistle the manufacturer could add and few more beyond that. After a voyage of over a thousand miles from its native boat yard, it was now docked in the shadow of the World Trade Center at an exorbitant cost, especially when one factored in that the boat left the dock perhaps only twice a month. Its owner just didn't have the time. A hedge fund manager by title, he had more money than he knew how to spend.

While he often entertained guests on board after a day at the office, he rarely asked Hugh to take the boat out. So, his Captain spent his days taking care of the boat, keeping it spotless and well-maintained. Ready to go at a moment's notice, should the man ever call and want to journey out. Most days Hugh was reduced to only a few hours on board, the rest of his time spent watching the man or listening to his conversations over one of the many bugs he had planted throughout the craft. Conversations that only made him despise his employer and his friends even more.

The owner was only a few yards away from him at the moment, having drinks with one of his Wall Street cronies, as Hugh guided the boat around Liberty Island for the umpteenth time. It was a trip so familiar that he could do it in his sleep. Other than avoiding the traffic in the bay—

mostly tourist boats—it was just a matter of keeping the boat on the path the GPS told him and stroking the man's ego whenever it was called for.

On the boat, small meetings had been happening more often lately. Especially with one man in particular. A corporate raider. The kind who liked to buy up large shares of a company, to the point that he could pressure its board of directors into making the changes he wanted, changes he was prepared to profit off before they even happened. The war had provided many such opportunities lately, and Hugh had found himself sailing up and down the Hudson on many evenings while the two of them plotted in what they thought was a secure location. Hugh had recorded it all and forwarded it to William. A few months back the corporate raider had been added to the list, and Hugh became the only Shepherd to have two Rubicon targets. It was something he had no issue with.

The two men were now sat forward of him, in the main salon, out of the wind and its winter chill. As usual, they were getting louder as the scotch took hold and the wind increased. Hugh noted its direction as he spun the wheel to round the island. Now on the more favorable wind, their words were swept toward him, and he caught the percentages and dollar amounts being bantered back and forth. Tonight, there were no other crew on board; the owner didn't want too many ears around, and the men rose only to visit the head or to refill their own glasses.

Hugh didn't worry about the words he was missing, confident that the microphone he'd hidden in the table between them would pick it all up for his review later. The two men didn't seem to notice him or even acknowledge his presence anymore. He was a worker bee, someone beneath them and nothing to be concerned about. They laughed as the boat cut through the shadow of the giant statue and turned farther north. Hugh had become the proverbial fly on the wall.

If they only knew. By dismissing him they were making it that much easier for him to plot their demise. Hugh's face was impassive as he piloted the boat back up the river. The lights of Manhattan were starting to glow off to his right. The GPS guided him, and he crossed a waypoint he had marked months ago. From this spot, the current flowed directly back to the island they had just passed. He estimated the journey to be less than two minutes. Setting the autohelm, he examined the water behind him, measuring the tide and current with a trained eye. He picked out two landmarks and used them to locate a rock in the seawall. It had a small spot of graffiti in a place not visible from the shoreline.

It was something that would become important someday soon.

"Sir, he's on line two."

"Thank you." The president flicked the privacy button on the intercom, before glancing at the door leading to his chief of staff's office. He pictured the man on the other side listening, before punching the button and picking up the phone.

"Charles?"

"Yes, Mr. President. How are you, sir?"

"It's been a busy day. How's the family?"

"All very well. David still insists on staying in Kansas for some reason; I still can't get him to join me here in the Big Apple."

Trying to tell me he's alone, the president thought. Bullshit.

"Can't blame him; I prefer the country myself, as well."

"I manage to avoid it as much as possible," the man replied with a forced laugh.

"You'll never change, neither one of you. Wish I could chat, Charles, but I have a budget meeting in ten minutes. Is there something I can do for you?"

"Well, there is. I'm told we have some action being taken in Syria, and I wanted to check in with you on that."

Check in with me? How subtle.

"It has to be done, Charles. I can't leave the boy hanging."

"You realize this will jeopardize many things."

"I do. But the choice was a clear one." *Take the bait, you bastard.*

"Are you sure?"

"What are you suggesting, Charles? That we leave the man in place?"

After a short silence, the man's tone changed. "We'd like you to reconsider the rescue. The pilot serves a purpose, one we can profit from greatly."

"We can deal with that afterwards."

"We don't feel the same, Mr. President. The pilot needs to stay on the ground. He's one man. We lose that many a day to training accidents. If the people are to be convinced to keep this war going, then certain ... sacrifices ... need to be made."

"I don't—"

"He's a catalyst! A rallying cry that we can use for the next five years and beyond. Opportunities like this must be seized when they represent themselves! If he dies at their hands, we'll have the justification we need to extend and escalate the campaign in the Middle East. Not even the Russians would vote against it. You have to look beyond what's in front of you."

"He's a soldier, the son of congressman."

"All the better."

The reply was cold, and blunt, and set the president back in his chair. He chose not to reply, waiting for the man to speak again.

"Call the SEALs back, Mr. President."

"And if I don't?"

"We cannot ignore this. If you cannot see the situation as we do, re-election will become ... most difficult."

The president paused for a long moment before replying.

"I'll give it some thought." He severed the connection before the man could reply and then voiced the time and date aloud.

Working quickly, the president disconnected

the device from the phone and slipped it in his pocket. He rocked silently in the chair for a few moments, before triggering the intercom.

"Yes, Mr. President."

"After this meeting, I need some time in the residence. Could you ask the first lady to join me for lunch, please?"

"Yes, sir."

"CNN IS DOING IT, too. Check this out."

Danny thumbed the volume higher to the annoyance of a few of his co-workers in nearby cubicles. Where Danny had gotten the remote for the overhead TV was a mystery, but now that he had it, they had been subjected to the sound of babbling commentators whenever he felt the need.

In order to see the screen better, Steve kicked his chair back and rolled to the entrance of his own cubicle. A short video of Jack Randall and his wife leaving the Robert Moses power plant was being shown. Jack was battered, bruised, and soaking wet, as he walked toward the waiting vehicles. His wife had streaks of blood on her face and hair. It was replaced by video of Sydney Lewis escorting former senator Prescott from the same building. Police and several SWAT team members milled around in the foreground, and the footage then widened to include the damn itself and the lake behind it.

"Man, are they giving Jack the full-court press," Danny observed aloud. "What do you think brought this on?"

"He's your buddy, isn't he? Why don't you ask him?"

"It's not that kind of relationship. Answer the question."

"Who knows? I think they're just putting a familiar face to the public on the investigation. Deacon was more of a title, but Jack's a known entity. It's PR."

"The American hero thing? You think that's it?"

"They're trying to counter the good press that the Shepherds were getting. You can't blame them."

Danny didn't answer; he was too busy watching the footage. It was becoming a regular thing. At first, it was Jack's face and the story of the encounter with the drug runners in Florida. Then they had pulled stuff from the archives and revisited that. Every day, they seemed to have another Jack Randall story in the rotation. It had all started at once, too, he had noticed. Several stations with different owners had all run basically the same type of story. It was as if they were working together. Those which hadn't had quickly picked up the ball and run with it to catch up. Now it was not hard to find Jacks face on every channel.

"Something's going on, that's for sure."

"What?"

"Nothin'."

Steve went back to his desk, and Danny continued to stare at the screen. The story switched to coverage of the protests. They too had become a regular thing. The difference here was that they were sustained. Groups would come together and form a large protest for a few hours outside some government building, and then fade away into the surrounding streets, only to congregate again elsewhere a few hours later. And not just in DC and New York, or even the bigger cities on the east coast, it was happening in state capitols across the nation. As if an unseen force were guiding them. Most reports focused on the protests only when they gathered; nobody had run a story yet on how they seemed to be operating. Was he the only one who had noticed? Surely not, but why no story from anyone?

Maybe he should write one. He thumbed the

sound off and got a sarcastic "thank you" from the adjacent cubicle. He ignored it and brought up a new blank document on his computer.

***

CAPTAIN JENNIFER DEHART was five feet ten inches tall. Just enough to meet the minimum set by the air force. As such, the pilot seat in the V-22 Osprey was at its maximum height setting. Something she took a lot of good-natured flack for at the academy, but that had quickly ended when she outflew all her classmates.

Her peers had all wanted jets. Supersonic air superiority fighters that fought at razor sharp envelopes and crushing G-forces for ownership of the sky. She could have joined them, and for a short time she did, but the romance of aerial combat soon gave way to her fascination with developing technology. And after a year of test-piloting, she was introduced to the latest the air force had to offer.

The V-22 had seen a troubled start. Several crashes had prompted questions about its feasibility, and most pilots with her credentials were more than happy to steer clear of it in favor of the new Lockheed Martin F-22 Raptor or even the developing F-35 Joint Strike Fighter. But there was something about the hybrid plane-helicopter that drew her in. While it lacked the speed and power, or even the sexiness, of a fighter jet, its potential and flexibility for multiple missions intrigued her. The capabilities only improved as the design was refined, and she found herself lobbying hard for a position on the development team. As a result, she was one of the first pilots to enter a combat zone strapped into a V-22.

A series of favors and some outright pushing on her part had gotten her an assignment with the 455th Air Expeditionary Wing. First in Afghanistan and now here, tucked into a corner of the Ayn al-Asad Airbase in northern Iraq. The accommodations were good when compared to Bagram, but she was sure her old classmates and their Raptors had it better. Still, she didn't regret her decision.

Its official designation was the CV-22C, and there were two occupying the hangar in front of her. The latest of many models, and the most flexible by far. The C model was specifically designed for special operations, and she had chosen the list of priorities herself. The brass had agreed, and the engineers had delivered. The standard chassis had been lengthened by over a meter and then strengthened to handle the armor plating surrounding the cargo area. Sixty-six plates were now fitted along the interior bulkheads and deck, adding 800 pounds to the aircraft's weight. It affected the aircrafts payload and unrefueled range, but she considered that a payoff worth having. The V-22's two Rolls-Royce AE 1107C-Liberty engines had been augmented to compensate, and were connected by an improved drive-shaft system to a common central gearbox so that one engine can power both proprotors if an engine failure occurred. Either engine could power both proprotors through the wing driveshaft. It would not be enough to allow a hover, but it if they were in level flight, they would be able to keep going. The cargo hooks and their required hardpoints had been removed to offset the added weight of the armor and some other items.

There were now two pods tucked into the fuselage just above the sponsons. Normally, the pods could be swapped out for whatever mission the aircraft was called for, but these had been permanently installed. She walked around the aircraft inspecting both. From the outside, they were indistinguishable from any other pod, but what was inside was unique to the V-22C. The right side held an M-230 Chain Gun. It was slaved to either the pilot's or copilot's helmet and could spit out thirty-millimeter armor piercing shells at a rate of 625 rounds a minute. It could be reloaded from inside the aircraft in less than thirty seconds. She patted the pod assuredly as she walked around the nose of the aircraft. It was studded with protrusions. Refueling probes, forward looking cameras, terrain following scanners, and radars, all crowded for space on the aircrafts front. The aircraft had one mission: get in and out of enemy territory as fast and as safe as possible. To do so required every tool they could carry.

She found the pod on the left side similarly stowed. It contained four AGM-114 Hellfire and two FIM-92 Stinger missiles in a rotating magazine. The missiles allowed her to engage both land and air threats from up to a few miles away. Like the chain gun, it too could be reloaded from inside the aircraft, where they carried eight more.

The armament was rounded off with a M2 .50 caliber machine gun mounted on the rear ramp and manned by the crew chief during the pick-up and offload of personnel. She had lobbied for an upgrade to a M134 Minigun but had been told not to push it. She had done so anyway, and the guns were supposedly on their way. The chief had assured her that he could make the changes quickly. Until they arrived though, they waited.

It was something they had become good at. She and her crew had been slotted for rotation back to the States over a month ago, but operation Valkyrie One had stopped that. They had been in stand-by mode ever since. Hurry up and wait, it was the same in militaries all over the world.

A sound behind her made her turn and she found her boss, an Army Colonel and pilot of the second Osprey walking toward her.

Sean Daniels was her exact opposite in both sex and appearance. His six-foot six frame towered over hers, and his constant grin worked to counter her "resting bitch face." His skill with the aircraft, however, rivaled or exceeded hers in every way. A search-and-rescue man, he had come to the Osprey from the opposite direction. A helicopter pilot his entire career, he had made his way up through the Pave-Lows and Jolly Greens to the Blackhawks of the 160th Special Operations Regiment.

Wounded in Somalia, Sean had become an instructor for a time and then was scooped up by the program at Groom Lake. He held the honor of being the first pilot to crash a V-22 while on a test flight in the Nevada desert. He and the crew had been found sitting on the crumpled fuselage of the prototype, smoking cigarettes and pondering what had happened when the trucks had arrived. Legend had it he had sent his report from the emergency room after being ordered there for evaluation. His cool had impressed the General in charge, and he'd been the lead pilot ever since, picking and choosing from a large menu those who he thought would fly the V-22 into the future. One of his first picks had been Jennifer.

"Kicking the tires?"

"Gotta do something. This waiting is driving me nuts."

"Part of the game."

He joined her for the rest of their walkaround, and soon they were standing at the rear of the aircraft at the bottom of the ramp. The black non-skid tape had been scuffed here and there by men wearing black soled boots. Beyond the doorway there were twenty crash-worthy seats. They were often only half-full, based on mission requirements. Valkyrie called for fourteen men for each bird to go in and secure the landing zone for the arriving SEALs. Or SEALs plus one, to be exact, but they wouldn't know that until they arrived. She had gone over the plan several times, each time weighing the ratio of soldiers to fuel. Soldiers meant firepower. Fuel meant more range and maneuverability. The mission called for each. Eventually, they had settled on a number all parties could live with, but the final decision was always Colonel Daniel's to make.

"Still concerned about the fuel?"

"Not as much. As long as the tanker doesn't go sour, we should be all right. If we have to ditch or land short of the base, the A-10s can be over us pretty quick. If you think the four extra marines are necessary, then that's what we do."

"It's not so much me but the Gunny who thinks so. He convinced me, so I found a way to make it happen."

DeHart could only nod in agreement. Asking a pilot to give up fuel was like asking a marine to give up his weapon. It just didn't compute. When the Colonel had ordered the extra missiles off, she had immediately balked, but after thinking about it, the order made sense. If they needed more than the eight missiles already in the pod, they had really screwed up. The missiles had come off and been replaced with marines, and there was no further talk of it.

"The Miniguns?"

"In transit. Germany, last I heard. They'll be coming in on the next C-5. Clayton says he can have them mounted in a day. The weight change is negligible."

Before she could reply, a private appeared in the doorway. He spotted them both and ran over, a folded paper in his hand.

"Colonel, a message from SOCOM."

The Colonel opened the paper and read it quickly before silently handing it to DeHart.

"Valkyrie is a go. Let's get it on."

14

---

*"Journalism is what we need to make democracy
work."*

—*Walter Cronkite*

"Okay, what is it?"

"I thought we might have lunch before you left to ... Just what are you doing today?"

"I'm going to the Norfolk shipyards to christen a new hospital ship. Its name is the Recovery, and I get to smash a bottle of Champaign over its bow. You knew this already. A lunch? Last minute, like this? What's going on?"

The president deflated. The woman knew him too well. That was both a good and a bad thing. He rounded the table and sank into the chair, before waving her over.

"Is your phone on you?" he quietly asked.

Her brow furrowed at that, and she silently took the device from her pocket and walked into the bathroom. She returned empty-handed and shut the door behind her. Neither of them harbored any illusions as to whether or not they were being monitored. The daily intelligence briefings alone had redefined their ideas of privacy. About once a week, they performed a midnight search of the room for any listening devices or cameras. So far, they had found nothing, but the thought was never far away. The first lady checked the door and then took a seat across from her husband. Her worry now matched his troubled face.

The president reached into a pocket and pulled out the recorder. His wife raised an eyebrow at it as he set it on the table next to her salad.

From his other pocket, he produced a set of earphones.

"What's this?"

"The first is James talking with Charles," he whispered. "The second is Charles and I a few hours later."

"James?"

"Yes, my friend and loyal Chief of Staff. At least that's what I thought. I'm not so sure any longer. Just ... just listen."

The first lady did as instructed. The food went untouched as he watched her reaction. She listened closely, rewinding several times to get it all. Eventually, she but the device down and pushed it away.

"How did you ... ?"

"Henry. My body man, he's a good kid. James has no idea."

"I see." She picked up her fork and then put it back down, trading it for the glass of water. She set this down, too, with a shaky hand.

"My god."

"Indeed."

"The nerve. You're the President of the United States. Who does he think he is, ordering you to leave that boy in the desert like that?"

"Evidently, he feels he's the man in charge. He may be right."

"What? Walt, you need to set that man straight. He and his brother need to know that they can't—"

"It's not that easy."

Her mouth fell open.

"I didn't want you to be involved at the time. But during the election, I found myself in a room with ten men. The Trust, they call themselves. I won't get into names, but I'm sure you can guess half of them. They broke the news to me that over ninety percent of the funding coming into the campaign was theirs. Sure, it'd been routed through a million little fronts and PACs and banks to get to us, but the sources were very few. They had also funded Martin's campaign in much the same way. I had to make a decision."

"You never told me."

"I didn't want you to know."

"Because you knew what I'd say?"

"To give you deniability."

"Deniability? We're in this *together*. How could you not include me?"

"There was no time!" He stopped himself and lowered his voice, "There was no time. It was either take the offer, or it would go to Martin. I did ... I did what I felt was needed."

"Needed? For what?"

"For this." He gestured at the building around them. "For the presidency! Was that not our goal the whole time?"

His wife rose from her seat as well and paced the room. The president watched her. He knew the look. He had seen it before. His wife had once been an accomplished lawyer, a veteran of several courtroom battles both for and against the government. Whenever she was ready to speak, it would be with a solution. His only choice was to wait, so he did. His eyes followed her as she wandered the room, and he noted that the office had not aged her as it had him. She was woman who welcomed stress, bathed in it. Drank it in and thrived on it, every day of the week. Her features were as beautiful as the day he had taken the oath of office. The dresses still fit her curves, and the hair was still a stylish cut one might find on a woman half her age. Yet, she pulled it off, as she did everything else.

Eventually, she stopped. With a glare at him she walked to the door. Outside, she found the usual Secret Service agent and a White House butler. She spoke briefly, and her voice brooked no argument. The uneaten meal was cleared from the room, and the agent took up his position as soon as the door closed behind him. As soon as it shut, she turned to her husband.

"Call your secretary and tell them to cancel your afternoon. You're not feeling well. And no calls."

To his credit, the president didn't argue; he simply lifted the phone and did as he was told.

Trough the frosted windows of the tiny apartment, Vasily gazed at the sliver ocean between the two buildings across the street. It wasn't much, but it was all he had. The windows were older than he was and did little to keep the New York winter out. The buildings superintendent had strict orders from the owner. The thermostat was located somewhere out of his reach and set at sixty-five-degrees year-round. This time of the year, he was lucky if it got within five degrees of that. Like the majority of his neighbors, he made do with a space heater at night to keep from freezing. In the warmer months, he would often venture out onto the fire escape to get a few more inches of ocean view. Again, it was not much, but it was all he had. At least until the mission was done.

The coffee in his hands was losing its warmth rapidly, and he cupped both hands around the ceramic before sipping again. The sunrise quickly faded, and the sky once again returned to a dismal grey. The buildings seemed to welcome the depressing tone, soaking up the color and adding to the city's bleak atmosphere. There were no neon lights here, no Times Square glamor, no tourist buses. This was Brighton Beach, and its acceptance of misery was a part of who populated it. In its shops and restaurants, the language of Russia was heard more often than English, and as such, it allowed Vasily to blend in.

He'd arrived over a year ago after enduring much hardship. It had been worth it, he decided. The pain of his parent's death and his flight from the Russian mafia in St. Petersburg had come full circle. He had come a long way since then. First hiding by joining the US military with forged papers, he had volunteered for repeated deployments in order to stay out of the country and off their radar, only to be recruited by the Twelve Shepherds when his real identity was discovered by William.

He had endured the facial surgery and then

overcame the fear of discovery to get himself back into their midst. The rat hole apartment and the ever-present danger of discovery had tested him, but he had endured it all to get close to the target. The job of a waiter was a simple one, and he had obtained a position at the restaurant after cultivating a repour with the owner's friends. They had stupidly vouched for the young man, and he was soon working for less than minimum wage at a job that offered barely enough to last to the next paycheck. He had played the part and kept the owner happy enough to get him even closer. He became an expected feature of the restaurant. A fly on the wall. A familiar piece of furniture. Unlike those he worked alongside, it was exactly what he wished to be.

Watching the man who had ordered the death of his family eat, and drink, and laugh with his mafia cronies had been a slow torture. One he had endured for over a year. But soon, that would be over.

He allowed himself one last look at the ocean before finishing his coffee and leaving the window. He rinsed and stacked the cup in the small kitchenette before checking the multiple locks on the door and then retreating to the small closet. Inside, under a cardboard box of junk, he removed a floorboard to retrieve the laptop and gun. Finding a seat at the one small table, he quickly connected to the Internet.

The communication was there. Rubicon. He read it three times before deciphering its message and then quickly consulted a calendar for the date and then sat back with a sigh.

After all this time, it was here. The day he'd been waiting for. He tapped out a quick reply before stowing the laptop in its hiding place. After returning to the table, he began to strip the gun down and clean it. The plan he had formed months ago now occupied his mind. He went over every step, every detail—there would be only one chance.

He knew it was wrong for him to do so, but he couldn't help but smile.

PARKER THREW himself out of the red nylon seating and made his way aft. The Lockheed C-130 Hercules had been packed by his SEALs at the direction of the load master, and the men were taking care of last-minute personal issues as they gained altitude over northern Syria. Each man had his own ritual. Some bobbed their heads to heavy-metal music blasted through their earbuds, while others studied maps, tied and re-tied their boots, or even read a book. Whatever it took to keep the pre-mission adrenaline under control.

The seats were anything but comfortable. Thick nylon stretched over aluminum tubing that was attached to the walls and floor with removable hardware. Deep enough to seat a paratrooper with his chute and other gear on, the seats were cursed by all who used them for the duration of whatever mission they were on. Most troops were more than ready to jump out the door into the slipstream after an hour of torture in the seats. But like most things in the military, the comfort of the troops was secondary to the mission. The seats could be rapidly installed or removed to fit whatever the mission called for, and that would always be the number one priority.

Parker stalked the deck and nodded to the crew chief sitting in the back. The drone of the four massive engines outside made conversation futile. The air was already starting to chill, telling Parker they were still climbing. Soon, they would be too high to be heard by anyone on the ground, and the combination of their camouflage paint scheme and the lack of running lights would make them invisible to any ISIS fighters on the ground below.

But the altitude brought its own dangers. They'd be jumping from over 22,000 feet, well above the height where the partial pressure of oxygen in the air was adequate. Forty-five minutes before their planned exit from the aircraft, they would all have to don their oxygen masks. This, when combined with the bitter cold, brought the risk of the mask freezing up and its wearer to lose consciousness due to hypoxia. They would all be checking on each other regularly until it was time for the ramp to come down. Then they would all line up in the faint red lights of the aircraft, staring out into the black void beyond the end of the ramp, until they got the green light. The charge off the end and into the abyss was a silent one, and their training would fight to overcome their natural instinct to ball up in the frigid temperatures.

Tonight, it would be twenty-two to two. They would plunge straight down through the blackness from twenty-two-thousand feet to open their chutes at two thousand. It was enough time for the main to deploy, and maybe enough time to pull the reserve if there was a problem before they meet the ground. The running joke was that it gave the jumper time to go headfirst. The thought being that it got it over quicker, and that it was easier to pull you out of the ground by your legs. When jumping from a perfectly good airplane, it helped to have a morbid sense of humor.

The wave of the crew chief prompted Parker to make his way over, and the man held up three fingers and then switched to a thumbs up. Phase three in place was the message, and Parker returned the gesture to acknowledge. The V-22s were taking off. If all went well, they would meet them in a little over an hour. He watched the crew chief speak into the mc of his helmet, before relaying another message. This one needed no pre-arranged codes. The man simply pointed to his oxygen mask before putting it on.

Parker turned and nudged the closest SEAL and then pointed to the man's example. He then nudged his neighbor and on up the line. Parker began moving back up the line toward his own mask. Before reaching his seat, he passed a small round window in the side of the aircraft. A thick nylon cover was Velcroed around its edge and he peeled a bit back to get a look outside.

The lines were well-defined. If he didn't have the context, he'd have easily confused it with being over a large city on the edge of the ocean. The manmade lights dotted the landscape for miles on one side of an invisible line, while on the other they simply ceased to exist. One side was southern Turkey, the other northern Syria.

They were already on the dark side.

"It's the only way I see."

The president nodded and continued to stare at the fire. The dancing flames did little to sooth his thoughts. What his wife was telling him was bold—bold and dangerous—but it was either this or a continuation of the status quo. That was something neither of them was willing to tolerate.

"You can't be a puppet-President, Walt. You have to take them down."

"And then what?"

She shrugged. "We go back home."

"You really think they'll just let us do that? You don't cross men like this and just walk away."

"This isn't Russia, Walt."

"Kennedy would disagree."

That gave her pause, but only for a moment.

"I don't care. I'm not going to stay here knowing this. And if we allow it to continue, then we're no better than them."

The president chose not to reply. He continued

his examination of the flames. What was it about a fire that drew one's attention? He could watch for hours without losing interest.

"Walt?"

"You think it will work?"

"I ... I don't know. With the recordings ... maybe. With the venue, I think so. This is crisis management 101. Break the story first, get it out there fast, control the narrative. We'll have all three at once."

"And if they come for us?"

"Then the chips fall, wherever they may."

The president continued to brood. This was outside his normal way of doing things. There was no staff to consult as in the case of a domestic policy issue. No Joint Chiefs to convey for the handling of a crisis situation. There was only himself and his wife of thirty-three years. Even then, the decision would fall on him. He would be the one held accountable by the people. The Presidency was indeed a lonely occupation.

"Okay."

"What?"

He repeated himself louder, and with conviction, "Okay. We'll do what you're suggesting ... and the chips will fall."

There was a knock at the door and a voice called. It was Henry.

"What is it?"

The door cracked, and the young man stuck his head in. "Sir, I'm sorry, but they need you in the situation room."

The president shared a look with his wife.

"The pilot. I have to go. We'll work on what we discussed after."

"I'll be right here," she assured him.

15

____

"*The revolution is not an apple that falls when it is ripe. You have to make it fall.*"

—*Che Guevara*

His name was Lee, and like the other Shepherds, he lived a life in secret.

It was also one of solitude. His growing disdain for crowded cities had resulted in his immigration from the largest one in the country to a series of ever-smaller towns, until he eventually landed in a small cabin in the mountains of North Carolina. The trails in and around the over two hundred acres he had acquired had once held only his tracks and those of his dog for weeks at a time. The waterfalls in the area had gone undisturbed for years. It was the kind of place where a man could get lost in himself. A place of peace.

Then the movie people had come. The scenery and rugged terrain had been perfect for the post-apocalyptic story they had adapted for the screen, and the area had been inundated with Hollywood film crews for weeks. The tiny restaurants and area hotels had enjoyed the novelty, as well as the boost in business, for a few weeks. But then the crews and the famous faces had left as quickly as they had arrived, and the town returned to normal. Life at the cabin returned to its once-peaceful state.

Then the movie had hit the box office. In a matter of days, the area had been jammed full of tourists seeking out the waterfalls and picturesque landscapes they had seen in the movie. The trails were now crowded with people, and several became lost enough to find their way to his doorstep, where they seemed to have no qualms about knocking on the door and asking for directions. Lee had stopped answering after the first week and let the dog handle things. Now he sat on his porch and watched groups of mountain bikers zip by every day. After a few months with no sign of it slowing down, he'd started looking for a new cabin.

Despite his physical isolation, he was still connected. A satellite dish mounted on a nearby timber served him Internet and TV on the rare occasions he wanted them. Unfortunately, it was one of the necessary tools of being a Shepherd.

He'd just finished his coffee, and the dog was giving a half-hearted growl at yet another passing biker, when he checked his watch.

"Time to check in," he informed the dog. "You watch the door."

The dogs tail thumped twice in reply as Lee rose and made his way inside. The cup was refilled before he made his way to the tiny back bedroom and opened the ancient roll top to exposed the new computer. He was online and checking his mail a minute later.

The coffee was quickly set down when he saw the message. The code phrase burned into his retina, and he read the passage again to make sure.

"I'll be damned," he mumbled. "Rubicon."

Grabbing a pencil, he wrote down a coded date and time before setting it aside and sending an acknowledgment of the message to its sender. He sat for a moment thinking about the date, before making a quick phone call and then getting up and walking to the small bathroom. He gazed at his reflection in the mirror before shaking his head.

"Time to change your look."

Finding his trimmer, he attacked the beard and then the hair, taking his time to get it even and styled in the manner of his former life. The moustache was also tamed and trimmed into a goatee to reflect current fashion trends. A set of contact lenses was brought out from a drawer, and he selected the green tinted ones, before cleaning them and inserting them with a practiced motion. He rubbed his freshly shaved jawline and turned his head from side to side, examining his new look.

"Handsome devil."

A trip to the closet revealed a number of suits, all of them sealed in plastic to keep them free of the cedar odor. He selected three, before adding ties and shoes to match. Socks. Underwear. Jewelry and a pair of Rolex watches, all went in the suitcase with them. When he returned to the porch an hour later, the dog leapt to its feet and growled at him, before catching his scent through the expensive cologne and laying back down with a grumble.

"I'll take that as a vote of approval."

Glancing around the area, he determined it was free of trespassing bikers and lost hikers, long enough to hide a plastic bag containing a wad of bills and a key under a large rock next to the steps. Taking in the view again, he let out a sigh, regretting that he was leaving it, before returning to the dog and giving him a long hug.

"Jimmy'll be by to feed you. Watch the place until I'm back. Okay?"

The dog again growled his disgust but surrendered to the act. It wasn't the first time his owner had left him. He'd be back; the dog just never knew when. Until he did, he'd sleep in the barn or on the porch, eat when the neighbor kid came and fed him, and continue his job of warning lost hikers away. He stayed on the porch when Lee headed for the barn, knowing he was not going with him this time.

Inside the barn was a six-year-old truck. A four-wheel drive Chevy with more than a few scratches on its side from the tree-lined rural roads. It was parked over a trap door, which led to a room no other person had ever seen. Lee stopped just long enough to retrieve the 9mm automatic from under the driver's seat, before moving to the car next to it.

Pulling back the cover revealed a late model Mercedes with all the bells and whistles. The cover slide across its waxed surface with ease, and he bundled it up neatly before placing it in the trunk. Sliding into the leather seat, he fired up its eight-cylinders and let the engine purr a bit before easing it outside. He paused long enough to shut the door behind him, before starting the car down the mile-long driveway. He honked at the dog as he passed the house and got a yawn back for a reply.

Lee punched up the map but ignored the GPS—he knew exactly where he was going. Rubbing his jaw again, he guided the car through the tunnel of trees and down the mountain, until he met a two-lane blacktop road. From here, he would blend in with the tourists—at least here they served a purpose he could take advantage of. Two miles later, he passed a neighbor he knew. The man didn't even glance his way.

It was a few hundred miles to Kansas City, about eleven hours last time he had driven it. He had plenty of time. If he drove at the speed limit and stopped for the night, he'd reach his destination sometime in the morning. Plenty of time to access the storage unit and retrieve the tools he'd need.

With a tap of the accelerator, he was speeding down the country road. He'd keep it under the limit until he reached his destination. According to the timeline the General had selected, he'd be in place early.

Yet, he couldn't wait to get there.

"Stay seated."

The president barked the words as he entered the situation room, and the men sank back into their respective chairs. He avoided looking at his chief of staff and instead pointed silently at the chairman of the joint chiefs.

"Sir, operation Valkyrie One is in progress. The V-22s crossed into Syrian airspace thirty minutes ago, and the SEALs will be over the target in ten."

"Any issues?"

"No, sir. Everything so far is proceeding as planned."

"The pilot?"

"We've seen no activity on the ground that might indicate that he's been moved."

The president nodded and quietly rapped his knuckles on the mahogany table. The map on the far wall showed every element of the mission. The C-130 carrying the SEALs was moving in from the west. The flight of V-22's from the southeast. The pilot's location was still marked with the tiny green dot. A pair of A-10 ground attack planes circled to the southwest, ready to enter the fray if called. A lone drone did the same just north of the pilot. Everything was in place. He watched the C-130 turn and head straight for the tiny green dot.

"I'll need your GO order, sir."

Cook leaned in and whispered. "Sir, there's still time to—"

"Proceed, General," the president spoke.

The General pretended not to see the exchange and nodded to the Colonel holding the phone. The man spoke three words and then listened, before nodding to the affirmative.

They sat in silence, each of them with their eyes glued to the screen. It switched to a view facing out the back of the C-130. Rough men bathed in red light sat with the tools of war strapped to their bodies before the open ramp. Beyond it was only darkness. As they watched from half a world away, the men struggled to their feet and lined up.

"Ten minutes," a voiced crackled through the radio.

They all leaned forward. All except one.

The White House chief of staff sat with his head bowed, an expression of regret and fear on his face.

It did not go unnoticed by the man seated next to him.

"We get a lot of the newly homeless in here. They still have email addresses and cell phones. Some might have cars they live out of. The phones disappear after a few months, but the email seems to stay with them longer. For some, I imagine it's their only way of keeping up with others. Nobody knows you're homeless when you're online. That and his size were the only things out of the ordinary."

Larry nodded as he scribbled in his notebook. So far, the woman had been overly nice and very patient. She had obviously answered these questions already several times, yet she appeared perfectly happy to do so again for him. He glanced sideways to see Sydney looking over the shoulder of a computer man from the local office. They were trying to determine where the man had visited on the computer.

"Out of the ordinary? How so?"

"Well, he'd obviously been on the streets for some time. I say that based on his appearance and, well, his cleanliness, alone. The homeless tend to go blind as to how bad they smell after a while, and he was there. Not their fault, but it tells you things about them. He was well past the time where most lose their phone and email, yet he still had it. That usually means someone else is paying the bill for them."

"I see. Anything else you can tell me?"

"Well, no. Just that he was polite. I mean, he seemed to know that his size was a bit intimidating, and I think he took measures to counter that. But I've seen that before. After the initial contact, I went back to work. Most of them check their email and just go, at least in the summer. Soon as it starts getting colder, we'll see them hanging around more."

"And you'd never seen him before?"

"No, he was new. I know all the regulars."

"Okay. Sorry for all the repeated questions. Thank you for your time."

"No problem. I'm here all day if you need me."

Larry smiled another "thank you," as the

woman picked up a stack of books and made her way to the shelves. A quick check through the glass told him Sydney was still engrossed in the computer, so he headed back outside.

The detective waiting for him finished his cigarette and stubbed it out on the top of the trashcan before tossing the butt inside. He'd met Larry at the airport and told him what they knew so far on the ride in. Professional courtesy that he was unused to, and he'd pointed it out. The man then admitted that his dad had been a G-man for Hoover years ago, and he didn't want a lecture from him at Christmas. Whatever the reason, Larry had decided to like him.

"Anything?'

"No change in her answers. Nice lady."

"Joe's wife. He's a good cop. What next?"

Larry tapped the notebook on his opposite palm and glanced up and down the street.

"Any coffee around here?"

"I know a place." He set off, and Larry quickly followed.

A block later, they entered the Amethyst Coffee Co., a local joint with a good following. The lunch crowd was just breaking up, so the detective and Larry were able to find a small table in the back. Larry sampled the coffee and labeled it good. He wasn't surprised—cops always knew where to get good coffee.

"So, what are you thinking?"

Larry opened his notebook, ran a hand through his mop of hair, and laid it down. He wasn't worried about prying eyes—nobody could read his shorthand but him.

"Newly homeless, but maybe not," he read aloud. "Not a local."

"Yeah, I caught that too."

"Our guys were unable to gauge from the picture how long the beard growth would've taken. Too variable by person, they said, but it's likely he hasn't shaved since he escaped."

"I wouldn't."

"Yet he's covered about a thousand miles to get here and done so in that condition."

The detective shrugged.

"What are the local homeless like? You familiar?"

"Oh, we have the usual. They mostly hang around the mission over on Park and Broadway. They hang out there and in the parks and wooded areas down by the rivers. Our skid row is more of a river, actually. They camp out in the green areas along the banks, and the highway near the rail-yard. Plenty of abandoned buildings and vacant lots for them to shelter in. The hospitals fill up when it gets cold. There's always a few over by the Coors Distribution warehouse. They'll report a theft now and then, and we follow the empty cans back to the culprits."

"All this within walking distance?"

"Heh. Walking distance?"

"Sorry. I say something wrong?"

"No-no. It's just that the homeless have a different definition of walking distance than most people. They've got nowhere to go and all day to get there, so they don't mind a few miles. Especially the migrants. They arrive here and walk all day to get where they're going."

The comment brought Larry's head up. "Migrants?"

"Yeah. Mexicans mostly, looking for agricultural work. They show up during the growing season, work a few weeks, and then move west to California."

"How?"

"How what?"

"How do they get here?"

"Cars and trucks, mostly. They'll cram as many as they can in and drive all night so they don't get seen and stopped. Some come in on the trains and some—"

"Trains?"

"Yeah. The rail yard is just on the other side of the highway." He pointed out the window with his cup and then took another sip.

Larry examined the view and then fell silent. The detective studied his face.

"Newly homeless, but dirty. You think?"

Larry finished his coffee. "Let's go see this rail yard."

16

"A revolution is a struggle to the death between the future and the past."

—*Fidel Castro*

Parker was first, as it should be.

The black hole of the Syrian night was ten feet in front of him, framed in the red glow of the plane's interior. But he had no time to think about that. All that mattered was the tiny green light that had just come to life. The jump-master stepped out of the way, and Parker jogged forward until the greasy ramp was behind him and he was falling through the blackness.

Twenty-two thousand feet below him was the hard desert earth of Syria, but he was too far away to see it yet. He'd have to fall over four miles before that would happen. At the moment, his only concern was the icy slipstream tugging at his body and the threat of collision with one of his own men. As soon as he felt himself stabilize, he craned his head around in an effort to see anything.

But it was a futile effort. After eleven seconds, he reached terminal velocity, and the sensation of falling diminished greatly. The high clouds masked the dim light provided by the remaining sliver of the moon, and the blacked-out plane had already been swallowed up by the night sky overhead. If it weren't for the roar of wind in his ears, and the hiss of oxygen in his mask, he could have been twenty-two-thousand feet underwater and not know the difference. He scanned the sky around him for any of his men, but they were dressed in black just as he was. They carried no lights or anything that might reflect the moonlight. It was the world's largest sensory deprivation tank.

Parker gave up trying to see his men and focused on the ground below him. He worked to control his breathing and divided his time between the altimeter on his wrist and the one on his chest. They matched. One less worry. He had about a minute and a half of freefall left.

The air grew warmer as he descended, so his muscles relaxed. The polypropylene underwear and leather gloves, which had kept him warm for the last few hours, and now kept frostbite from claiming any exposed skin, would become a burden once they landed. But there was nothing he could do to change that. The mission demanded surprise, and a HALO jump straight into the target was the best way to achieve that.

At the one-minute mark, he concentrated his gaze below. Land features were visible now. Dips and rises in the earth, and roads reflecting the scant moonlight. As much as they might have shielded them further, he was happy to see no clouds between him and the rapidly approaching rock. Despite what his twin altimeters were telling him, he never fully trusted them. The nagging question of whether it was clouds or fog always entered his mind. If it were fog it would be too late to take action when he realized it. Fog was never welcome. Fog was bad.

Another glance at the altimeter made him tense. Like the kick of a well-aimed sniper rifle, the opening of the parachute came as an expected surprise. Parker was yanked skyward by the opening canopy, and he bit off the grunt that threatened to escape his lips. He bounced twice before settling upright from the hanging risers and immediately grabbed for the guidelines and tugged, making sure the chute was full of air.

No rips. No holes. He had survived part one.

The harness now made itself known as it dug painfully into his crotch. The hundred pounds of extra weight he had brought with him was now making itself known. Most of it was metal and quite lethal in his hands. A 9mm pistol was strapped to his right thigh, along with eight extra magazines of hollow-point ammunition. Strapped to his left side was a modified Heckler & Koch MP5, with another four-hundred rounds of 9mm to go with it packed away in the thirty round magazines that encircled his leg. Added to that were the radio and throat microphone, a variety of grenades, strobes, IR light sticks, wire snips, an eight-inch Tanto dagger, combat bandage, and a satellite phone. All this over a layer of body armor.

Adding to this were the clothes, boots, and 220 pounds of muscle Parker had, and the chute was near its weight limit. He wouldn't complain though; the medic and the machine gunner had it even worse.

But there was no time to think about that. Parker tore off the oxygen mask and took his first breath of Syrian air as the ground got closer. Ignoring the altimeter on his wrist, he turned his hand over to reveal the compass beneath it glowing in the dark. He was going the wrong way. Tugging on the guidelines, he brought the chute around 180 degrees. Unfortunately, this had him running with the wind. The forward motion of the chute would now be added to the winds speed. It was going to be a hard landing. But the little tritium-fueled pointer could not be denied.

The sound of fluttering nylon moving through the air was all around him, but he ignored it as he looked for landmarks. The drones had provided pictures from every angle, and he examined the buildings below in an attempt to match his current position to one of them. He saw the orchard first, and then the road, and determined he was south of the intended target.

Good.

Parker made small adjustments and then

aimed for a spot between the trees. Behind him and slightly above, he knew his team would be S-turning in an attempt to space themselves out and avoid a collision on the ground. Now committed to his fate, Parker watched the tops of the trees as he barreled in at high velocity. When his feet were even with the tops, he flared hard, trying to lessen his impact as much as he could.

But it wasn't meant to be. The edge of his canopy snagged on a tree and the air was immediately dumped. Without lift, Parker hit the ground hard and rolled left to try and avoid planting his face in the rocky soil. Instead, he was yanked sideways by his own chute and planted firmly into the trunk of a tree, knocking the breath from him. Figs rained down on him as he struggled for air.

He soon had it back and moved to get on his feet, only to discover coils of parachute cord wrapped around his feet. His hand found the tantō, and he slashed himself free as a figure approached.

"Okay, boss?"

It was Waltrip, his alpha team leader. He held out a gloved hand and Parker took it, letting the big man yank him to his feet. The knife went back in its sheath and the H&K replaced it. Waltrip yanked on Parker's chute twice before surrendering it to the tree.

"Count?"

Waltrip hissed into his radio, and dark shapes appeared out of the blackness one by one. Parker counted them until the number matched the number they had left the plane with. He let out a sigh of relief. They had all made it. Without him saying anything, they formed a tight perimeter around him and fell silent, each of them facing out and probing the darkness for any indication that they had been seen or heard arriving.

"Switch."

The men quickly donned their night vision goggles and stood when they were ready. Parker paused only long enough to send a pre-arranged code on the sat phone before glancing at his compass and gesturing to the north.

"Let's go hunting."

LARRY HUFFED a bit as they climbed the embankment. The detective had made a few calls, and the railyard had been closed off by the uniform cops. After talking with the few workers present, they had been pointed to the wooded area on the hill overlooking the trains. There was one currently pulling out after having been inspected from end to end. In the woods they had found several men. They were now lined up on the ground, waiting for Larry.

A uniformed man walked up and motioned the two of them over. Keeping his back to the row of tramps lined up on the ground behind them, he spoke in a whisper.

"See the guy on the end wearing a red coat? He's evidently the gatekeeper here. He's the one you'll want to talk to."

"Gatekeeper?" Larry asked.

"Sort of an unofficial mayor. He keeps the bums separated from the tramps. Sounds the alarm if anyone is coming. That kind of thing. He'll know if your guy passed through."

"You know him?"

The cop shrugged. "In passing. He's not one to cause trouble. Computer says we've hauled him in a few times for being drunk and trespassing. The usual stuff. You'll have to find a way to win him over—he doesn't trust us locals. Even then, he's more likely to protect his friends first, if you know what I mean."

"Yeah, okay. Thanks." The cop turned to go.

"Wait a minute." Larry motioned him back. "You two got any cash?"

The detective and the officer shared a look, before pulling out their wallets.

"I got ... two twenties and seven ones."

"I got nineteen bucks."

"Gimme the small bills." Larry pulled every one dollar bill he had from his pocket and added it to the officers' cash.

"Drinks on me tonight." He wadded up the cash and left the two of them behind.

The two cops watched as Larry approached the line of men. He greeted each of them warmly and handed the cash out. He got a few mumbled thanks and suspicious looks, but the deed did not go unnoticed by the man at the end of the line. Larry worked his way to him slowly, even shaking hands with a few of the men on the way. The man did not miss a move he made.

"Mr. Mayor," Larry greeted him.

He got nothing but a suspicious nod for an answer. Larry didn't blame him.

"Nobody's going to jail today," Larry said. "Not why I'm here."

The man looked over the dozen officers standing off to the side and shrugged. "Not what it looks like."

"Well, I'm with the FBI, and today I say nobody's going to jail. These boys here are helping me out today is all. I was wondering if you might do the same."

The man eyeballed the wad of cash in Larry's hand.

"What ya want?"

"Looking for a man. A big guy. Stranger to you all here. He might have passed through recently." Larry fished in his pocket while he spoke and pulled out the detective's pack of cigarettes. He shook one out and lit it up, before offering the mayor one. The man took it and held still for a light.

"Mind if I join you?" Larry asked, before lowering his heavy bulk to the ground next to the man. The mayor eyeballed Larry's suit, and then the dirt under them both, before dismissing it and taking a drag on the smoke. If the man didn't mind getting dirty, then he was okay in the mayor's book.

"Here, I got a picture of him." Larry dug in another pocket and unfolded the mug shot. He smoothed it out on his leg before handing it over. The mayor squinted at it with myopic eyes, and Larry's hope sank, but the man fished in his own pocket and produced a cracked pair of glasses.

Donning them, he selected the best angle and gave the picture a look.

"Maybe." He handed it back and eyeballed the wad of cash again.

Larry didn't pretend to notice. "I don't mind that. But I need to believe what you tell me."

"Got no reason to lie."

Larry fixed him in his eyes, and the man was trapped. "He hurt a little girl. You gonna help him or me?"

Larry held his breath and waited. He was taking a chance with the lie, but even the homeless had kids.

The mayor took a drag and then nodded. "All right. Lemme see that picture again."

Larry watched his face while he examined the picture again.

"Yeah, the jerky boy. Got me a fist full of it from him. He was here. Showed up the other night. Said he just got in, I think, but I didn't believe him. He's got a beard now, trimmed up neat, and he was clean when he got here."

"Clean?"

"Yeah. Clothes was clean and new. He din get um from no Sally. He'd just had a shower, too. His hands were clean, nails were white." He held up his own filthy hands to emphasize, his nails long and black with dirt under them. "If he was a tramp, he was a new one, I'd say. Knew the lingo, though."

"How's that?"

"Said he was running counter. To a rail tramp, that means he's heading north out of here. Up to Montana or Washington, then back down to California. Unless he gets off somewhere to winter over." He shrugged.

"Heading north, huh? He alone?"

The mayor took a long drag and cocked his head before replying, "Not sure. He left with another guy, but they could have just been heading the same direction. Yeah, maybe I saw em come in together, nowz that I'm thinking about it."

"They came in together?"

"Train come in and woke me up. I seen two hop off and head into town. One big, one small. Could have been them. Didn't have my glasses on. The big one come back alone and wearing new clothes. Jerky boy. Yeah, must have been him. Went into town and come back clean. Magic trick."

"When they leave?"

The mayor shrugged. "Dunno. Two, three days ago, maybe? I'm not big on keeping track."

"Right."

They smoked for a bit, and Larry played with the pack and the cash while they did so. The mayor's eyes didn't leave them.

"This other guy, what did he look like?"

"Just a tramp. Old and black. Just like any other."

"Got a name?"

"Heh. No, we don't do no names."

"Got it."

They both watched the trains in the yard creaking and groaning. A yard engine was making one up on track three.

"That one heading north?"

"Probly. Tracks two and three usually do."

Larry was about out of cigarettes and quickly searched his brain for anything else he might ask the man. Deciding he had exhausted what he could hope for, he made a show of tucking the cash into the remainder of the soft pack and handing it over.

"Much obliged, Mr. Mayor."

"Good luck, G-man."

"When dictatorship is a fact, revolution becomes a right."

—*Victor Hugo*

"The SEALs report they are on the ground and code green, sir."

"Very well."

The men around the table relaxed only

slightly. A few of them knew first-hand what the SEALs were going through. Surviving a HALO drop intact was no easy task. Code green meant they were still operational, and the mission was not compromised. That didn't mean that they had all made it, nor that some of them weren't injured. As with all their assignments, it was mission first and welfare of the men second. They wouldn't really know if they had lost anyone until they were on their way out. And they were far from that point.

"Move the drone in. Keep it high," the General ordered.

The president watched silently as the mission played out on the screen. The C-130 was now leaving the area, its presence replaced by a dot indicating the SEALs. They were very close to the target.

Sat next to him, his chief of staff stewed, wiping his palms on his pants and only glancing at the screen. His mind was obviously occupied with more than just the mission on the screen. The president kept his eyes forward and followed the events there.

He'd already made a decision on the man next to him.

CARTER PULLED the heavy coat tighter around him and planted his feet wide in the open doorway. The train was snaking its way up another mountain and had slowed to a walking pace. Outside, the high plains were covered with a fresh layer of snow for as far as he could see. The wind had entered the two open doors of the boxcar at every hairpin turn, and he and Tye had huddled together in the forward section on a double layer of scrounged cardboard to silently suffer through it.

Hours earlier they had endured the Moffat Tunnel. A six-mile-long tube of total blackness which had driven them both slightly mad. The darkness had been total and seemingly without end, and Carter had finally managed to light a candle to drive it back. The fumes had become thicker the more they traveled, and they had soaked their sleeves in water to hold over their mouths and noses until the train emerged out the other side, their burning eyes blinking in the sun. Carter could still smell the fumes, and the headache persisted. It was one of two reasons he was currently braving the cold and wind.

The other was in his pocket.

With a glance over his shoulder, he confirmed

that Tye was still asleep. Why he had chosen to travel farther north with him, Carter didn't know.

"One direction as good as any other." had been Tye's answer.

Carter had given it some thought and concluded that, when one had no home to go to, staying mobile was the best alternative. To stay in one spot would be admitting that you had no place to go. The moving train provided a false sense of progress, even it was a never-ending roll to nowhere. Tye had offered the excuse of keeping Carter out of trouble, and he had let the subject die. The old man now slept, warmer and more comfortable in the new clothes Carter had gotten for him. He'd blamed the windfall on the generous friend in Denver, and Tye had accepted the story without any further question.

He turned away and dug into his pocket. The GPS was a little too much to blame on a generous friend, and Carter had decided to keep the device hidden from his traveling companion. The tiny screen came to life, successfully linking with the satellites overhead out the open boxcar door, and he navigated its buttons to find what he wanted to see. The rail lines were depicted as very thin tracks across the map. Its manufacturers had obviously favored the people traveling in cars over the well-financed tramp riding the rails. Nevertheless, he was able to measure their progress and estimate his arrival time to the tiny town to within a twelve-hour window.

West Glacier, Montana was small, even by mountain town standards. But it was the closest departure point to the General's ranch Carter could see. From there he would part ways with Tye and travel overland by foot. His biggest worry now was the temperature and depth of the snow. But if that became a problem, he would have to find a way to overcome it once he got there; there was nothing he could do while on the train.

The train leveled out, and Carter soon heard the jangling sound of the warning bells. He stepped back from the door and pocketed the GPS as they drew closer, the bell's sound changing in both pitch and volume as he got closer. He struggled to remember the name of the phenomenon. Doppler something. It was the same as the sound of a passing car on the highway, only he was the one traveling and the crossing was stationary. He waited patiently for his car to meet the crossing. The jangling bells got their loudest just as they passed and then faded away at the same rate they approached. Tye grumbled a bit and turned over but otherwise had no reaction. Carter spotted one man in an old pickup waiting at the crossing, but otherwise the view was free of other humans.

The train's speed stayed unchanged, despite the somewhat level ground, and Carter soon heard another crossing. They were passing through a town. Outside, he soon saw the usual assortment of warehouses and small factories. Storage lots and rusty overgrown sidings holding the occasional abandoned railcar. The engineer slowed the train a bit further until the buildings began to dwindle, and the car rocked as they changed tracks to head farther north.

Carter wondered about the engineers; if they had the same drive to travel, to be constantly moving, as the tramps they hauled with them had. The engineers had no real choice in the train's direction. Their path was determined for them by the control towers in the yards and the schedule of the clock. The job was considered prestigious by Tye and the other tramps Carter had spoken to, yet he didn't see the difficulty of the position. The man upfront had nothing to do with steering the train. Granted, it was millions of dollars' worth of cargo and equipment, but the man's job still boiled down to faster or slower. A simple throttle and brake was all that was really needed. He tried to remember the hundreds of buttons and switches he had seen in the engine they had rode into El Paso on, but the memory eluded him. There was obviously more to the job than he could imagine, but he had no one to ask.

Carter's breath clouded his view of the mountains. Their snowcapped peaks stretched out behind him, and he stamped his feet to warm them as he took in the view. The train began another slow climb, and Carter wondered how high they were going to go. Not that it mattered; he had reduced his options to few, and right now walking to where he wished to go was out of the question.

Where he wished to go. Carter repeated the thought. While he knew his destination, he was still unsure what he hoped to find there. An explanation? Or was it confirmation? They were not necessarily one and the same. A confrontation, perhaps? Was he spoiling for a fight? He wasn't sure of that, either. Or was he on a fool's errand, looking for something that wasn't even there? He didn't know.

Answers. Maybe that was all he needed. Answers, so he could move on. To where was a subject he had been avoiding. Like his traveling companion, he was without a home. But he couldn't build a new one without satisfying the questions haunting him. One needed closure before he could get past some things. Perhaps that was what he was after: closure—and his purpose for being. He hoped to get both when he arrived.

He let out a deep breath and the fog clouded his view again. It matched the picture in his mind.

SEALS ATTACK the village Part I

Parker moved from tree to tree until the wall was in sight. It was something he had studied repeatedly over the past month. The wall was low and made of stones pulled from the fields since the land had first been settled. About waist-high now, it stretched from one end of the orchard to the other. He had pondered its purpose for days but had not found one. Perhaps it was just a convenient place to pile the rocks? He didn't know. What he did know was that it provided cover for himself and his team as they approached. While the darkness of the trees behind them offered concealment, the wall offered a bulletproof barrier, and that was something men in his line of work always looked for.

It was also their exit. The V-22s would be landing on the opposite side of the orchard. Parker had planned it that way in the event they were exfiltrating under fire. He and his team could use the wall and the trees to help them reach the birds, which would also be shielded from the buildings by the treetops. That was the plan, anyway.

Using only hand signals, he and his men spread out and hunkered down behind the wall. Parker let his mouth fall open and he listened. Some low voices could be heard in one building. They traveled to him from behind a tattered curtain showing the flickering light of a candle around its edges. He counted four voices and then confirmed the number with the man next to him.

"Sit-rep," he whispered into the microphone.

"Bravo One. I've got the tent in sight. No lights. IR showing three inside. One of them is small, maybe the boy. No guards."

"Bravo Two. One Toyota truck under the roof of building two. No other vehicles. No one in sight."

"Bravo Three. LZ is clear. Setting up the music."

"Bravo Six. Acknowledged. I have four tangos in the lit window. Nothing else. I—"

"Movement! I have a guy just outside building one!"

The team all froze in place, their weapons up

and ready. The safeties had been off since they hit the ground. They all held their breath waiting.

"One guy with an AK ... he's ... he's taking a piss," the man whispered.

"Nobody moves."

"WHY ARE THEY STOPPING?" the president asked.

"I can't say, sir," the Chairman replied.

The SEALs were on their own frequency, one they were not listening in on, and all the men had to go on was the fuzzy green image provided by the drone a mile overhead.

"Everybody stay calm," the General spoke, "They'll work it out,"

He was stopping them all from speculating out loud. The president saw it and realized he was guilty of it himself. They had to have faith in the men on the ground. But faith wouldn't stop the V-22s from coming. The SEALs would have to do something soon, or the Ospreys would have to be ordered off. The president watched the mission clock tick on as the planes grew closer. He silently urged the SEALs to move.

But they refused his wish, and the men began to squirm in their seats.

Waltrip watched silently as the ISIS fighter retied his pants and then pulled out a cigarette. The flare of the match illuminated his face and flashed bright in the night vision goggles of the SEAL. The man puffed hard, sending the smoke across the small courtyard to travel directly into Waltrip's face only twenty feet away. Its acrid stench made his nose twitch, but he remained frozen in place, watching the mans every move over the barrel of his H&K.

The ISIS fighter took his time, enjoying the smoke as he took in the night sky out over the orchard. Waltrip kept the sights centered on the man's head, watching his face closely for any sign he'd been discovered.

But the man's gaze was focused somewhere else, something out in the orchard had caught his eye. He stepped forward and lowered the smoke, squinting as he tried to make it out. The clouds cooperated and cleared enough to provide him a tiny bit more light.

It was a parachute. Snagged on the top of a fig tree and flapping silently in the faint breeze. Waltrip watched as the man's eyes grew big while he sucked in a lung full of air.

Before he could shout, the H&K spat twice. Two 9mm hollow points slapped into his face and out the back of his skull, and he crumbled in place, the AK rattling as it impacted on the stone path.

"Shit. One down," Waltrip hissed the message into the microphone and then vaulted over the wall.

Parker cursed silently and spoke into the microphone, "Go, go, go."

The buildings had been divided equally among the team, and they all knew their targets. Without a reply, they all sprang up and ran to them in pairs. Any thoughts of land mines, hidden sentries, barbed wire, or booby traps were tossed aside. It was now a full-on attack before they lost the element of surprise. The SEALs had to strike hard and fast; there was no time for a drawn-out engagement, and time was on the enemies' side. They didn't have the ammunition for a prolonged firefight, and they certainly couldn't afford to get pinned down.

But now they were ahead of schedule, and that was a bad thing. The V-22s weren't just coming to give them a ride out; they were heavily armed and carrying Marines in the event they were needed. Now the SEALs were committed to their attack, and the cavalry was still fifteen minutes out.

But Parker had no time for that. He followed the man next to him over the wall, and they stacked under the window on both sides. He'd pulled the flash-bang from his webbing as soon as his feet were under him and now pulled the pin, counting down the four-second fuse on the beer-can-sized device. At two, he stood and tossed it through the window.

Screams in Arabic immediately sounded from inside, but Parker hunkered down and squeezed his eyes shut just as the grenade blew, the million-candlepower flash and the concussion blast effectively blinding and rendering deaf anyone inside the small room. Three more explosions quickly followed as the rest of the team did the same.

Parker stood and stuck the snout of his H&K into the room. He double tapped the man standing in front of him first, before sweeping left and taking down a second man in the corner. The two SEALs then scrambled over the sill and into the house proper, before clearing each room one by one. The suppressed coughs of other H&Ks filled their ringing ears, and the shouted directions from SEALs as they advanced echoed through the once-quiet night.

Parker stopped at the exit and pointed to his shadow. The man fired a round into a downed ISIS soldier to assure he stayed there and then took up a position at the door.

"I'm good, skipper. Go."

Parker went. Running back through the house, he yelled into the radio, "Parker coming out!"

He dove through the curtained window, rolled to his feet, and immediately ran in the direction of the tent, the H&K up and trained on its entrance. A pair of hands emerged, palms up, and he almost fired. The hands waved as he got closer, and he risked turning on his flashlight.

The hands were white.

"Friendlies inside! Friendlies inside!"

The English was pure American, but Parker was still careful. He held the light away from his body and grabbed the flap, whipping it open and playing the light around. A fellow SEAL joined him, ready to spray the entire tent from the opposite side.

Parker found a man just inside and flat on his back. On the other side knelt an Arab-looking man and a twelve-year old boy. Both of them had their hands up and were clearly terrified.

"Don't shoot! I'm Navy," the man on the ground said.

Parker looked down at Archie with a grin. "Me too."

Up on the ridge overlooking the small village sat The Rebel. He'd awakened to the sound of the flash-bangs, and he cursed his men until they lowered their guns and hide themselves. He now followed the movements of the SEALs with a broken pair of binoculars as they moved through and around the tiny homes. The white light of the flashlight at the tent brought a smile to his face.

"We must kill them!" a soldier hissed.

"Silence! Not yet. More are coming. Get ready."

Without another word, he sank back into the hole he had dug on the ridgeline. He had kept only five men with him, but they would be enough. He tore his eyes away from the tiny flashlight in the distance to find his gunner standing in his own hole ten feet away. The long tube was already on his shoulder and his eyes were searching the sky.

"From the south, you think?" he whispered.

"There is no way to know. Watch your sectors and stay down. They can see you in the dark. And listen. They are coming. You will hear them long before you can see them."

The men did as they had been told. The Rebel palmed the device in his hand. At the first sound of the helicopters he was sure were coming, he would activate it.

Like a moth to flame, he thought.

18

"In every revolution, there are winners and losers. Every dystopia is a utopia for somebody else. It just depends where you are. Are you in the class that benefits, or are you in the class that's not?"

—*Ken Liu*

"**N**o!" Parker paused at the man's outburst.

He'd stepped in the tent and removed a pair of zip-ties from his belt, with the intention of binding up the man and small boy.

"What?"

"They're prisoners too."

Parker shook his head. He didn't have time for this. Another SEAL, a medic, entered the tent and immediately began checking Bunker over.

"I'm fine. The leg is broken. He fixed it." Bunker told him as he gestured at the man across from him.

"You fixed him?" Parker asked, the warm muzzle of the H&K inches from the man's head.

"I ... I, yes. I'm a doctor. My name is Waqas. I'm ... I'm from Pakistan."

"Bunker?"

"It's true man; he fixed me up. The kid, too. They gotta come out, too."

"I'm here for you."

Bunker summoned what strength he had and shoved the medic away. The man was shocked and raised his hands to combat his patient, but he was cut off by the man's tone.

"No! All three of us, or I'm staying here!"

The medic looked to his team leader. This was not in the mission profile. Parker just shrugged. They would sort it all out later.

"Fine. They come, too. Now get him packaged up!"

The medic broke out a collapsible liter and began setting it up. Parker shook his head at Bunker, before leaving the tent and snagging the satellite radio.

"Bravo One to Caesar One. Expedite. We need pick up now. Package is secure."

"Roger, Bravo One, Caesar One. Copy your expedite. We are ten, one-zero, minutes out."

"Copy. Bravo Four, start the music."

Parker got two clicks of the microphone for an answer and then turned to check the perimeter. SEALs were prone on the rocky ground or behind the cover of the wall, in every direction. With the Ospreys were ten minutes out, and they would have to move fast to get to the other side of the orchard in time.

From a building down the street, a burst of AK fire ripped through the air over their heads, and the team spun as one to return fire. With a steady stream of three-round bursts keeping the AK bearer pinned down, Parker pointed to the left. Two SEALs sprinted for the side of the nearest building and disappeared around its corner.

"Get 'em moving!"

The medic and Waltrip emerged from the tent,

with Bunker on the stretcher. The doctor dragged the boy behind them, as they ran for the wall. More AK fire zipped past them, and Waltrip let out a yelp as they ran into the darkness.

Parker located the flashes of the rifle and sent a few bursts its way. Sparks flew as they chipped stone from the wall of the building.

"C'mon, guys. Where you at?"

He'd no more than said the words, when the boom and flash of a frag grenade exploding filled his sight-picture. He raised his head to see two shadows sprint across the street, the muzzles of their submachine guns spitting rounds in the direction of the ISIS fighter.

"Two more down, skipper. They must have been hiding somewhere."

"There may be more. Get to the wall and cover our exit."

"On the way."

THE PRESIDENT EXAMINED the face of his chief of staff, out of the corner of his eye. The man looked sick, as if his emotions were taking a toll on his stomach. He read his face clearly now. It was fear. And not fear for the lives of the pilot or the SEALs that were rescuing him. It was fear for himself. He had failed to stop the president from this action, and he would be held accountable. Not by him, but by his true masters.

It made his decision that much easier.

The chairman of the joint chiefs of staff watched this play out silently, wondering what it all meant. But he dismissed the thought when the radio traffic increased and concentrated on the screen.

Whatever it was, he would find out soon enough.

"You are bleeding."

"You think?" Waltrip replied.

He didn't slow down, and the doctor, not understanding the soldier's flippant reply, struggled to keep up. The man was twice his size, carrying what must be close to fifty kilograms of gear, and the end of a gurney holding a man who weighed twice that, yet the doctor was being outpaced. He stumbled once, and the boy helped him up. They followed the soldiers through the darkness of the orchard, tripping on roots and dodging low hanging branches. Where they were going, the doctor didn't know, but they were in a big hurry to get there. His breath was becoming ragged, and his legs began to ache, but he pushed on.

And then they stopped. The boy crashed onto him, and they almost fell on Bunker, but a soldier snagged his tunic and tossed him toward a tree.

"Take cover."

From what? he thought. The other SEALs threw themselves prone and aimed their weapons back the way they had come, while two others were creeping around the open area south of the orchard. They seemed to be placing something on the ground.

"You really a doc?" Waltrip asked him

"Yes."

"How bad?"

"I'm sorry?"

"The ear, doc. How bad?"

Waqas crept closer and examined the side of the man's head. Between the black face paint and the dark hat, he could see a wet shine. The man had been shot in the ear, its lower half was missing. He quickly tore a piece of his tunic away and slapped it over the wound.

"You will live."

"Excellent. Here, tie this around my head for me."

Waqas took the offered bandana and did the best he could, while the soldier scanned the tree line over the barrel of his rifle.

"What do I do?"

"Just stick close to me. There'll be more soldiers here soon, and, well, you aren't dressed for the part."

Before he could inquire any further, a sound interrupted them. A low drone that got steadily louder. Then the chop of rotor blades. Waqas searched for the source, but the sky was black.

"That's our ride. Grab the kid and be ready to move."

Waqas did as he was told, pulling the boy away from the tree and forcing him down next to Bunker. He grabbed one end of the stretcher, while the medic nodded in approval from the other side. If the doc was seen doing so, it would keep him from being shot, not to mention freeing up a SEAL for other issues.

"Light 'em up!"

The yell sounded doubly loud after all the whispering, and the two SEALs in the open jumped up and ran for the trees. Waqas could see nothing different, but they had obviously performed a task.

"Infrared strobes and a beacon," Bunker told

him. "Tell him to cover his face; those birds are going to land right here, and they kick up a shitload of dust."

Waqas moved to do so but stopped short.

"A beacon? Like yours, Archie?"

"Shit! Get the SEAL! Now!"

A rapid string of Arabic made the boys eyes widen even more, but he swallowed his fear and did as he was told and ran for the SEAL who had brought them. Waqas threw the end of his tunic over Bunker's face, just as the Ospreys appeared overhead.

A HUNDRED METERS AWAY, Parker scanned the buildings over the top of the wall. Next to him was Bones, his machine gunner. His M249 Squad Automatic Weapon moving left to right, as he scanned the village for any opposition.

"It's wrong."

"What, skip?"

"It's wrong," he repeated louder. "Too soft. I don't like it."

"What's not to like?"

Parker didn't answer. The intelligence guys had estimated a three-to-one enemy ratio. They had encountered a fraction of that. Where were they? Had they run? If so, that was great—he'd take it and not complain—but his gut was telling him that wasn't the case.

The sound of the Ospreys coming in behind them reached his ears. His men were split evenly now, half of them at the landing zone, the other here on the wall. It was time to change that.

"Left peal," he ordered.

Bones immediately swung his machine gun to the middle of his sector of fire. A second later, they heard a pair of running feet approaching and passing behind them. Then another, and another. From the left end of the line, the SEALs were leaving their positions at the wall, one by one, slapping the man next to them as they passed. Eventually, Parker himself was slapped, and he grunted as he threw himself to his feet.

"Let's go."

Bones fell in behind him as best he could, moving backwards into the orchard. The sounds of the turbine engines and heavy rotors slapping the air now dominated his senses. The circles of static electricity they produced making them look like UFOs in the dark sky.

THE REBEL SMILED as the aircraft drew closer. Now. Now was the time.

"Be ready!" he yelled.

Spinning in place, he aimed the large flashlight at the base of the ridge and flashed it three times.

He got three in return.

ABOARD THE INCOMING V-22C, DeHart nudged the stick to center the direction indicator. The heavy helmet fed her a grey-green picture of the terrain passing under the belly of the aircraft, as she held it just meters above. Her copilot hands hovered inches away from the controls as he followed her every movement, ready to take over should the need arise. Three times, the red glow of tracer rounds had reached out for them, but DeHart had dodged the deadly streams with a cool hand and placed them back on course without a word.

"I've got music times two," DeHart said. "Confirm your location."

"We're at the south end of the orchard," a SEAL replied. "Four strobes."

"Roger."

"Two degrees right."

DeHart made the correction without comment. The "music" her copilot had spoken of was the beacon activated by the SEALs. If all had gone as planned, they would be gathered just south of the orchard neighboring the target and ready to roll. The plan was for her to set down and take on the team and their cargo, while the second bird circled and provided cover. Unless its load of heavily armed marines was needed. Now there was a second beacon, one that was from an unknown source.

"Code One. We are Code One for extraction. LZ is cold."

"Caesar One. Roger Code One," she acknowledged. "Caesar Two, I have a second beacon four-hundred meters north. Can you investigate?"

"Caesar Two breaking off."

"Copy, Caesar Two. Caesar One remains inbound. Two minutes."

DeHart double-clicked the microphone, before addressing her copilot, "Open our presents."

"I'm on it."

The copilot's hands flew across the armament panel, and DeHart felt the thumps and clicks of the pods being deployed and locked into place. The added drag forced a small correction in their angle of attack, and she compensated without thinking.

"Caesar One, Two. Your target is lit."

"I see it."

The flashing of infrared strobes was now visible ahead, and she added them to her scan as they rapidly drew closer. The strobes soon separated into four individual lights, and she measured their distance from the nearby trees. Closer than what she would have liked, but doable. Couldn't really blame the SEALs; she wouldn't want to be standing out in the open desert either.

She was setting up her approach and had begun the transition to level flight. The aircraft pitched up, and on the ends of the wingtips, the nacelles began to rotate to the vertical, slicing through the dry air and creating a halo of static electricity. The airspeed bled off rapidly. DeHart did her best to ignore the flashes of light in the corners of her eyes and focused on the strobes below her. Twisting the throttle to max power, she dumped the nose and dove straight into the landing zone. At a hundred meters, she brought the nose back up and flared the aircraft to slow down directly over the strobes. The prone bodies of the SEALs lay in an awkward semi-circle around them, and she kicked the tail around to rotate and set down the aircraft so the ramp was pointed at them.

"I've got eyes on them," she heard the crew chief inform her and her copilot over the intercom. The steady whine of the rotating barrels of the minigun was being transmitted through the tiny speakers, and she pictured him hunkered down behind it, ready to return any incoming fire. DeIIart was too busy to acknowledge. She completed the turn and set the aircraft down hard, its heavy-duty landing gear soaking up the impact as they bounced on the flat earth.

"Caesar One is on the ground."

"Do they have him?"

"We'll know soon, sir."

The president made no reply, he simply stared at the screen on the wall along with every other man in the room. The picture was split. He had views from the cameras of the aircraft and of the drone circling overhead. The signal from the drone would occasionally freeze, only to catch up a moment later. The camera from the circling V-22C was forever changing due to the needs of its pilot. As frustrating as it was, they all remained silent, urging the men on the screens to move faster. Several exhaled loudly from held breaths, only to take in another. The drone stayed fixed on the few buildings while the circling pilot focused on the aircraft now on the ground. Shapes could be seen moving all around the aircraft, and the twin engines glowed white hot in the enhanced view.

"Bravo team. Load up."

"The SEALs?"

"Yes, sir."

The president watched as the green blobs of light disappeared inside the rear of the aircraft. He scanned the surroundings but saw nothing but blackness. Did they get him? He forced himself not to ask again. The circles of static electricity formed again and washed out the view as the aircraft got ready to leave the ground. The radio chatter reached them through the hidden speakers.

"Caesar One. We're at the LZ, negative incoming."

"Caesar Two, roger, orbiting at one mile. I have the second Beacon location. We are inbound."

19

---

*"You can jail a Revolutionary, but you can't jail the
Revolution."*

—Huey Newton

"Patience. Wait for them to load."

His men were all hunkered in their holes, with only the tops of their heads showing now. They didn't know how the Americans could see them in the dark, but they knew better than to doubt The Rebel. They had seen aircraft like them before. The stream of bullets they could belch had captivated them, reminding them of a mythical beast, one that breathed fire and death on those below its spread wings. The memory froze them in their holes.

Except one. The man with the Stinger missile on his shoulder sat slightly higher, with just enough of his head and upper body out of the hole to operate the weapon. The Rebel looked over to see him sighting through the scope, centering it on the red-hot engines of the twin rotor aircraft. The faint tone barely reached him, but it was all he needed to hear. The weapon had a lock on the heat source and was screaming its readiness.

"The other?" the man asked.

"It circles. Ignore it until I say otherwise. Stay on target."

"But—"

"Stay on target!"

PARKER DUCKED his head into the onslaught of dust and debris thrown up by the landing V-22.

The ramp was down, and the marines were emerging before it was fully settled, and he hoped his SEALs had communicated that the LZ was cold. The last thing he needed was a nervous marine mistaking him for an ISIS fighter. The four marines fanned out around the aircraft, and he could see the pilots in the red glow of their cockpit instruments scanning the ground outside the angry bird.

He passed the supine form of Bunker lying in the ground and, with a wave of his arm, gave the "follow me" signal. He stopped to take a knee next to the ramp and began counting men as they ran past him and into the gapping interior. The doctor and the boy stayed close to Bunker, both wide-eyed and nervous as they entered the red lit interior.

"Almost there."

He traded looks with the crew chief sitting behind the spinning barrels of the mini-gun on the other side of the ramp. The barrels were now pointed at the sky as the SEALs moved in from all directions. It was the worst part of the mission. They were in a big noisy target that was announcing its presence to all within earshot. Even worse, with every SEAL boarding, they lost another rifle from the perimeter. Soon, they would have only the Minigun and the skill of the pilot to protect them.

"THEY WHAT?"

"They took my beacon!" Bunker yelled over the scream of the engines. "Tell those pilots to ignore anything but yours!"

"Awe, shit!"

He left Bunker and ran for the crew chief. Getting directly in his face, he screamed to be heard. The man quickly repeated it to his pilot.

DEHART KEPT her eyes out the windshield, and her hands on the controls, ready to yank her Osprey skyward as soon as the word to do so sounded in her ears. The vibrations of the SEALs pounding the metal deck reached her through the metal frame, and she waited for them to stop.

"C'mon, TJ. Talk to me," She spoke to her crew chief.

"I got a SEAL here that says they compromised the pilot's beacon. Tell Caesar Two to back off!"

"Roger, that. Caesar Two, ignore the second

beacon. Repeat, ignore the second beacon. Break off!"

"Copy, Caesar One."

DeHart exchanged a look with her copilot. He shrugged. They'd figure it out later.

"Almost there." A few more vibrations and they stopped.

"That's it!" Parker yelled.

"We're all in." TJ informed the pilot.

"Roger."

The last SEAL was aboard, and since it would lighten the load, TJ lowered the spinning barrel and depressed the trigger as the aircraft's engines spooled up. The gun shook violently in his hands, and the sound of ripping canvas filled the air as a tongue of flame spewed forth from the rotating barrels. The flash was so bright he could barely make out the tree line through it, but he guided the cone of tracers into the orchard and swept it across the trees. Trunks splintered and severed branches were launched into the air, only to be blown aside by the powerful rotors carving their way skyward. The dust blew up around them, as the pilot banked the aircraft around to the south, allowing him to expend more rounds on the trees behind them.

"She's sluggish," DeHart commented as she

brought the Osprey around, the few tons of newly added weight now straining the available power. She allowed the aircraft to skim the ground until she had built up some airspeed and then thumbed the controls to adjust the nacelles forward. The aircraft responded, and they were soon climbing above the trees.

THE REBEL CURSED as the second aircraft broke away and circled behind them. It was soon out of sight behind the ridge. The plan had failed.

Or had it? He returned his gaze to the first aircraft, only to hear its engines screaming louder. It was taking off.

"Now!"

The man was ready. As soon as the aircraft rose above the trees, he stood and centered the closest engine in his sights. The weapon screamed its readiness in his ear, and he obliged it with a squeeze of the trigger. The missile left the tube and raced across the sky over the orchard, its exhaust momentarily blinding them all.

The Rebel stood and watched, his eyes wide as the gap rapidly closed.

"Allahu Akbar!"

COLONEL DANIELS HAD JUST COMPLETED a second orbit and was tightening the circle in preparation for Caesar One's departure. They had scanned the area around the LZ for two miles without seeing any additional threats, and were now approaching the LZ at a right angle just as the first Osprey was taking off. The question of the second beacon was in the back of his mind, but they would clear that up later. Right now he had a mission to complete. They would fall in above and a half mile behind Caesar One until they started their climb out of the area.

The flash caught his eye, and by reflex he triggered the microphone.

"Missile!"

THE ONE-WORD WARNING cut through the background noise like a knife, and DeHart reacted immediately by dumping the nose. The V-22C responded, and the men in the back felt their harnesses dig into their shoulders as the aircraft rapidly sank. DeHart struggled to keep the nose from digging into the ground as yells sounded from the rear. A cloud of debris was thrown up by the rotors, and she grit her teeth as they powered through it.

"Where?" was all she had time to voice before an explosion rocked the aircraft.

THE REBEL HAD WALKED AWAY from his shelter without caring when the aircraft dove to the ground, ready to rejoice in the coming explosion. The shouts of his men abruptly stopped as they watched the strange plane dive into the trees. The missile dove after it and exploded, its proximity detector mistaking the trees for the target and detonating early.

But it was close enough. The expanding ball of shrapnel expelled by the tiny warhead shredded its way into the right nacelle. It immediately began to fail, and the sound of rendering metal echoed across the desert. The aircraft spun to the left rapidly and sank lower.

The Rebel seethed. His mind focused on the aircraft and its path, enraged by the possibility of it escaping.

"SHUT IT DOWN!"

"I need more revs!"

"Screw the revs! We gotta shut it down!"

"Okay ... now!"

DeHart had somehow kept the aircraft upright after the impact and now steered them south. The aircraft had been in transition, its weight in the process of moving from the rotors to the wings, when the missile had shredded her right engine. She had coaxed a few more revolutions out of the failing engine and gotten the nose down in time to gain some ground effect and increase the lift from the wings before it failed altogether. They were now skimming just a few feet over the rocky surface on one engine while she labored hard to keep the mechanism from destroying itself.

Fortunately, DeHart had memorized the map of the target area and was now using the descending grade of the terrain to keep the airspeed up as much as possible. The aircraft was fighting her every step of the way, and her hands were going white on the controls as she struggled to keep them airborne. The radar altimeter was screaming in protest as they raced across the earth.

"I can't maintain! Cross-couple!"

"What if—"

"Just do it!"

The V-22C had the ability to run both rotors from one engine, but they had no way of knowing if the mechanism was damaged. If it was, they could lose the power from the engine they did have and never get it back, and the V-22C was not much of a glider.

The copilot reached up and yanked the lever. The linkage mechanism protested, and they both held their breath as they slowly lost altitude. DeHart was about to sound the impact warning when the linkage engaged, and the right rotor came to life. DeHart made use of a draw in order to keep the nose down, and the combination gave the engine time to catch up with demand. The low RPM alarm stopped screaming at her a few seconds later, and she coaxed a few meters of altitude from the wings. Only when the aircraft refused to sink did she allow herself a breath.

"Damage?"

"The right engine is gone. IR is out. I've got a gear alarm on the nose wheel. TJ?"

"Couple of these guys are wounded, but the SEALs seem to have it handled. I've got a hydraulic leak to the ramp line, and the right pod is jammed. It'll have to stay out. A few holes in the wall, but other than that, she's holding together. The package is fine."

DeHart caught a strain in his voice. "You okay, TJ?"

"Just a scratch. I'll be fine."

She swallowed that for the moment.

The radio squawked. "Caesar One?"

"This is Caesar One. I've lost the right engine, but we've successfully coupled. Ramp, nose gear, and starboard pod damage. Rudders a little sluggish. I'm underpowered, but okay. Three wounded on board, including my chief, nothing life threatening. The package plus two is secure."

"Roger all. You okay?"

"It's like holding a greased pig in the air, but I think we can make it. What was it?"

"Looks like a shoulder-fired missile from the ridgeline. It's being addressed."

DeHart shared a look with her copilot. He just shook his head; whatever that meant, they didn't have time for it right now.

THE REBEL STARED into the blackness, waiting for the explosion that never came. His rage built and consumed him, cancelling out all other input. His men addressed him twice, and not getting a reply they left their holes and began making their way down the ridge to the village, leaving the cover of their carefully constructed holes behind.

"I GOT at least four coming down the ridge. Maybe one's still on top," The drone operator reported. "They must have been dug in deep to not be seen on the IR."

His fingers typed in the coordinates while he spoke and sent them to the pilot half a world away. He then turned on his laser designator and slaved it to the man bringing up the rear.

"Music is playing."

"ROGER THE MUSIC. ROLLING IN HOT."

The A-10 pilot pulled back on the stick and aimed his bird directly at the spot now indicated in his heads-up display. Rolling himself upright, his fingers worked the switches of the armament panel, and he selected a single GBU-39 Small Diameter Bomb. The weapon located the laser from the drone and informed him of its readiness. He allowed the plane to drop a bit closer, before triggering the weapon's release switch. The aircrafts computer took in a variety of data, decided the plane was "in the basket," and kicked the weapon free. The pilot pulled up and banked sharply to the left, in order to see the impact.

The flash was silent and gone as fast as it had appeared. His only clue was the voice of the drone's pilot half a world away.

"Hit. Four down. Repeat, four down. Nice job, Tiger Six"

"You will be fine," Waqas told the boy.

The hot metal had pierced his arm after passing through the side of the aircraft. The boy had been so scared and bewildered by the experience that he had not even noticed the wound until they had settled into level flight. Waqas now tightened the bandage and then tied it off, before offering a reassuring smile. The boy returned it in a show of bravery he clearly did not feel. But the doctor was smiling and couldn't stop, and that told the boy much.

Waqas turned his attention to the SEALs. They all watched him with curiosity when he released the straps to join the medic. Waltrip waved one of them back into his seat who had risen to stop him.

The SEALs were good at identifying friends or foes; if Waltrip said the man was okay, that was enough for them.

"It's broken, isn't it?" TJ was asking the medic as he examined his arm.

"Yeah. Not too bad, though. Just the radius; the ulna seems intact." He probed the man's wrist, and he winced.

"Can you wiggle your fingers, please?" Waqas asked him.

The crew chief shared an amused look with the SEAL, who nodded that he should.

"Excellent. Did you fall or, perhaps, put out your arm to catch yourself?"

"Exactly. Broke it on my own gun, a brand-new one, too. Who are you?"

"I am Waqas. A doctor and fellow prisoner. I was in the wrong place, as you say."

He turned to examine Lt. Bunker, who was now strapped to the floor and being questioned by the team leader.

"Or maybe the right one."

20

"You cannot make a revolution with silk gloves."

—Joseph Stalin

"What the hell happened?"

"It appears the lead bird took a missile to the right engine. They are still in the air and reporting they are airworthy. Whoever launched the missile was taken out by the A-10. Caesar One reports that they have the package, and that they are going to try to make it to Al Asad"

"His condition?"

"Unknown yet, sir. Let's give them time to get that aircraft back home. I imagine the pilots are rather busy."

The president fumed but nodded in agreement.

"A missile?"

"Perhaps, the missing Stinger?" the Air Force General offered.

The president's jaw tightened at the information, but he said nothing.

"How long?"

"They should clear Syrian airspace in about thirty minutes at that speed and be on the ground at Al Asad within the hour, sir."

"Very well. Well done, gentlemen. If something changes, I want to know. Call me the second they are on the ground."

"Yes, sir."

He stood and the men stood with him.

"I'll be in the oval. James?"

The chief of staff quickly stood and followed the man out. The chairman watched them go, wondering what was about to happen.

When the door was shut behind the man, he turned back to the screen.

"Colonel, I'll need the contact information for Lt. Bunkers next of kin, please."

"Yes, sir."

The chief frowned. The president would make the first call, followed by him and a few others. He just didn't know whether it was going to be good news or bad news yet. His eyes found their way to the mission clock. It was counting down agonizingly slow.

He would know soon enough.

———

"DAMN, IT'S COLD."

"Those boots workin'?"

Tye stopped and looked down at his new boots. They were a size or two too big, but he'd stuffed some newspaper in the toes to compensate. They were a far cry better than the pair he'd discarded back in Denver.

"They work. No holes."

Carter smiled at the understatement. It was what he had come to expect from the man. His one-day-at-a-time attitude wanted for little. A little food, a little shelter, the occasional cigarette, and the means to stay mobile. That was all he asked for out of life. There had been a few moments over the past weeks when Carter found himself thinking that it was Tye who had life all figured out, and it was Carter was the one on a fool's errand.

"Good. Mine are working, too."

They started off again down the side of the tracks. The train had stopped in an unknown yard, and Tye had stuck a head out long enough to see the brakemen crawling under and around the second engine. A few minutes later, they had heard the engineers walking past their boxcar complaining about a mechanical issue. One that was going to cost them a few hours. He and Tye had decided to make a trip into the town in search of food.

"Where you think we at?"

Carter knew exactly where they were, but didn't want to reveal how to Tye.

"Not sure. Wyoming, maybe. Idaho? You don't recognize anything?"

"Nah. Never stopped here before. If I did, I probly stayed in my box. Too cold to do anything else. Nice view, though."

Carter turned his head to the east and took in the view of the rising sun coming up over the mountains. It was indeed a beautiful sight, even if they had to see it standing in the snow on the side of a railroad track. They watched for a full minute before silently moving on.

Some evergreens blocked their view of the yard until they were almost on it, but Carter's height gave him just enough of an advantage to see the cars pull up to the engineer's shack. He grabbed Tye and tugged him into the trees.

"Whas matter?"

"Cops. A bunch of them."

Tye dropped any protest and followed the bigger man into the trees. The snow covered their branches, and two of them dumped their loads on them as they worked their way into them. Carter looked behind them and cursed their tracks in the snow, but there was nothing he could do about it.

"Stay here. I'll take a look."

Leaving the older man sitting on his pack in the snow and grumbling, Carter stole his way through the trees until he could see the yard again.

The cops were mostly State troopers and what looked like a local sheriff. They had the yard workers and the crew of the train gathered around them and were passing out papers. Carter couldn't make out what was on them, but he had an idea. Wanted posters. Probably with his face on them.

The group broke up as quickly as it had arrived, and the men fanned out to check every car in the yard.

Despite the low temperature, Carter began to sweat. His eyes examined the cars the cops had driven in, and he took a slight bit of comfort when he saw no canine units. A good dog would pick up their trail and lead the men right to him.

Were they looking for him? Had they put two and two together and determined he was using the rails? Had his encounter with the cop in Denver tipped them off in DC? He had no way of knowing.

A cry went up from the men on the train. Carter looked and counted. It was not the car he and Tye had used, so he watched carefully as a man was pulled from the dark recesses and out into the snowy yard. Another tramp, one that he and Tye—and evidently the crew of the train—had been unaware of. The troopers quickly surrounded the man. Several seemed to be asking him questions, while the others rooted through his belongings. The paper was shoved in his face many times and the man repeatedly shook his head to the accompanying inquiries.

"What they doin'?"

Carter flinched and then cursed himself. Tye had followed his tracks through the trees, and with the snow muffling the sounds of his travel, he had managed to sneak up on him. He'd gotten too focused on the goings on in the yard.

"Get down. They lookin' for somebody."

"Us?"

"Dunno." Carter chose the safest reply. "They found another guy on our train. Whoever he is, he's not the one they after. One thing's for sure, though: They aren't gonna let him get back on that train."

"We go back in that yard, we gonna be here a while. Been to jail before." He stopped there as the thought needed no additional explanation.

"So, what we doing? Wait till they leave and try to sneak back on?"

Tye thought that one over for a bit and shook his head. "I wouldn't."

"Then what?"

Tye examined the yard one last time and then turned to do the same with the woods they currently occupied.

"Let's go for a walk. We stay in the woods, though."

Carter was open to ideas. The officers looked like they were being very thorough, but the crew, not so much. He wasn't sure what to make of that yet. With a last look at the men in the yard, he turned and followed Tye back the way they had come.

THE PRESIDENT SAID nothing as the two men climbed the stairs to the west wing's main floor. With the State of the Union speech now locked, the staff were scrambling to prepare for its delivery. The communications staff and the press secretary were wearing out the carpet between their offices. A few of them saw the president passing through and almost voiced a question, but a look at the man's face, and that of the chief of staff behind him, quickly erased that idea. They traveled on until they reached the oval office, and Mrs. Lancaster wisely shut the door behind them. She knew that look, and it wasn't something she wished to be part of.

The president stalked across the room, while stripping off his suit coat. He flung it on the chair and then fixed himself a drink at the sideboard. He didn't offer one to his chief of staff.

"Explain it to me, James. I want to understand."

"Sir?"

"Why are you not with me?"

"Sir, I support you in every way you—"

"No. Not on this."

Cook fidgeted and looked away for a moment. The president sipped his scotch and waited. He expected one of two answers, and he had a decision tied to whichever one he got.

"Sir, the Republicans—"

"Will go for military action. They always do. I can give that speech myself: 'This President has a duty to support the only true democracy in the region, and help it defend itself against these terrorist threats. These threats to Israel are also threats to America and bring instability to an already volatile area, blah, blah, blah.' I've heard it a million times and so has the American people. It's not just bullshit; its recycled bullshit."

"That's exactly why we have to do what's best for the long term, sir. The countries in the region, they only allow us in for a short period, and that's a mistake. We need to keep a presence, a stabilizing force, if we want this to work out. I know its counter to what we wish, but we have to commit to the long term. This may take decades before its truly over. And for that to happen, we will need the backing of the people."

Decades of war, the president thought, just what they want.

"And you feel the pilot was the key to that support?"

"I ... yes."

The president drained his glass and walked to the windows behind the Resolute desk. Outside, the protestors marched in the light snowfall, their signs clearly visible through the tall fence. Despite the freezing temperatures, their numbers had only increased. He held his breath and listened. Their shouts barely penetrated the thick glass, but they could be heard, if one truly chose to try and listen.

"I'll need some names for your successor. We'll announce after the State of the Union."

Cook stood frozen by the words. He waited for more, but the man was silent.

"Yes, sir."

Cook hesitated, but finally left the room through the main entrance, not through the one leading to his office.

The president never turned.

COOK WAVED the inquiring look of his secretary off as he approached.

"Hold all of my calls until further notice."

"Yes, sir. Is everything—"

"I just need some time."

He shut the door behind him and then stood in place, examining the room. It was a modest office for a man of his accomplishments and power. Barely large enough for a desk and a small conference table. He'd had the maintenance staff wedge a couch into the corner, so he could spend more time here. The walls were covered in pictures, most of them of him and a slew of politicians. Some of them domestic, some of them world leaders. His desk held few other than the required family photos. The rest of its surface was covered in files and briefings, the contents of which he constantly previewed.

The view was of the garden outside. He'd found it odd when he'd first seen it. Every view out his office window for the past three decades had been one of high-rise buildings. Always in two directions, as that was keeping with a man of his position. It was only one of the two ways this office was different.

The other was a door. A simple item, but one that represented something few could aspire to. It led from his own modest office to that of the most powerful man in the world. He walked around his desk and sat in the leather chair before examining it closely. He doubted he would ever walk through it again. The man no longer wanted his council. The door was shut and would stay that way.

And it had been his own doing.

The man on the other side of the door was not the most powerful man in the world. Cook had learned that some time ago. Exactly when this had happened, he wasn't sure, but it could not be denied. Somewhere along the way Cook had been compromised, he had found himself under the control of the true master of the nation, and he had excepted his fate.

But the man with the title had not, and he had just let Cook know that. What the next move was, he wasn't sure, but he knew he had no choice in what to do next.

With a sigh, he unlocked the bottom drawer and opened it. The phone sat where he had left it, and with a degree of unease, he dialed. It was answered by a gruff, yet familiar, voice.

"What is it?"

"He launched the mission."

"And?"

"It was successful. The pilot should be on the ground in Bagdad within the hour. I tried to stop him, but he refused to listen."

"I see."

"How do you want me to proceed?"

"Do nothing. I'll be in touch."

The line went dead, and Cook palmed the device before securing it back in its place. He then opened the drawer above it and pulled out a pad of paper. #From the office of the White House Chief of Staff# was boldly emblazoned across the top.

The message was short and to the point. He signed it without pausing and then folded it carefully before placing it in his jacket pocket. A few days from now, he would place it on the president's desk after he left for the Capitol building. With the eyes of the nation focused on the president, no one would see his chief of staff leaving out through back door.

***

"THAT'LL DO."

Carter followed Ty's pointed finger and saw an abandoned warehouse. Its roof, fenced in yard and parking lot held several inches of snow, and there was no sign of a human visitor anywhere. They had stayed in the woods paralleling the tracks and then stolen their way through town without being seen for about two miles before Tye stopped. The train had not passed them, and Carter held out hope that whatever Tye had in mind would get them back on it. He now examined the building, taking note of the heavy doors and their locks. The windows were high and would require something to boost him up if they wanted to get inside. Carter had seen easier choices for shelter behind them, and he said so.

"Not to stay the night," Tye explained. "To get us back on our train."

"How?"

"See that loading dock? It lets the cars right up to it."

Carter eyeballed the concrete platform. It was about forty meters long and maybe twenty meters deep, and he imagined it was thick enough to hold a large forklift and its load with ease.

"I don't ... You mean catch it on the fly? Thought you said that was a bad idea?"

"It is. You gotta better one?"

"What if they button up the train?"

Tye shrugged. "Can't help that. But they can't close up a flat or a canopy."

"Freeze to death."

"Maybe."

Carter examined the idea for a moment. The only way he saw it working was if there was an open boxcar.

"That first box we looked at in the yard in Denver, the one with the busted door, you think it's still on?"

"They may have set it off here, but I doubt it. Something wrong with that engine, thas why we stopped."

Carter measured the concrete again, and then the levelness of the track. It looked flat, but it was hard to tell. Was it slightly uphill? If so, how fast would the train be moving when it passed by? Could they just hop on, or would it require a running start and some good timing? A slip on the snowy concrete could put them under the wheels.

"What about the roof?"

"What about it?"

"If the trains buttoned up, we could hop off the roof there and onto the top of a box."

"And then what?"

"I don't know; just thinking out loud."

Carter rubbed his hands together and tried to picture them jumping from the roof of the warehouse onto a moving boxcar. The roof of which would be angled and covered in a layer of snow and ice. It was not an attractive option.

"Let's wait and see."

21

"No real social change has ever been brought about without a revolution ... revolution is but thought carried into action."

—*Emma Goldman*

The president opened the door to find his wife seated in bed with her laptop. A few legal pads were scattered around her, and she had a pencil stuck behind one ear. A habit she had tried to break for many years and failed. She grabbed the top of the screen to close the device, if need be, but relaxed when she saw her husband.

"The pilot?"

The president shut the door behind him and crossed the space between them, before replying, "The SEALs have him. One of the Ospreys took a missile as they were extracting, but they are expected to make it to Al Asad in a little over an hour. We'll know more then."

"Oh ... good. A missile?"

"A shoulder-fired one."

"The missing Stinger you told me about?"

"I think so."

"How in the world did they ever get—"

"I fired James."

She looked back up from her screen and examined his face, before reaching out to grasp his arm. "I'm sorry."

"I told him he could wait until after the State of the Union. Said I'd need some names to consider for his position."

"What did he do?"

"He called Charles. Told him about the pilot, but he left out that he'd been fired."

The first lady removed her glasses and thought about that. "Maybe he just needs to accept it himself, first."

The president rose from where he'd sat himself on the edge of the bed and paced. The sideboard called to him, but he dismissed it. He'd already had one, and it was not a time to drink.

"What happened to him? I wanted to ask, to understand. He was my best friend. A statesman. Ever since I've known him. I ... I don't understand. I *want* to understand."

"I hope you never do."

He spun to face her. The look on her face was difficult to define. Worry? Relief? Sadness? Resignation? Only then did he see it. How close he had come. They had gotten James.

They wouldn't get him too.

"What's that you're working on?"

"Come and see."

She moved the legal pads aside, and he crawled across the bed to join her. She handed the laptop over and then watched him as he read.

"It's good."

"You're sure? I can work on it some more."

"No. It's good. Let's keep it short. It's not a time for flowery speech. Short and simple is best. It's what they deserve to hear."

The first lady took the laptop back and read her own words, soon to be his, a final time, before saving the file to a secured location. She would print it off in her office later and have it back to her husband soon after. She looked back at her husband when she was done, to find him resting, his eyes closed.

"I love you."

"I love you, too."

———

"I trust you've heard?"

Haney had been expecting the call. He'd almost made it himself, but chose to wait, buying him some time to think.

"Yes."

"If that pilot comes out of there alive, our whole campaign is in jeopardy."

"I don't think so; we can always fan the flames in other ways."

"With something better than this? A downed pilot held captive by the enemy? A congressman's son! If they behead him on the internet, the people will beg us to step up the war. Hell, they'll demand it! We could carpet bomb Damascus, and nobody on the security council would dare to protest! Iran would start rattling their sabers, and that would set us up for the next one. This was a golden opportunity, and the man is letting it slide! You have to stop that SEAL team from bringing him out."

"And how do you propose I do that? You think I can just countermand a presidential order, from my office here at home?"

"You told us the man could be controlled."

Haney bristled at the rebuke and paused to take a breath, before responding, "There are no guarantees here, and you know that. The office changes them. The power they yield gets more comfortable and easier to apply every year they're in office. He's in his first term and polling well. Re-election is not his primary problem. He's forgotten how he got there."

"Well, I sent him a reminder."

"You spoke with him?"

"Yes. He said he'd take it under advisement. Obviously, he did not. The bastard thinks he can brush me off? He better think again."

"Charles, that was a mistake. You can't bully men in his position. He's still the President of the United States."

"Because of me! My brother and I put him there!"

"You can buy the office, but it doesn't always come with the man in it."

The statement cut the man off and silenced him. Haney waited. It wasn't long.

"The Vice President is a good man?"

"One of our best."

"I want a meeting of the Trust. Set it up immediately."

"Charles, let's slow down a bit. Take a day to think about this and—"

"Set it up."

The line went dead, and Haney palmed the phone for a few moments before shutting it off and dialing another number. Harper answered on the first ring.

"Yes?"

"I need you here."

"On my way."

***

"Hey, boss."

Jack climbed the last two steps and sat down on the cold aluminum next to Eric. They were both dressed for the weather, this time, but Eric's hair somehow managed to exit his knit cap in all directions. The fleece had been traded for a down jacket and heavy boots, while Jack sported his heavy wool trench coat over his office attire and black tennis shoes. Eric noted the tired eyes and pale skin as Jack sat down and examined the field.

"They gotta be about done for the year, don't they?"

"They're in the running for the finals. If they win this one, they could go all the way."

Jack examined the scoreboard and saw that the home team was well ahead. Their helmeted heads lined the sidelines, and their breath formed clouds in the chilly air as they watched the action on the field. Not a butt was on the bench. The coach screamed from the sidelines, and the crowd kept up, and Jack envied them. He wished he had time for such things. The local things. The things they all considered normal.

"Your face healed up nicely."

"Thanks. Not that anyone would notice, with all the makeup they have me wearing."

"Yeah. What's that all about?"

"PR. Public relations always wins with the politicians. With the Director in the hospital, and Deacon running the show now, they wanted a face to put on the investigation. One that the public already knows. The president decided that I was their man."

"Saw you on the Sunday shows a couple times. You're good at saying nothing," Eric remarked with a grin.

"That's the job: say nothing, while giving off the appearance that there's more you just can't say. The problem is, it's true. We haven't found any trace of our fugitive Shepherd, nor have they made any recent attacks since the guy in Florida. I've got nothing. The techs are still going through the items we salvaged from the storage locker in LA, but other than that we haven't gotten anything new. It's been, what? Almost two months? They've never gone this long without doing something. It's making me wonder."

They both paused the conversation to stand and cheer for the running back as he made a move. After a thirty-yard run and several slipped tackles, he was brought down just short of the goal line. The clock and the position on the field told Jack the game was over. But nobody in the crowd was moving to leave. Jack and Eric made themselves comfortable again.

"So, why do you think they're quiet?"

"I don't know, really. Exploring some theories."

"Such as?"

"Well, the State if the Union speech is coming up. Maybe they want to see if the man is going to acknowledge them?"

Eric thought that one over and then shook his head.

"Not seeing that one, boss. They've never waited for anything, especially politicians."

"True. But ultimately their mission is a political one, so perhaps their leadership wants to pause and let the people think about it. I don't know." Jack shrugged and buried his hands deeper in his pockets.

"You said theories. Plural. What else you thinking?"

"Maybe they're taking a break, because they're gearing up for something big."

"That's a pleasant thought."

"Sydney's, actually. I'm not sure whether I agree or just don't want to."

They watched the game for a bit in silence, before Eric spoke again.

"I wish I had some good news, but I'm afraid I don't. So far, it's all dead ends. The phone number was traced to a burner sold at a Wal-Mart. I checked the security tapes, but the archive had been purged already. No picture of who bought them. We need to have these companies hold the information longer. Most aren't keeping them for the full six months, but we only find out when we go to get something from them. The fine is a fraction of what it costs them to keep the tapes longer, so they just don't."

Jack frowned and nodded. It was an old problem. The cost of compliance with the Homeland Security regulations was often more than the fine for not doing so. Most companies did a simple cost-benefit analysis and opted to pay the fine. It was something he had railed against several times, but the changes were coming slowly.

"The letter?"

"Nothing there, either. All I have is the origin of the mailbox. I pulled security footage from three businesses in the area, but only one of them could give me license plates. The ones I ran came back clean. A couple rental cars, but they traced back to an elderly couple and a family on vacation. I was able to get a few shots of the drivers in the other cars, but they were all profiles, so the facial recognition software wasn't able to offer anything. I have the best shots here."

Eric tapped his leg, and Jack saw a manila envelope under it. Eric would leave it when he got up, and Jack would take it from there to examine later.

"The number?"

"Just a number. It's lost in the flood."

"What's that mean?"

"Six digits. It could be so many things that there's no way to track them down. Is it a license number? Maybe a locker combination? Somebody's old address? Who knows. It's a dead end. Even if it is significant to the sender, it could just be six random numbers they pulled out of their ass."

Jack sighed. He'd expected the answer, but was hoping Eric had stumbled across something. They both watched the quarterback take a hit from the linebacker, for a loss of three. The game was over; they were playing for the scouts who might be in the stands now.

"You said you had something?"

"A mystery, really. What's the word *rubicon* means to you?"

Jack shrugged. "A river in Italy. Or is it Greece? I forget. Something that one of the Caesars crossed, and by doing so, committed the empire to war. Synonymous with the point of no return now. Why?"

"I should have stayed in school, I guess—I had to look it up. Anyway, the NSA programs crawl the net and flag words they see having a large increase in usage. It's mostly to see breaking news from around the world and automatically consolidate it."

"So, you're seeing the word Rubicon?"

"Yes. A lot. But it's mostly in emails and personal text messages. And it's always in a passing way. Never the title of anything or as the subject line. A lot of group texts, and what you'd call junk mail. It's odd, and we can't figure it out."

"You're tracing it?"

"I wanted to, but there was no reason to justify it beyond my gut and that of a few others, and the S&U people don't listen to us. You know that."

Jack grimaced at that. S&U stood for Suits and Uniforms, the people who ran the NSA and other intelligence services. Most were still having a hard time seeing the young computer nerds who worked for them as real soldiers. It was something Jack had warned them about, but the inclination to do so was buried deep.

"I'll make a few calls. Anything else?"

"The protesters."

"What about them? They seem to be behaving."

"They are. They're also very quiet."

"Quiet how?"

"When Occupy was in New York, they were

chatterboxes. It was how the feds knew what they were planning and who the leaders were. Between the phone traffic and the Internet, we were deluged with conversations. It was actually hard to keep up, because we didn't have the people. These protestors, they hardly talk at all."

Jack shrugged. "So, they learned."

"Yeah, but—"

"They're doing nothing illegal, Eric. Constitution? Perhaps you've read it?"

"True. It's just very ... odd."

"We need more than odd—at least I do."

They both stopped as the quarterback took the last snap and spiked the ball to run out the clock. The benches cleared, and the lineman turned to be mobbed by their teammates. The bleachers vibrated with the stomping feet of the fans, and they rose with them to cheer along. Jack used the opportunity to grab the envelope and tuck it inside his coat.

"Call me if you find anything," Jack shouted over the din. He took a step down before Eric stopped him.

"Hey Jack?"

"Yeah?"

"What if the Shepherds being quiet, and the protesters doing the same, is somehow related?"

Jack stopped and considered the question. He didn't have an answer, so he just nodded as the crowd got louder, before moving down the steps and into their numbers. He was soon lost from sight. This time, Eric sat back down and let him leave first.

22

"If we don't make earnest moves toward real solutions, then each day we move one day closer to revolution and anarchy in this country. This is the sad, and yet potentially joyous, state of America."

—Louis Farrakhan

The sound of the engine's horn woke them,

and they immediately scrambled to their feet.

"Stay down."

Carter kept a hand on Tye's shoulder, keeping the man down and out of sight as the train approached. The sheet of plywood had been scrounged from the trash piled up in the corner of the parking lot, and Carter had carried it through the tall drifts of snow and planted it against the wall of the warehouse where it met the leading edge of the concrete platform. He'd then chipped a small hole in the wood, just enough for him to see down the tracks toward town.

That had been several hours ago. Now he and Tye rubbed their arms and stamped their feet in the small space to build a bit of blood circulation. They'd likely get only one chance at this, and they'd prepared as much as possible. Most of Tye's pack was now crammed into Carter's—the bigger man could handle the extra weight without losing his agility on the slippery surface of the concrete platform. Tye had assured him, several times, that he could move fast enough, and Carter tried to remember the man's surprising speed when they had hopped the engine back in Arizona. Whether the older man could make it or not, they would just have to see.

The light of the engine rounding the curve focused right at him, and he turned away so as not to be blinded. The air was filled with snow flurries, and they reflected the light in every direction, cutting visibility to maybe fifty meters. That could help them. The track straightened where it met the warehouse but then curved again soon after leaving it. If the engines were around the bend, and the trees lining the tracks were tall enough, there was a good chance they could get on the train unseen.

A lot of ifs. Carter was hoping they were stacked in their favor.

The three engines chugged by, and Carter measured their speed while examining their windows. The units were buttoned up tight, and condensation fogged the windows. The engineers were no doubt running the heaters on high until the tiny space and its windows were warm enough to overcome the moisture. Good for them.

Carter turned his attention to the approaching cars. Canopy cars mostly, heading north empty to pick up raw materials of some kind. Some tankers that he ignored. Some boxcars came around the curve, and he tapped Tye's shoulder.

"Get ready."

The first fifteen boxcars were shut, and Carter's hope started to fade.

"It was farther down. Toward the end, I think."

"You sure?"

"Not sure of anything, but I think so."

They watched the cars pass now from the open. There was no use in hiding at this point.

"Was that?"

"The red one?"

"That door's half-open. Thas not good."

"Why?"

"Broken. They probly wedged it. If it comes lose, it'll open and shut on the hills. Cut a man clean in half."

"Looks like our only option."

"You say so. Just don't hit it or nuthin' getting on."

"Got it. You ready?"

"As I ever be. You say 'go.'"

Carter measured the train's speed again, and thought it was gaining speed. That probably meant the engine was outside of town and past the speed zone. They'd have to move fast.

"Ready ... Set ... Go!"

Tye took off across the ramp, his legs pumping hard through the foot of snow. Carter waited a full second and then followed, both of them angling toward the edge where the boxcar was approaching. Tye matched the car's speed for three paces and then leaped.

But the snow worked against him. The foot he'd pushed off with lost traction, and he landed hard in the car's doorway. His feet dragging behind him and building up snow, as they traveled along the concrete. Carter cursed as he pulled alongside. With only five meters left, he threw himself over Tye to land inside the car.

"Git me in!" Tye said.

Carter scrambled on all fours across the floor and grabbed Tye's hand just as he started to slip away back out the door. The heavy metal door bounced on its hardware, and Carter cringed, waiting for it to come loose and slam shut on the man's belly.

"Git me in!" Tye wailed again.

Carter grabbed his other hand and rolled toward the middle of the car, pulling the older man inside and over his own body. The door banged hard again, as if protesting their actions, but Carter didn't care; they were in, and that's all that mattered. The two men lay on their backs and sucked in the cold air in rapid succession.

"Heh-heh. I never was very graceful." Tye remarked.

For some reason that struck Carter as funny, and he chuckled along with him. The chuckle turned to a laugh, and soon they were both roaring as loud as they could manage in the cold mountain air.

Eventually, the cold floor forced them back to reality. They both rose and examined their surroundings. A few large crates occupied one end of the car. The name of a major farm equipment manufacturer stamped on their side. A few sheets of cardboard and some trash were stuffed in the rails along the sides, and the floor held its usual coating of grimy railyard dirt.

"Seen worse. Let's see if there's room behind the crates, knock down the wind some." Tye tossed his pack down against the larger one and then moved around the side. Carter was about to follow when something caught his eye.

It was just a wadded-up piece of paper. Like any other one might see in a pile of random trash, it moved around the floor in a circle, propelled by the swirling wind coming through the open doors. But this one was white and without the layer of dirt it would have normally acquired bouncing around the inside of a railcar. This one was new. He stepped over and retrieved it before it could blow out the open door.

He smoothed it out on his leg and examined it.

He'd been right. The paper was a wanted notice. His mugshot from LA, both front and in profile, was portrayed prominently at the top. The list of charges was vague, but somehow managed to sound dangerous. Anyone who might see him was instructed that he was armed and extremely dangerous and to not approach. The numbers for the FBI and the State Troopers offices were displayed at the bottom.

Carter thought about what it meant. There was no mention of him being a member of the Shepherds. Nor had they gone so far as to give him a most-wanted status. There was also nothing suggesting he might be on the trains. Yet they had been specifically targeting the rail yard. Perhaps the information regarding the trains had been discovered after the flyer had been printed? Either way, this was a problem.

"Whatcha got there?"

"Oh, nothing. Just some junk mail advertising." Carter wadded the paper back up casually and tossed it out the open door.

"What you find back there?"

"Enough room for both of us. Couple sheets of cardboard. Not too bad, really."

"I'll take it. Long as it's not in the snow."

"Heh. I hear dat."

"HOW LONG ARE you in Boston for?"

"The contract is for six months, but it might run over that; they usually do. No more than eight months, I should think. Is that a problem?"

"I don't think so; we have a few units available around that time. Mostly retired couples that head south for the winter. Here we are."

Will followed the woman out of the elevator and paused briefly to inspect the foyer before moving on. He saw three doors. One to the adjacent apartment, and the other to the fire escape. The agent sorted through her ring of keys to find the one which matched the number on the third door. 902. The ninth floor. That put it in the middle zone, one that people accustomed to living in tall buildings were familiar with. It was high enough to escape most of the traffic noise from below, yet still within reach of flying insects. Not that this would be a problem. The freezing New England temperatures outside made bugs the least of his worries. Despite what he was telling the real estate agent, he would be gone several months before the bugs showed up.

He half-listened to her banter as she led him through the condo. The area he was in was on the west side of the city and home to several large corporations. Money was everywhere. To fit in, Will had been forced to clean up his act. Gone was the long hair and the scruff of beard. He now sported the gelled hair and goatee of a Gen X mercenary consultant. The scars and the muscles were hidden under an expensive tailored suit, and the sunglasses and gold watch only served to cement the look of money he was trying to portray. He'd seen the woman sizing him up and had no doubt the price she would quote him had been adjusted upwards. He didn't care; she wouldn't be getting anything beyond the initial six-month deal, and that was well within his budget.

He wandered behind her as she walked him through the rooms, inspected the refrigerator and sink for appearances' sake, and then tested the water in the bathroom. It was a condo, like a thousand others in the city, nothing to get too excited about. A one bedroom with a balcony off it and the large living area. The features were new, and Will politely smiled as the woman went on about the granite countertops and wood floors.

"The kitchen's a bit small, but you could

handle meals for two quite easily. Four or more in a pinch."

"It's very nice," he humored her.

'The rent's 2,800 dollars a month. That's obscene to most out-of-towners, but on average for the area. They've actually held steady, this year. Have you worked in Boston before?"

"No, no. My first time. I travel a lot." He walked to the window and wiped the condensation from the glass. Outside, there was a small table and a pair of chairs. They both held a dusting of snow.

"What kind of work do you do?"

"Consulting, mostly government but also the occasional Fortune 500 company. I'm afraid I can't go much beyond that."

"I understand. Are you used to the cold?"

A snowcapped outpost made of rock on the top of an Afghan mountain flashed through his mind.

"It won't be a problem."

To drive the point home and hopefully end the small talk, he opened the slider and stepped out into the frigid temperatures. Grasping the railing in his gloved hands, he peered over the side. The building was one of four, all rising to the east of an exclusive gated community. He compared the view with the map in his head and traced the streets to the home of his target. It was a straight line-of-sight.

"Braver than me," she commented. "I'm not a fan of the high places."

He offered a disarming smile and returned to the condo. After shutting the door behind him, he began asking questions just to keep her from doing the same.

"The neighbors?"

She dropped her voice to a whisper, as if she were betraying trade secrets. "I only know a few. I sold the unit next door to the Johnsons last year. He retired from the military a few years back, and now only works for some contractors over the summer. A lovely couple, but they do have a small dog. The man upstairs lives alone; he lost his wife to cancer a few months ago, and he's called me twice about putting the unit back on the market. Always changes his mind. I know he probably can't afford it with her gone, but I think he feels he'd be leaving her if he moved. So sad."

"I see. That is sad." He paused for the appropriate amount of time, before asking, "Security?"

"A doorman, who doubles as a guard, is here twenty-four hours a day. There are cameras in the lobby and the parking garage. Each occupant has a pass card and code that is good for every entrance and all the amenities." She went on about the buildings pool and gym and the library for several minutes, and Will let her, happy to let her babble away while he sized up the rest of the room.

If she only knew he would be using it for a short time, she certainly wouldn't have bothered. Will continued his survey, until the woman ran out of steam and stood clicking her pen while she waited. He stopped again at the window and examined the view again.

"We have another unit available on the other side? Two bedrooms, but it gets more sun from the southern exposure."

Will turned to her and smiled. "I don't need the extra space, and I'm a bit of a night owl. This will be fine. You've sold me; I'll take it."

The agent smiled and pulled out a rental agreement. Thirty minutes later, Will left with a key in his hand. He walked her down to the parking garage and helped her into her aging Volvo. He'd parked his new BMW next to hers for appearances' sake but waited until she had backed out and was driving away before moving toward it.

In the trunk were two suitcases and a large cardboard box. It was everything he would need for the mission. It would take him a few trips to get it all upstairs. He grabbed the suitcase with the wheels and pulled it out. He'd come back for the rest later, after he had taken off this damn suit.

The first thing he unpacked was an electronic scanner. Using the device, he checked every inch of each room, looking for any hidden bugs or cameras. After finding none, he checked several broadcasting frequencies. Most were clear, and he jotted the numbers down before moving back to the balcony.

The bedroom offered a slightly better angle, and he moved some furniture around to give him the best view from the bed.

With any luck, he'd be able to perform the mission without leaving the room. He stowed the scanner, and then stripped off the tie, and heavily starched shirt, and tossed them on to the bed. He rubbed his neck while walking back to the slider. He hated wearing suits; they reminded him of his uniform. The same one he had worn for the parades and medal ceremonies he had attended for years. He'd hated those too; hours of pressing, and creasing, and measuring, to make sure the blue suit was perfect, only to stand at attention for hours on end in the hot sun. He had tolerated them in exchange for the shiny piece of metal.

Back then, he had believed it all to be worth it.

But then the war had been declared over. He

had been ready to finish his enlistment and go home, but they had convinced him to stay. The re-enlistment had come with a promotion, and that led to a higher security clearance. With that had come more missions, ones that came with classified code names. Will was soon flying his General Atomics MQ-1 Predator drone into places the maps told him they were not supposed to be. The war had changed. His targets were no longer black and white. The word "suspected" began to appear in front of many of them. And suspicion alone was enough to earn a visit from his drone and its million-dollar missiles.

The day had finally come when he had refused to pull the trigger. He'd been immediately replaced and had watched from the back of the small room as the two vehicles traveling on the desert road were obliterated. The little girl's face that had been pressed to the glass, disappearing in an orange and black cloud.

They had tried to talk him back in, and when that didn't work, they had sent him to the shrinks. Neither had changed his mind, and a month later he found himself standing in the airport with discharge papers in his hands. A month later, he had cut his hand on the glass he was holding in a tiny bar on the city's south side, the overhead TV showing leaked footage of drone strikes similar to his last one.

He'd walked out of the emergency room with eight stiches and the intent of going right back to the bar. Leaning on his car in the parking lot was a man who called himself Dayton.

That had been over a year ago. Will now pursued a life of ever-refining balance, each mission getting him a little closer to finding his center again. Hopefully, this one would complete that process.

Opening the balcony door, he ignored the blast of cold air and walked through the snow to the railing. He gripped it hard and stared off to the east. Out there was the man whose company made the missiles. A man he was told had taken steps to see that more of them were needed.

Will was here to do something about that.

23

"*We know what the birth of a revolution looks like: A student stands before a tank. A fruit seller sets himself on fire. A line of monks link arms in a human chain. Crowds surge, soldiers fire, gusts of rage pull down the monuments of tyrants, and maybe, sometimes, justice rises from the flames.*"

—Nancy Gibbs

L ike the others around him, he shouted the slogan back and waved the sign at the building. His wife was a few yards to his right today, and they kept tabs on one another as they worked their way around the perimeter. Today the sun was shining, and he welcomed its warmth, as well as its brightness, as it allowed him to wear his sunglasses without raising suspicion.

As they walked, he took note of the men manning the fence today. They were DC policemen, and he knew most of them by name and badge number. During the first few days, he had wandered close to them, one by one, and his body camera had gathered the info without the men. It had been copied down, encrypted, and then sent to a PO Box somewhere in Virginia. A few days later, files on each man had arrived in the couple's mailboxes, and they had taken a few drives around the city to locate the policemen's residences. The husband now ticked them off from memory as he encountered them. So far, he had seen no new people today, and that was good.

The men were alert but relaxed. So far, the protests were working as they were designed to. The crowd was loud but disciplined. Angry, but restrained. The result of which was a more relaxed police presence. The first sign of which had been a drop in their numbers. He now estimated that they held about half of what they had started with on the first day. Perhaps the overtime was starting to weigh on their superior's budgets? Good.

The riot gear was gone too, but he was sure there was a van full of armor-clad SWAT teams within a couple of minutes distance that could be summoned with a simple radio call. He dismissed that; that problem had no doubt been assigned to someone else.

He eyeballed the next cop. Regular winter uniform. Insulated jacket over the blue department garb. Thick soled boots to insulate his feet from the cold concrete. The Sam Browne belt held the usual suspects. Gun. Taser. Cuffs. A few had nightsticks, and others carried extra zip ties. The man met his gaze, and he returned it with a smile. The man's lip twitched before adopting its prescribed poker face, and he moved on without engaging him further. If the man was returning the smiles of the passing protestors, that meant the police were getting comfortable with them. Good. He tested this further, by grinning broadly at the next man and walking as close as he could to him. The man stood his ground with a nod, but took no action against him, even though only inches separating them. It was working.

A nudge from his opposite side revealed that his wife had joined him.

"That was close," she said.

"Yeah. If they all get as complacent as that guy, I think we'll be okay."

"Let's hope. Ten minutes to rotation. You thirsty?"

"If we go now, we can stop and grab something on the way and still make it on time."

They turned away from the White House and made their way north-east toward the Capitol building. It was a walk they were well familiar with now. A favorite coffee shop was only a block away. They nodded at other protestors as they made their way down the street.

"How's the vest traveling?"

"Heavy, but at least it's warm. Anybody say anything or bump into you?"

She was referring to undercover cops. It was well-known that the DC police sent plain-clothed officers out into the protest. They would ask seemingly innocent questions and bump into people in an effort to learn what they had under their coats. Most had been flagged and then followed by one of their people with specially worded signs announcing who they were. If the cops had caught on, the couple had not yet seen any sign of it. Today had been a day to try the vests. It was colder, and the added bulk would not be found unusual. It was time to let the cops get used to their size and shape.

"No, not so far. I only saw one warning sign today, and it was on the other side of the crowd."

"Just don't show everybody what you got on under there when you reach for your wallet."

"Yes, dear."

They entered the coffee shop and stowed their signs next to the door while he went to stand in line. She watched out the windows as the protest left the White House and made its way down the street on both sides. They were careful to step aside for passing pedestrians and also to stay out of the street. A few cops escorted them along without any trouble. Her husband was right: They looked relaxed.

"It's working."

"Excuse me?" the man next to her asked.

"I'm sorry; just talking to myself."

The man nodded and went back to his paper. The *Washington Post*, she saw, was only a few blocks away. She remembered the reporters and their editorial and wondered what they were doing now. What did they think of all this?

THE MOOD WAS evident as soon as they entered the house. There was no light banter taking place. No cigars. No rattling glasses of amber liquid. There was only the smell of damp hay and the rustic decor of the rural farmhouse. Their drivers waited in the barn with the horses, and the men were forced to brave the rain in order to reach the house itself.

The air was thick with tension as they sat down. At the head of the table was the elder brother, with Haney now sitting at his right side. Something had happened. An event worthy of them being summoned for an emergency meeting. The private jets gathered at the airport had been an unusual sight, even for Teterboro. What was even more unusual was the drive north, rather than into the city. But they had learned not to question such things anymore.

The last of their members silently arrived and took his seat, raking the rain from his face and frowning until the tension around him became known. Haney nodded to acknowledge his presence and got started.

"We have an issue. The President has launched a mission to retrieve the pilot from Syria. As you know we were counting on his ... demise, to fuel the call for further action in the area, with the hope of leveraging that across the entire region. The instability we seek may be compromised by this action. The President has—"

Charles cut him off, "The President can no longer be counted on. I'm proposing that he be removed."

The men all spoke at once, and Haney waved for their silence.

"Somehow, the President was convinced to go against our plan. I'm looking into how and why that happened, but for now, Charles, David, and I are considering alternatives."

"The Vice President?" the banker said. "Seriously?"

"You have an objection?"

"The man's a placeholder. We had him say and do everything that was needed to fill the holes in the President's resume just to lock up the base voters. Beyond that, he's a caricature. Do we really want him in the oval?"

David placed a calming hand on his brother's

arm before he spoke up, "The issue isn't his character or his lack of spine; it's his pliability. The Vice President has proven himself to be a man that will do as he's told."

"That's what we were told about the current President," the banker added.

Haney's head snapped around at that and he fixed the man in his gaze until he looked away and sat back. He then turned it on each member at the table, before addressing them all, "I installed the man you chose. He didn't come with a guarantee. If you don't like my services or my way of doing things—ways that have delivered for so long that you've come to take them for granted—you can all go fuck yourselves and find someone else."

The following silence was deafening, broken only by the flash of lightning and the roar of the thunder outside. Haney's face was a mask of evil in the reflected light, and the others quickly remembered their place. Haney was their dog, but he was a dangerous one—one that could turn on its masters at any time, with deadly results.

The elder brother broke the silence, "The mission cannot be retracted. We need a substitution."

"What are you proposing?"

"We have two threats. The delay of our mission in the Middle East will take some time to overcome, and we will make arrangements to do so. The threat of the President cannot be ignored. He needs to be weakened. We feel it best to accomplish two goals at the same time. Ratchet up the fear levels of the public, while showing the current man in office as ineffective.

"Just what is it you're proposing?"

"Threats from overseas only work if they strike a chord here at home. Americans didn't give a damn about Syria until a few of their people lost their heads on the Internet. The few lone wolves they've managed to inspire have done more for us than anything happening overseas. The Boston marathon. San Bernardino. The nightclub in Florida. The idiot shoe bomber. That's what gets the fear factor working for us. Each one of those attacks resulted in billions in profits. If we keep this on the TV, and in their heads, they'll elevate it to a priority, no matter how low the odds of it actually happening to them."

"You have some of these lone wolves in your quiver?"

"Normally, I would steer away from this domestically. But the time may be right to arrange an ... incident."

"An incident? You mean another attack, here in America?"

"Yes, and very soon. Something that will get the public's attention and hold it. Something that shows them that the President is not keeping them safe. Something close to home."

"New York or DC?"

The brothers exchanged a look with each other and Haney, before agreeing to reply.

"DC."

"THEY DON'T NEED to know the specifics," Haney said.

The two brothers and Haney were now alone in the small house. The Trust had been dismissed, all of them warned where not to be when the time came. They had reluctantly agreed to the plan, despite Haney's unwillingness to reveal its details. Each of them had chosen a place that would provide them both safety and deniability, should either be needed in the future. Now the three men were alone to work out the details.

"The attack in DC? You'll make it appear as if it was the Shepherds who made it?"

"I believe I can do so, especially if we make it a two-pronged attack. We'll remove the opposition and repaint the Shepherds as a terrorist organization, all at the same time. But I think I can do more than that."

"Explain."

"I know who their leader is."

"You what? Have you been keeping this—"

"I've just obtained some evidence from the Shepherd case file. It's only a few days old, and it's not conclusive, but it makes sense.

"Who?"

"General Nils Marr."

"Marr? He's done. Sure, he has some influence, and he throws a bit of money around, but it's a fraction of what we do. He hasn't been a player since he got blown up in Iraq. What makes you so sure it's him?"

"My gut. It's just too convenient. The more I think about it, the more it makes sense. He never stopped, even after I put him in that chair. He just went underground. The information I have points to the Shepherds' operations using property and accounts which trace back to the General's corporations. It's a loose connection, but it's there."

"That's not much."

"Exactly. But it's precisely how I would do it."

The two brothers exchanged a look after hearing that. Haney was their fixer, the man who got the things done that they couldn't. He also had decades of experience in his field. He was telling them something he believed to be a danger to them, and they had learned long ago the fault of doubting him.

"What do we risk by removing him?" David asked.

"It depends on who's doing the asking. After tomorrow, I don't think that will matter."

"What are you proposing?"

"Our friend the General lives in a remote location. One that's far from the prying eyes of neighbors or the law. If I'm right, reaching him won't be easy, but if done right, we can isolate the action. We'll remove both him and the Shepherds in one swift strike."

"And then?"

Haney smiled.

"Erase the fact that it ever happened."

The brothers said nothing, and Haney waited while they weighed the pros and cons. It wouldn't take long; they were men used to making decisions rapidly and decisively.

"Inform us when it's done."

Haney watched the men leave, each of them driving themselves away in a generic car. Each of them thinking they were kings of their world.

Haney knew better. Who was more powerful? The king, or the man who controlled him?

Footsteps approached behind him and stopped.

"You heard?"

"Yes," Harper replied.

"Make it happen."

24

"You don't have a peaceful revolution. You don't have a turn-the-cheek revolution. There's no such thing as a nonviolent revolution."

—Malcolm X

His name was Simon, and he'd been a Shepherd for some time.

Like many of the others, he'd been a

soldier once, but that was many years ago, and when not working as a Shepherd, he now worked to help his fellow veterans. The injuries he saw at the Veterans Administration hospital were horrific, and each one of them only cemented his resolve to continue.

It had started in Iraq. After the initial attack, and the president's foolish *Mission Accomplished* speech on the deck of the aircraft carrier, the call had gone out for men with his skills and education. Like many young people, he'd been galvanized by the events of nine-eleven and abandoned his pursuit of an advanced degree in microbiology in favor of joining the military. After basic training, his education had been discovered, and he's been sent to OSC and then on to NBC school. There, he'd become an expert on Nuclear, Biological, and Chemical weapons. By that time, the war in Iraq was gearing up, and he found himself deployed with several Special Forces units as they scoured the country for weapons of mass destruction.

It took him several months, and a bullet through his thigh from an enemy sniper, before he saw the truth.

He had been sent on a fool's errand. His mission was nothing more than a show. One put on to appease the international community and justify their reason for being there. He'd watched the war continue while lying in the hospital bed. With countless men and woman on both sides paying the price for an old man's vengeance. Many without their arms or legs. More with their lives. A countless number paid with their sanity, a wound they would never recover from, and the truth of why they were there burned into Simon's consciousness to smolder just under the surface.

But then Dayton had found him. Just in time. He gave Simon both an outlet and a focus for his rage. He had kept him from returning to the hospital as a patient and transformed him into one who helped instead. He now spent his time and his knowledge helping the soldiers he couldn't save. Between that and the Shepherds' mission, he had found the balance he so desperately needed.

Tonight, that balance called him. His daily check-in with William had prompted an early morning exit from his home in Norfolk. A visit to a storage unit had resulted in the van being stocked and the motorcycle loaded. He now drove up I-95 toward New Jersey, past the line of aircraft carriers at the shipyard. He'd be across the bridge-tunnel complex and into Delaware in about an hour. Plenty of time to get in place.

As he crossed the bridge, he couldn't help but notice the black water of the Atlantic off to his right. The ocean churned, and the whitecaps looked cold as they lapped against the patches of snow on the sand.

If everything was still in order, he'd be walking in that cold water soon. Despite its frigid temperature, he welcomed the idea.

HARPER FOLLOWED the map on the GPS and cursed the men who had sent it. He was travelling through the worst part of DC he had ever been to, and that said something. The job was bad enough without unnecessary risks, but he wasn't the one who picked the drop-off point. The item was prepared as he had requested and delivered on time, and that was all that really mattered. The men who had fabricated it had asked no questions, and he didn't even know their names or where they came from. He had offered nothing in return, either—just a bag of cash and a time. It was business as usual for him, even if it was inside the nation's capital.

The car got a few curious glances, but they quickly turned away, and Harper chalked it up to the crime kingpins in the area driving similar vehicles. Maybe the high-dollar Mercedes hadn't been such a bad choice. At the last intersection, he'd seen a man at the corner sizing it and him up, but in the end a shake of his fellow dealer's head had killed the idea of robbing the strange white man.

"Leave this one alone," Harper said for him. He laughed and then drove on.

The warehouse had a fence. Twelve feet high, with a barbed wire top. It was par for the neighborhood. The row houses around it were mostly abandoned, and he scanned their windows for anyone watching as he worked the key into the lock. He drove the car through and pulled the gate shut behind it, leaving the chain together but unlocked in the event he needed to leave in a hurry. The car was parked in the middle of the lot, and he paused for a few seconds to address something, before exiting and locking it behind him. The same key worked on the garage door of the warehouse, and he left it open behind him as well.

Inside, he found it. A delivery truck. Brown in color and displaying the logo of a well-known shipping company. Its surface had been newly washed and wiped clean of any smudge or fiber. The cockpit was as clean as the outside. Not a trace of anyone's presence was to be seen. Harper examined it carefully without touching it for a full minute before walking to the back, donning a pair of gloves, and opening the rear.

Inside were cardboard boxes. All different sizes. They lined the sturdy shelves on both sides and covered the floor. Prominent among them were four big ones, each about the size of a trash can. They were sealed up with shipping tape and bore all the usual stickers and bar codes of the packages one would expect to find. On the floor in front of him was an electronic clipboard, and a small box with a coded address prominent on its front. Harper pulled a knife from his boot and sliced the seal open.

Inside was a remote detonator. It had a dial that he could adjust to count down from any number he chose under sixty minutes, and a master switch to override that if needed.

Perfect.

Underneath the detonator was a uniform wrapped in plastic. He held it up for size and then rapidly changed into it. It fit as had been promised, and he only needed to adjust the ball cap a little to complete the disguise. The keys to the truck were in the pocket of the jacket, and he palmed them before shutting the door and returning to the front.

Starting the truck, he listened for any mechanical complaints. The fuel gauge read almost a full tank of gas. He'd only need a quarter of that, but the rest would not go to waste.

He pulled out of the warehouse and past the car without stopping. A light tap on the gate shoved it open, and he was through and gone before it stopped swinging. He retraced his path through the streets for several blocks until he was stopped by a red light. There, he pulled out his phone. The number was already queued up, but he double-checked it and then the clock on the dash, before moving his thumb over the call button.

The car had been in the warehouse lot for maybe fifteen minutes. Long enough for the two open jugs of gasoline he had left on the floor of the backseat to fill the interior with fumes. As much as he wanted to wait and add this to the confusion of what was to come, the chances of someone moving into the warehouse's open gate and attempting to steal the car were too great. He pushed the button.

In his rearview mirror, he saw it first. An orange flash of billowing cloud suddenly sprang into view over the rowhouse roofs behind him. A second later, the sound reached him, and his fellow drivers gazed about to find its source. By the time they did, the cloud had turned black and was rising rapidly into the cold air and drifting east.

The fire, fueled by the two gallons of gas inside and the contents of the cars own gas tank, would burn hot and fierce for the next several minutes, engulfing the car and erasing his existence from it. The burner phone he had used for a detonator would be melted, and only a detailed examination would reveal what it had been used for. By the time the fire department reached it, the car would be little more than a charred frame of steel.

He dismissed the car as the light turned green. He had more important things to worry about. With a lurch, the truck moved forward, taking him back toward the district.

THEY WERE CLIMBING AGAIN.

Carter pulled the coat tighter around his neck and watched the snow-covered peaks out the open door of the boxcar as the train struggled up the mountain. He looked for familiar terrain, but nothing had jogged his memory yet. Perhaps he was looking in the wrong direction. The overcast sky hid the sun, and with the constant twist and turns in the track, he had lost direction. They had not passed through a town in some time, it had been nothing but snow and pine trees for the last several hours.

He leaned forward enough to see around the edge of the crate. Tye was bundled up in his new coat and boots, and sleeping in Carter's sleeping bag, which they had placed on the stacked scraps of cardboard scrounged from the corners of the boxcar. Every square inch of skin was covered, and Carter could only see the cloud of each breath in the cold.

Assured that his companion was out, Carter pulled the GPS from inside his coat and held it out toward the open door. It took a change in the train's direction before it got signal, and Carter soon had a map showing his position and that of his destination.

It was close. It was time to go.

He shut the device off and got to his feet, flexing them inside the boots to get some warmth back into them. He stuck his head out into the cold breeze for a quick look ahead, but seeing nothing but the snow and the trees, he quickly pulled it back. Rubbing his cheeks with both hands he checked for frostbite. He thought his nose might have a bit, so he gently rubbed it until it tingled. While he did so, he contemplated the man sleeping at his feet.

A part of him didn't want to leave him. In their time together, he had come to like the old man and his simple life. The words of Dayton had kept coming back to him. *You need ordinary people in your life; they'll keep you grounded.* It was true. Tye had helped him define his situation. He'd reduced it down to the bare minimums. It had taken Carter until yesterday to realize that the monster was at bay.

The simple acts of staying alive and moving had relegated its thirst to a lower priority. Carter had explored the how and the why that had happened for several hours. Had he become to obsessed with his past? Did his addictive personality just need a different outlet? Could he replace the gym and the missions with something else, and still keep the monster at bay? He didn't know, but he had plans to find out. If Rubicon was indeed in play, he would soon lose his identity of Number Six, and he wasn't sure what would happen to him after that. Could he function in the world without being a Shepherd? He hoped so. The alternative frightened him. He was afraid of what he might become. Without the missions to balance him, the monster might take over. He had to find a way to stop it.

Later.

He first had to complete the mission he was on now. For that to happen, he needed to travel undetected. So far, the trains had allowed that to happen, but where he was going there would be no trains. Or sixty-year-old tramps to guide him. It was time for him and Tye to part ways.

Carter silently walked to the corner and grabbed both of their bags, before returning to his seat on the other side of the crate. Digging deep into his own, he found the stacks of cash and pulled one free. Ten Thousand dollars. Was it too much? He tried to picture what Tye would do with ten thousand dollars. Would he leave the rails and try to start over? Would he use it to go find his family? Or would he just stick it back in his bag and ride on? Carter didn't know.

He found himself hoping Tye would simply ride on. It gave Carter some comfort knowing Tye could do so a little easier, and Carter selfishly admitted that he might join him again someday. Either way, he didn't need the money nearly as much as the old man did. He stuffed the stack into Tye's bag and zipped it up.

Leave a note? No. What was there to say?

Would Tye see a police flyer soon and wonder who the man was he had shared a railcar with for a few weeks? Maybe. Would he fear Carter's return? He doubted it; Tye didn't seem to be afraid of much.

The boxcar lurched as the train swung into another curve. Carter shuffled back around the crate and left the bag next to his traveling companion. Carter would leave the sleeping bag and a few other items behind, as well. He hoped to be long gone before Tye woke.

"Good luck, old man," Carter whispered.

Without a second look, Carter made his way to the door. The wind had a bite to it, and he squinted ahead as the train began to climb again. He could now see up ahead, and the lights of the approaching town made the sky above glow in an orange haze. It was the top of the pass; on the other side of town, the train would start its descent into the valley. That meant more speed. If Carter was going to leave the train, he had to do it now.

He tightened the backpack's straps and scrapped any snow from his boot's treads, before examining the snow and the trees on the side of the tracks. The drifts were deceiving. Were they just snow, shaped by the wind into drifts as tall as a car? Or were they hidden trees or boulders, covered with just enough to hide them? If Carter made the wrong choice, he could lie injured, possibly for days, until someone happened across his frozen body, or he was seen by the conductor of the next train passing through.

Unless the animals found him first.

Carter shook off the morbid thoughts and kept his eye on the tracks. A large snowbank was his first choice, followed by a small group of pines or a combination of both. He estimated it to be a ten-foot drop from the deck of the railcar, over the raised bed of the track, and into the snow. He planned to do a PLF, a Parachute Landing Fall, into the snow. Rolling with the impact, and letting it be absorbed at multiple points of his body. With any luck, he would only get a little cold and snow-covered.

That was the plan, anyway.

The glow of the town was getting closer, and the grade was beginning to decrease. Every meter the train traveled now brought him closer to being to discovered. He had to go.

A break in the trees was up ahead. He examined the opening and saw a large drift had built up in the gap. Beyond it were some dense pines, where he could hide until the train passed. It was the best option he'd seen so far.

Backing up a few paces, he watched for the gap

to appear. When it did, he took a last look at the sleeping shape of Tye before launching himself across the boxcar and out the door. The cold wind found its way into every gap in his clothes as he sailed through the air and landed in the soft snow. He rolled his body as it approached and braced himself for impact.

But it never came. The soft snow swallowed him up, and he sank deep into its clutches without resistance. Day quickly turned to night as he disappeared from sight. It was as if he had dived into a bowl of milk. He let out the held breath and forced himself to lie still, as the sound of the passing train and the vibrations of its weight on the tracks traveled through the snow to his ears. After a few moments, it began to fade, and he cautiously moved to escape the snow.

It was harder than he had expected. The snow was soft in every direction, and it forced him to swim to his freedom. Eventually, he struck solid ground and got to his feet.

The snow was over the top of his boots. He stood still and cleared it from his neck and eyes, before brushing it off his body. He couldn't afford for it to melt and get him wet. With no way to get warm other than his own body heat, he would quickly succumb to hypothermia. In the process, he examined himself for damage. He was surprisingly intact, as was his gear. The bank now showed a large hole, marking his impact. His first reaction was to hide it, but he dismissed the thought. The wind and the coming snow would do that for him before the next train arrived. He needed to move.

The train could now be seen traveling on the other side of the bend, and Carter saw the last boxcar disappear into the haze under the lights of the small town. He hoisted his pack and made to follow.

HARPER PULLED into the small parking lot and shut off the engine. Through the fence he could see the entire facility. The runway was small, and the planes it serviced matched. The single runway was barely long enough to accommodate the small jet that was to arrive at any minute. But that had never stopped the man before. He had flown in and out of tighter spots on six continents for the majority of his life; today was nothing new.

The urgency of the request had determined the meeting place. The late hour would assure their privacy. The amateur pilots with their tiny

Cessnas and Pipers had long since departed. The placc was a graveyard.

The runway lights came to life before he heard the plane. It descended out of the clouds and lined up only seconds before hitting the runway. Harper left the car and let himself into the building, only to exit out the other side and wait where the man could see him. The plane pulled up forty meters away, and the man in the cockpit took a good look at him before shutting the engines down.

As usual, he had come alone, and his large frame crossed the tarmac directly to Harper.

"Aaron."

"Harper. Long time."

"C'mon. We can talk inside." Harper turned and headed back inside the building. The man hesitated only long enough to scan the area before following.

Harper smiled at the man's paranoia, but it was well-earned. Aaron King was a mercenary. Oh, he had a different, more politically correct way, of saying it, but they both were past that. A former SEAL, King had been one of the first to see the opportunity for private security companies to profit greatly at the upstart of the Iraq war. Using his family's money, and the long list of contacts he had made while in the spec-ops world, he had quickly built the largest security company in the United States. Soon after, he had over a hundred different contracts signed.

After milking the government for every dollar he could get from that war, he had changed the name of his company twice before branching out into Africa and other parts of the Middle East. Today, if you were a wealthy Saudi who needed your family guarded from rival factions, or an African tribal leader who needed his enemy removed, it could all be handled with one call to Aaron King. He and Harper had known each other for over a decade, and work often got passed back and forth when needed. As it would today.

Harper led him inside, and they grabbed a seat across from each other in the tiny lounge. Harper reached into his jacket and removed an envelope. He tossed it on the table between them. King glanced at it but left it alone.

"What's the job?"

"Need a man removed."

"Foreign or domestic?"

"Domestic. Montana."

King frowned at that. He hated working in-country. But if the money was right ...

"Who?"

"General Nils Marr."

King's eyebrows shot up on hearing the name. Everyone in the military— past and present— knew the name of the General.

"You're serious?"

"Yes."

"You know what kind of heat that will bring down? The kind that's worldwide and never-ending."

"Never scared you before."

"Don't be stupid. If you're *not* scared, you're too dumb to be thinking about it. You don't just pop a guy like that and walk away. He's got soldiers of his own."

"His army of misfit toys?"

"No, he's got more than that."

Harper was caught off guard. Did King already know about the General and the Shepherds?

"Explain?"

"A few of my older guys heard he had some Delta guys on the payroll now."

Harper shrugged "So? You do too."

"If all you want is a secure place, you can do it for a lot cheaper than what those guys cost."

"So, what are you saying? Can you handle it or not?"

King looked away and recrossed his leather boots on the table.

"At his home? That fucking castle in the mountains?"

"Yes. You know it?"

"Checked it out, once. It's a fortress."

"But rural. Isolated."

"Assault on a place like that ... it'll take every guy I have. When do you need it done?"

"You have a bit of time to prepare, but the mission has to go off on the time set in the package."

King frowned and scooped up the envelope. He scanned the first page and frowned harder.

"That's a busy night. Is this just to assure that he'll be there?"

"Yes."

King shook his head and examined the rest of the envelope's contents. Photos. Maps. Some diagrams of the power and communication systems. He leafed through it and then stuck it back in the envelope. He tossed it back on the table and rubbed the stubble on his chin while he examined his old colleague. He was hiding something, but that wasn't unusual in their line of work.

"Well?"

"Ten."

"I was thinking more in the neighborhood of eight."

"Eight million, for this job? Make it twelve."

"Ten is fine."

"What I thought. In my account, no later than tomorrow night."

"And?"

King picked the envelope back up and stood.

"And nothing. Send the money. When I have it, I'll be in touch."

With that, he spun on his heel and stalked back outside to his plane. The little Cessna Citation Mustang came to life a moment later and taxied to the end of the runway. Harper waited until the roar of its engines faded, before pulling out his phone.

"Yes?"

"He agreed to the ten. Soon as it's in place, he'll get started."

"Excellent."

25

"Revolution is as unpredictable as an earthquake and as beautiful as spring. Its coming is always a surprise, but its nature should not be."

—Rebecca Solnit

An hour later, Carter came to the edge of town and found a good spot in the trees to look it over. A few people were out and about on the main street, but there were not many. He spotted several trails of smoke now coming from the chimneys and could follow to where the few roads went to by the smoke. It was an odd town. One that appeared to be in transition. He saw a lot of heavy logging equipment sitting idle in various lots. Warehouses near the tracks with snow covering their driveways and parking areas. Many of the homes had snow drifts blocking their driveways and piled up against the sides. The few stores he could see were gift shops and small eateries, most of them closed. It was logging town, one that was becoming a resort community. The closed houses were no doubt owned by seasonal owners. Retired couples who were now in Arizona or someplace else warm. The rest were year-rounders that kept the town in a dormant stage until they returned, or the back roads cleared of snow enough for them to resume logging.

The observation gave Carter options. He examined the few roads leading out of town and selected one which had only a few wisps of smoke rising from it. He set off to parallel it.

A couple miles later, he found what he had been looking for. The house was small—little more than a cabin—but it had a few clues as to what he might find inside. A rope with a hook hung from a large tree in the backyard, and Carter had no problem picturing a freshly shot deer or elk hanging from it while the hunter dressed his kill. A four-wheel drive Ford Bronco, several years old, stood to the side of the garage, with a foot of snow on its roof. That told him the garage was full of other things—and probably not vehicles. The drifts in the driveway and on the porch told him the home had not had a visitor in many weeks.

It was the home of an outdoorsman, one whose income was on the lower end of the scale, and therefore it would most likely not have a security system. Carter watched the home for an hour, before deciding it was indeed empty and made his approach.

The door was defeated by a key found hidden in a nearby birdhouse, and he was inside a moment later checking every room. It was as he had expected. The rooms were sparsely furnished with cheap furniture and covered in a light layer of dust. The closet revealed a selection of both men's and women's clothing, and the pictures on the wall were of an older couple posing with what looked like a son and his wife and kids. Another shot of grandpa with a deer hanging from the tree. A nice ten-pointer. The smile was big. Carter dismissed the photos and dug into the closets further, but didn't find what he was looking for.

The garage. He went back to the door he had come in and looked around. Opening the nearest kitchen cabinet, he found a key hanging off a thumbtack. He grabbed it and ventured out to the garage. A two-car, it had a side door that accepted the key and let him in.

Inside, he hit the jackpot.

An ATV sat parked inside with its battery pulled. The rest of the garage was filled with outdoor equipment. A small jon boat sitting on a trailer occupied the other side, and beyond that were several lockers. Carter opened the first to find a few sets of skis, both downhill and cross-country, with the boots to go with them. His excitement was shortened, though, when the boots proved to be too small. The clothing hanging inside, however, made up for it. Insulated hunting bibs with a woodland camouflage pattern. He quickly exchanged them for his current coat and was both warmer and more tactical as a result. The bibs fit as well, and his legs welcomed the down insulation. A set of gloves, which were a bit too tight, were pocketed and replaced with a pair of shooter's mittens. He stuffed them in a pocket as well and searched on. Socks. A black sweater and a set of thermal underwear presented, and he set them aside as well. He'd have to make do with the boots he had, but the rest of his wardrobe had just gotten an upgrade.

He closed the first locker and opened the second. The smile threatened to crack his chapped lips.

A gun safe. A large floor model that filled the space. One hidden inside the steel cabinet and no doubt bolted to the floor. He tried the handle and wasn't surprised to find it locked.

The combination lock mocked him. So far, he had been lucky, finding hidden keys with little effort. That was not the case here. While the crime level in the town was obviously low enough that the owner was comfortable with hidden keys and no alarm system, the safety of what was inside the safe was beyond that. He reached out and rapped on the side.

Steel. But not as thick as he had thought. There was more than one way to get into a safe.

He turned back to the garage and examined its contents more closely. It was the usual menagerie of tools, lawn care equipment, old furniture, and boxes containing a variety of discarded items. In the far corner, he found what he needed.

The two tanks were small and mounted on a

two-wheel cart. The hoses connecting them were wrapped tightly around it, and he was able to hoist the item out from behind the trash with ease. He rapped on the tanks with a knuckle but couldn't decide if they were full or not. Only one way to find out.

The striker was hanging on a convenient nail, and the helmet was on the one below it. He donned it and opened the valves on the tanks and then the handle. A slight hiss of escaping gas brought a smile to his face, and he ignited it with a scrape of the striker. Adjusting the valves, he soon had a blue-white cone at the tip of the cutting torch.

Carter flipped the helmet down onto his head and attacked the steel surrounding the hinges. The torch made quick work of the metal, and he traced a path around the bottom and then the top hinge, getting a pop as each one failed. He paused long enough to wedge a crowbar into the gap, and pry the crack open enough to see the steel rods that held the door in place. He attacked them next, and the door popped again as each one yielded to the hot flame.

Carter shut the torch off and examined his work. The safe had four bars, one in each corner. He'd cut through two of them, but the door was still in place. Would he have to cut through the other side too? He decided to try something else first.

Picking up the crowbar, he wedged it into the side which was still holding and applied some pressure. The door creaked but held. He adjusted his stance and pushed again, harder, adding his own considerable weight to the strength of his arms. The door creaked again, and then broke free, crashing to the concrete with a loud bang that echoed in the small space.

"WHAT WAS THAT?"

Hal Reiser was up on his roof, trying to locate the hooks for the Christmas lights under the snow. His son was standing below him, with a long line of lights they had untangled the night on his arms. They would do the untangling ritual every year, no matter how well he'd packed them away the year before. How it happened, he had given up trying to figure out. What mattered was that his wife and daughter liked the lights, so he risked his ass every year on the slippery ladder to make them happy. He vowed that this year would be his last. Next year, his boy would be old enough to man the ladder while he stood below and gave directions.

He looked off into the woods in the direction of his neighbor's house. With the leaves gone from the trees, he could just make out the peak of the roof from his elevated position.

"Did you hear that?"

Still not getting a reply from his boy, he looked down over his shoulder to see him bobbing his head to the song playing on his ever-present earbuds.

"HEY!" He tossed some snow at him.

The boy filched and then looked up. He pulled an earbud aside.

"What?"

"I heard something over at the neighbor's. Go see if something's wrong."

"What did you hear?"

"If I knew that, I wouldn't be asking you to go check it out. Now, hurry up!"

The boy frowned but knew better than to talk back. He set the lights down carefully in the trampled snow and moved off toward the neighbor's.

CARTER HAD BEEN WAVING the smoke away from the steel box, when the shout reached his ears. He immediately dropped the torch, pulled the gun from his belt, and moved to the door. He reached up and turned the lock and then wedged himself into a dark corner.

The smoke. It had spilled out of the safe when the door had fallen and now filled the room. A tiny flame could now be seen inside, and Carter cursed it as he threw himself across the room. He snuffed the flame out with a gloved hand and then closed the cabinet doors in an attempt to keep the remaining smoke inside. He looked at the safe's door now laying on the concrete. There was nothing to cover it with. What if someone looked through the window? It was high, so they would have to pull themselves up, but they would see the door if they did.

Cursing again, he looked for a spot he could see out. Standing on the workbench, he was able to get right next to the window. He stuck an eye to its corner.

Someone was coming.

JASON BOBBED his head to the music in his ears as he followed the snow-covered path toward the neighbor's house. His feet and lower legs were now covered in snow, and he hadn't worn his hunting boots or gators for the light-hanging chore. His wet feet were now starting to complain. As soon as his head came over the slight rise, and he could see the house, he stopped. He could see the top half of the roof and the garage, same as it always had been. The old couple wasn't expected back for another five months. He or his dad would check on the place if it got really cold for a spell or if the power went out, but otherwise they left it alone.

A noise? He didn't see anything that would make any kind of noise. He thumbed the music off and took out the earbuds and listened. Nothing.

The snow in his boots was melting now, soaking his socks. He worked his toes around to keep the blood flowing but made no move to go further. The snow just got deeper.

Jason glanced behind him and discovered his father had moved the ladder around the corner of the house. He could no longer see him. He turned back to the view in front of him. Would he rather hang Christmas lights, or go hang out at the neighbor's for few minutes?

CARTER THUMBED the safety off as he watched the man. His orange hunting hat made it easy for Carter to make him out in the snowy landscape, and Carter sat frozen on the bench when he stopped.

"Go away," Carter whispered.

He watched as the man—or was it a teenager—looked behind him and then back. He seemed to be considering what to do next.

"Go away," Carter whispered again.

The boy looked down at his feet and then back to the house he had come from. A loud tapping began, like someone pounding nails. Then a shout. The boy turned and headed back the way he had come.

CARTER LET OUT A HELD breath and watched until the boy was out of sight. The pounding continued, and Carter waited and listened for several minutes before deciding that the boy was not returning. He lowered himself to the ground and took stock of the situation.

There were people outside and close by. Close

enough for them to hear the door fall. He had forgotten to factor in how well sound traveled in this environment. The snow acted as a blanket, snuffing out a lot of the ambient noise which was usually found in the woods. As a result, sounds carried. He would have to remember this when it was time to leave.

He carefully moved back to the safe and opened the door. A small amount of smoke remained, and he waved it away to see what was inside.

His eyes were drawn to the rifles first. Three of them. He pulled them out and lay them on the concrete. A Savage hunting rifle in .300. It was old, but the action was sound. He found a box of shells for it, next to a charred box of .22 rifle ammunition. The .22 was a Ruger, also old but well cared for. The last rifle was a Winchester 30-30, but there were no rounds for it. Carter was down to two choices. He laid the Savage aside and returned the .22. The shells went on the buttstock, and the remainder into a pocket.

The safe had drawers, and he opened them, hoping for more ammunition. Inside he found a collection of knives and some paperwork for the guns. There were more rifles and a few handguns in the man's arsenal, but they had obviously traveled with him. Too bad.

In the bottom drawer, he found a scope and quickly discovered it matched the mount on the Savage. He mounted it and then zeroed the sights, before setting it aside again and searching further. A pair of binoculars went into another pocket, as well as a compass.

The bottom drawer held the best find. Maps. Carter pulled them and spread them out until he determined which ones he needed. They were well-marked up with several labels. Fire-pit. Bait stand. Salt lick. Tree stands one, two, and three. The man was a hunter and had the entire area plotted out. Carter smiled. The maps would tell him where to go and where not to. Deer season was over, but he was sure that didn't matter much to the locals. He'd have to be careful not to run into any on his way out of here.

He took stock of the situation. He was in shelter. Cold, but that couldn't be helped. Outside, he had left tracks in the snow, but they were being covered by more as he sat here. He was armed, reasonably fed, and clothed for the current weather. The climb out and into the next valley would be a hard one, but nothing he hadn't faced before.

The tapping outside reached his ears, again.

Whatever they were doing, it would not go on forever. But it drove home the fact that it was not the time to go out. Sometimes, the best thing to do was nothing. If he waited until dark, it would lesson his chances of being seen. Less people out. Less chances of a dog. Less visibility. He checked the watch and then the angle of the sun coming in the window. A few hours—maybe less, if the mountains shaded the house. He would leave then.

Carter pulled a lawn chair up to the door and planted himself in it. He settled in with his new rifle across his lap to wait.

He found himself wondering how Tye was doing.

26

"The seed of revolution is repression."

—Woodrow Wilson

"You're Lieutenant Bunker? I'm George Wahlburg."

Archie looked the man up and down, before sticking out a hand. The V-22s had somehow made it to the airbase, and the pilot had set the wounded bird down on the far end of a taxiway. It was an ominous sign for those that knew what it meant. They had not been out of danger. The pilot had feared the aircraft could still break apart while landing—or even explode—and with the ordinance they carried on board, the danger to anything in the area was a real one.

Fortunately, they had survived the landing intact, and the SEALs had whisked the three of them off the ramp and into a waiting ambulance in record time. But not before Archie had caught a look at the shredded engine nacelle and the wounded SEALs. He yelled at them to come over, so he could thank them, but they had disappeared as quickly and as silently as they had arrived.

The ambulance had taken them to the base hospital, where he had been poked, and prodded, and questioned by a number of doctors and medics. They had tried to separate the three of them twice, but the loud objections from Archie and his refusal to cooperate until they listened had been enough for the doctors to relent.

They were now in a large bay that could hold all three of them. The doctors had eventually concluded that they would all live and were now hovering together across the room. Waqas was talking quietly with the boy while a medic stitched up the wound in his arm. Archie kept a smile on his face to ease the boy's fear. The boy was in a land of strangers, ones he could not even understand, and Archie knew the feeling very well.

"Could you stand over there, please?"

Wahlberg was caught off guard by the request, but after looking behind him, realized he was blocking Archie's view of the boy. He shuffled a few feet to the right.

"Thanks. You the resident spook?"

"Yes, I suppose you could say that."

"I want an assurance from you that these two men are not classified as prisoners. No interrogation without me present. Understand?"

"I ... no, I don't. What are you afraid of?"

"They were prisoners as well. You're not required to believe that, and I don't expect you to, but they saved my life. If they get treated any different than me, I talk."

"Lieutenant, I have no reason to think—"

"You know who my father is?"

The man's face fell. That was all that Archie needed to see. He waved the man closer and lowered his voice.

"I know what they sent you here to do, but it's not going to happen. If you need to confirm that the doctor is with us and not them, clear this room and we'll talk."

"This is not how it's done," the man stalled.

"It is today."

"I can't—"

"Right now, in the White House, the President is waiting for the word that he can talk to me. What do you think I'm going to say?"

The captain stood straight and examined the two men on the other beds. One was a man his people were working hard to identify; the other was just a young boy, wounded and scared. The medic was now cleaning up his mess while the boy examined his new stiches. Archie gave him a thumbs up, and the boy returned it with a grin.

"All right, you win."

Archie watched the man walk across the room to the group of doctors. After a brief conversation, they left the room. The captain shut the door behind them. The quiet changed the tone in the room.

"Waqas? This man is with intelligence. He needs something, I don't know what ... something to prove—"

"That I am not of ISIS? I understand. You have

my picture and fingerprints. You are checking with my government, I trust?"

"They haven't gotten back to us," the captain replied with a glance at Archie.

"I see."

"Tell them about the woman," Archie prodded with a nod at Wahlburg.

"You mean Miss Valerie?"

Archie had been watching the captain's face, and his flinch was palpable. He looked to Archie for confirmation and got a nod. He reached in his pocket and pulled out a recorder.

"Mr. el Sal."

"It is Doctor, but you are forgiven," Waqas replied.

"I'm sorry. Doctor. You met a woman named Valerie?"

THE FOUR OF them sat in the General's private study. The walls were covered floor to ceiling with books and oil paintings of past presidents and generals. The leather and wood dominated the space, and the air held the faint odor of cigar smoke. They each sat with a tumbler of amber over three cubes of ice. Something the room seemed to call for. The fireplace roared and spit next to them as they held a final meeting.

"Is everyone in place?" the General asked them.

"All Shepherds report they are staged and ready," Dayton replied.

"And the others?"

"The leaders of every cell," William said, "report greater than ninety percent manned. That's ten percent more than what we estimated we'd need to be successful. I've sent every bit of intelligence I had. Unless something crucial comes in, there will be no more communication. It's up to the leaders and the groups being in place when the time comes. So far, they seem to be following the plan." William responded before looking at his shoes.

The General said, "You have something to add?"

William raised his head and exchanged a look with Dayton.

"Sir, I know I crossed the line before, one we all agreed on, but I feel we're letting a man slide."

"Personal revenge is not what this is about."

Dayton answered that one, "It's more than that sir; he's their muscle, their fixer. He needs to be addressed. It's not about what he did to us; it's what he does for them."

The General sighed and looked away, before his eyes found their way to Charlie. The man sat quietly, wiping an ever-present tear from his damaged eye. His scared face offered nothing.

"Charlie?"

"Yes, sir?"

"I'd like your opinion, please."

Charlie's lips grew taught, and he exhaled loudly before answering, as if he'd been holding in what the general was asking for.

"I've never known you to be afraid, sir."

"Afraid?"

"It's the only thing I can think of that's stopping you. You're afraid."

"Of Haney? I—"

"Not Haney, sir. Of yourself. You think if you target the man, it will amount to revenge, and that would make you a monster. The monster you warn us of all the time."

The General was shocked by the words. "I can't use the Shepherds to combat my own personal demons; that would be—"

"They're not yours alone, sir. Look at what the man has done. Not just the evidence right here in this room, but the trail of destruction that's followed him for the last three decades. Why does he get a pass? Because we're personally involved? It shouldn't matter. Who speaks for the others he's harmed? Who stops him from harming more tomorrow? It's not personal revenge, it's justice. Justice we rob others of, out of our own fear."

General Marr turned and examined the faces of the other two men.

"You feel the same?"

"Subtract the four of us from the list," Dayton solemnly replied, "and then ask yourself what the Shepherds should do."

The three of them watched as the man struggled with his thoughts. The sun was going down outside, and they sat silently as the shadows made their way slowly across the hardwood floor. Ice melted in glasses, and the fire slowly died as they waited.

Eventually, the man raised his head and spoke.

"Very well. How do you plan on proceeding?"

Dayton stood. "There's still one Shepherd left."

The others watched him leave without a word. A half hour later, the scream of the jet passing overhead rose and then faded.

THEY PASSED HIM AGAIN, and this time he returned their nod. The crowd was huge already and just getting bigger as more and more people seemed to appear out of nowhere. Entire trains of protestors streamed out of the station, and waves more walked into the area from the surrounding town. He and his wife had housed over twelve of them in their tiny home without complaint. The supplies they had stocked up over the proceeding months had proven sufficient, and the group had bonded over their tight quarters and common cause. No names had been exchanged, and nicknames had soon been required.

This morning, they had all left the house slowly, leaving in singles and pairs, until the home held only the two of them. With nothing to do but wait, they had cleaned and run several loads of laundry—anything to fill the time as they repeatedly walked past the TV, monitoring it all. They both hoped that their numbers did not change.

Some of them would not return. A few had jumped the gun and acted too early. The police scanner had already reported a few arrests for vandalism. A few more for auto theft. It seemed to be a popular crime today, and the police were a bit confused by the sudden uptick in petty wrongdoings. The chatter on the radio so far indicated that they had yet to connect the acts of misconduct to one another.

When the time came, the attack would happen in three places. Everyone had a mission. Phase two of theirs would start with the man they had just passed.

The thought had barely left his mind, when the phone in his pocket began vibrating. He yanked it free, as many others did around him, and gazed at the solemn message.

It was a single codeword. Within it was a date and time. He couldn't help but turn and find the man he had nodded to earlier. He was only a hundred yards away from them.

Soon, he would be much closer.

CARTER CRACKED the door open and listened. The wind had died, and there was a trace of moon now showing as the sun had disappeared behind the mountains. It was eerily quiet. Nothing moved.

He had almost left twice. Once after hearing the neighbors truck pull out and travel past on its way to town, and again when the cold had gotten to be too uncomfortable. But military discipline had won out, and he'd waited, pacing the small space when he got cold and packing and re-packing his gear to pass the time.

But now was the time. He shoved the door far-ther open, and it wedged itself on the snow. Avoiding making any unnecessary noise, he squeezed out through the gap and checked in all directions. His footprints he'd left in the snow were now shallow divots, the majority of them drifted over.

He'd found a way to keep them that way.

While roaming the garage, he had found a pair of snowshoes. After an hour of trying them on and stepping around the concrete, he was ready to try them in the snow. He strapped them on now, be-fore raising a leg and planting it in the snow. He sank into it, but not as far as he thought. He tried again with the other foot, and the shoes held him up. Carter thought he was maybe two inches into the soft snow.

He took a few steps toward the wood line. The snowshoes required him to lift his feet higher than he normally would, but the action was more than made up for, by keeping him on top of the snow as opposed to down in it. Examining his trail, he saw that it was minimal. With any luck, more snow would arrive soon and erase them completely. Either way, he'd be long gone before anyone discovered that he had been there. He moved on.

A half mile later, he came to the trail he had found on the map. He would follow it until he was out of town and then take up a heading straight up into the mountains.

27

"It is impossible to predict the time and progress of revolution. It is governed by its own more or less mysterious laws."

—Vladimir Lenin

ayton stared out the window at the passing clouds. The Citation X was at its max altitude and speed, but it would still be another hour before he arrived. The snow-covered landscape had faded, and he now saw more green-covered terrain the farther they flew south.

He'd been thinking for several hours already and was still not sure what he was going to say. Anna needed to be told—and not just about Rubicon or what had led to it, but about more than that. None of the other Shepherds knew his whole story. The General knew. William—and Charlie, he suspected—but she would be the first outsider.

His mind kept taking him back to the night in the mountains. They had not spoken a word, and she had stopped any attempt to the next morning. But it was there, a subject that refused to be ignored. So, what to tell her first? Rubicon? Would her reaction to that even allow for anything further? There was no way to know.

The Gulf of Mexico appeared below him, and then the west coast of Florida. Dayton finally pulled his gaze from outside and focused it on the GPS map on the wall. He counted down the minutes, and right on cue, the throttle was pulled back, the plane's nose dipped, and they began the long power-on decent into Miami.

He still had no idea what he was going to say.

THE TERRAIN WAS steep and only getting steeper. Between that and the thinning air, Carter was slowing his pace. He forced himself to stop every hundred meters and check his back trail. So far, he'd seen nothing following him.

Thankfully, the sun had come out, and he welcomed its warmth on his back and face as he climbed. He had hoped to be over the pass and on the western side before it got dark but now dismissed that as wishful thinking. The snow was just too deep. He had hoped that being in the trees would somewhat lessen that, but there was really no change. He wondered if it was due to avalanches and, after a careful look at the mountain above, could not rule it out. He'd adjusted course to avoid an area which looked dangerous and chosen a path which offered shelter.

He reached it with only two hours of sunlight left and sat down on his pack for a rest and a drink. While he did so, he watched his backtrail. Some of it was visible from the air, but there had been no helping that. His only hope now was that the combination of the snowshoes and lite snowfall would erase them. At least enough to thwart anyone trying to track him. He doubted that his theft of the cabin would be discovered anytime soon, but he couldn't rule it out. All he needed was

some state trooper or game warden on a snowmobile out looking for him.

His stomach growled, and he acknowledged it
with a pat on his belly. Soon. He had other things
to accomplish first. He heaved himself back to his
feet, collected the pack and moved deeper into the
trees. It was a thick stand of pines that butted up to
the exposed rock of a short cliff. Carter had chosen
it for its ability to block the wind, as well as protect
him from the sliding snow.

He dropped the pack again and pulled the .45
from its holster. If he thought the place was good
shelter, then it was possible others would too. This
was bear country, and while most would be asleep
this time of year, one never knew. He kept the
pistol out until he had circled the entire area. If he
had company, he couldn't find it.

The pistol went back in its holster, and he
pulled the pack over to a large drift. Removing a
snowshoe, he used it as a shovel to pile the snow
even higher, before donning it again to pack it all
down. He soon had a mound the size of a car. He
then pulled out a stainless-steel bowl he had obtained from the house and started digging.

The sun was almost touching the earth, when
he decided he was done. The cave was just big
enough for him to lay in with a little extra for the

gear. He spread the tarp out in a triple layer on the floor and then followed it with the sleeping bag.

"Now, eat," he told himself.

He'd paused his digging to find a few downed limbs that were dry enough to snap with his hands. He built a small fire and then a berm of snow around it, to both reflect the heat toward him and hide its flame from anyone looking his way. The fire was started with a piece of rag he had found in the garage, and he soon had a can of beef stew heating itself over it. His stomach growled in anticipation.

While the stew warmed, he thought about the remainder of his trip. His first estimate had been way off. He now recalculated with the map in his head, and the pace he'd been forced to travel on his climb up to his present location.

"Another day. Maybe two," he told himself. "Then you get some answers."

A quick mental inventory of his supplies drew a frown. He'd make it, but he'd be hungry when he got there.

Cold. With the sun sinking rapidly, the temperature was as well. He reached for the pack and pulled out the down blanket he had found at the house. His knife had made a quick twelve-inch slice in its middle, and he had stapled the cut closed on both sides after searching a kitchen junk drawer. He now unrolled the creation and slipped his head through the hole. A down poncho. He ignored the feathers sticking out around the staples and welcomed its warmth.

The stew was ready, and he removed it from the fire with a gloved hand. A drop landed on the rifle in his lap as he shoved it in his mouth with a cold spoon, but he ignored it in favor of feeding his stomach. The can was empty within a minute, and he let the warmth fuel him before chasing it with a full can of water.

Satisfied, he sat back and listened. The slight breeze rattled the trees, and a few pines shed their snow covers, but other than that, it was blissfully silent. The last bit of sun slowly sank from sight, and the sky was painted several shades of purple in its wake.

Carter found a smile on his face. It had been a cold night followed by an all-day journey up the mountains. He was exhausted. But there was no denying the beauty of the view. Tomorrow would be more of the same, but he could at least enjoy the sunset before facing that fact.

"Anna?"

"Yes?"

"I'm downstairs. Can you buzz me in?"

"Uh, sure."

Anna quickly hit the button and then ran to her bedroom to change. The comfortable yoga pants were exchanged for her last clean pair of jeans, and she ran a brush through her hair as she walked back to the door.

Why was Dayton here? With a start, she realized the papers were still out. She gathered them off the couch and table and stuffed them into a drawer just as she heard his steps outside her door. He had taken the stairs, but she wasn't surprised.

She checked the peephole, even though she knew his knock, and then let him inside. He took a few steps and then stopped, caught off guard by the condition of her place.

"The power just came back on this morning. I haven't gotten caught up on dishes and laundry."

"I saw that on the way in. There's power trucks everywhere. Didn't the building have generators?"

"It does, but they only do so much. I kept the refrigerator running, and the air on just enough to keep everything dry. They asked us to keep everything that drew power to a minimum. I wasn't here very much, anyway."

Dayton had not asked William about her, so the statement caught him off guard.

"What have you been doing?"

"Volunteering mostly. First by cleaning the streets so the trucks could get through, then by checking on everyone in the building. I ran a few of the more elderly people to the airport and got them out, but then I started getting low on gas, and I didn't want to get into my storage unit. So I switched to walking or using my bike to get around. I've been working down at the shelter for the past couple weeks. There's a lot of people with no place to live."

"Sorry, I didn't know."

"Normal people in my life. Isn't that what you said I needed?"

"True. I guess the situation called for it. Hard to believe we had a hurricane this late in the season. There's a foot of snow in the mountains already."

"Yeah. The weatherman can't stop talking about it."

An awkward silence descended, and they both avoided eye contact, until Anna broke away and began tidying up her place. Dayton stood still and watched.

"You did well."

"Is that from you or our boss?"

"Both. William reports that the cops have nothing as far as actionable leads."

"I see."

"The FEMA thing. That was a good idea."

"Thanks."

"I guess you haven't been able to restock. I could have brought you—"

"What do you want, Dayton?"

"I ... what?"

"What is this? An after-action revue? You telling me you flew seven hours just to give me a critique?"

"I ... No. There's something ... There's something about to happen. Something we don't share until we know the Shepherd is committed."

"No, wait. I want to talk about something else, first."

"Okay. What is it?"

"Valerie."

WILLIAM WATCHED as the progress bar slowly marched across the screen. The files were being compressed. Packed into tight little packages that could be sent much faster. Soon, they would go out to several server farms across the country. Each of them ready to pass the information on to a multitude of recipients ranging from major news organizations to millions of private citizens. No one would be denied.

Despite the work to compress the files, the process of sending them would still take a few hours. He had arranged the files to go in a specific order, first by identifying those that might take action against them, and then those who would support such action to save themselves. It would be a cascade of revelations. A wave of truth. And like the saying went, it would set them all free.

He hoped. But hope was what revolutions were born on. And this one was no different.

The progress bar marched on, much like a revolution should.

28

———————

*"Now and then, someone is able to look at an empty
space, conclude it would be a great place to start a
revolution, and bravely go forward."*

—*Henry Rollins*

"**S**he was good. Too good to just make a
mistake like that. William searched for
weeks and found nothing. Not even

Mossad had a line on what happened. But some things started happening. Things which could only happen if you knew what she knew. Somebody had her, and they were extracting the information ... " His voice trailed off and he sipped the beer again. It had long since grown warm, but neither of them wanted to stop talking and get another.

Anna had confronted him and left him no way out. The papers had been produced. The articles from the Internet. As vague as they were, there was no denying who and what Valerie was. Dayton's wife was a CIA agent, and he had no idea where she was, or even if she were still alive.

"So you think ISIS has her?"

"We thought so. We're not so sure, now. We may have been wrong from the start."

"What were you going to do?"

"I was ready to go charging into Syria to find her."

"Why didn't you?"

"The General stopped me. It was a suicide mission, at best. That and ... "

"What, Dayton?"

"The intel. The attacks. They stopped."

Anna wasn't sure what that meant, but she had an idea. "You think she's dead. That they killed her when they realized she was no good to them anymore."

Dayton shrugged, as if it didn't matter what he thought.

"Wouldn't they, you know, make it known?"

"A video on YouTube? Them carving her head off in front of a camera?"

"Sorry, but ... yes."

"They haven't done that in a long time. They learned. It made them more enemies than it did friends. There was some thought that they would try to trade her. You know, exchange her for something or someone they wanted back. Others thought she might become a shield. Something they could use to keep the bombs from dropping."

"Like the pilot they've just rescued?"

"Yeah. Or they gave her to Assad, or it was Assad who took her to begin with. Or the Syrians captured her, along with some ISIS soldiers. Nobody knows. Either that, or they aren't talking. I don't know."

"William can't—"

"He's tried. If there was something in the system, he would know it. He's been searching for the how and why that she was compromised. Whoever was, they hid their tracks. I'm not sure they can be found now."

They fell silent, and Anna watched his face as he stared out at the ocean outside. The wind was blowing, and a few strands of hair flew across his face. She saw it now, and it all made sense. His expression. The one she had struggled to figure out since the first day she had met him. It was both hard and soft. The jaw held a constant tension while the eyes were searching. She wondered if he saw her face at night.

She'd heard enough. There was nothing to be gained by questioning him further.

"You said there was something you had to tell me?"

His face changed, and he brought his gaze back inside. His answer was one word.

"Rubicon."

***

"I LIKE the P-7 the best. It fits my hand so well. I tried your Glock and your Browning, but they're just too big for my hands."

Jack was listening to his wife discuss her taste in handguns while he prepared two pizzas for dinner. It was a conversation he had never expected to have with her.

"H&K make a good gun," he agreed. "Are you sticking with the nine-millimeter?"

"I think so. Catherine tried hard to get me interested in the .45, but I just couldn't keep it on target after the first few kicks. The .40 was only slightly better. I guess they just didn't speak to me. Maybe if I had her hands."

Jack adjusted the temperature of the oven to pre-heat before returning to his chopping. Green peepers and onions for her, mushrooms and Italian sausage for him.

"Are you saying Catherine as man hands?" He smiled.

"Well, yes. But they fit her. On me, not so much. Although I wouldn't mind borrowing them when we're at the range."

"Your hand healing up okay?"

"Yes. Embarrassing."

"Did it myself the first time. You won't do it again."

Debra frowned at Jack's attempt to save her pride and then held up her right hand for inspection. She had made the rookie mistake of holding the automatic too high, and the slide had sliced twin grooves in the webbing between her thumb and first finger. Fortunately, they were shallow cuts, but the sight of it advertised her mistake. She would just have to own it until it healed.

"Did you talk with Frank by chance?"

"Oh! Sorry, I forgot to tell you. He said your new Browning would be in next week. He already has the sights and says he'll mount them the day it arrives."

"Frank's the man. Was Greg down there?"

"Both him and Laurie. They seem to be healing up okay. I've been watching Greg. Laurie is worried about his headaches."

"They getting any better?"

"She says they are. Not as frequent, anyway."

"How does she—"

"Really? I thought you were a detective, honey?"

"Ah, I see. Well, they are a good match."

"We should have them over sometime."

"Maybe when this Shepherds thing is over."

"And when might that be?"

"No telling. You wanted spinach, too, right?"

"Please."

Debra watched as her husband left the chopping block and dug into the refrigerator. Evidently, the case was not progressing, and he didn't want to talk about it. That was fine. It was something she had gotten used to. She now knew when she could pry into what he was doing and when it was best not to. This time, it was the latter.

Jack returned with a bag of spinach and resumed his chopping. She watched his work with the knife, his scarred and bruised hands still wielding it with skill. Always in motion, but precise, producing the results he wanted at maximum speed, with a dexterity that had him in constant danger without crossing the line that would produce a cut. It was metaphor for his life, she realized.

"How's Sydney?"

"Okay. Still sifting through the pile. She's convinced there's a clue in there somewhere and won't stop looking for it. Larry sent her home while he chases some weak leads. Lenny's in town, and I practically had to order her to stay away from the office. I even offered them the beach house, but she refused to leave town."

"Why?"

Jack sprinkled a healthy amount of cheese on the pizzas before examining what was left over and just adding it too. You could never have too much cheese in his opinion.

"I'm not sure. She just said she wanted to stick close to town."

"Odd. Does she think something is going to happen?"

Jack opened the oven and slid both pizzas inside, before letting it slam shut. He set the timer and then walked back to the counter, where Debra was sitting. After retrieving his glass of wine, he sipped while he thought about her question.

"I don't know. It's that damn nose of hers. Once she gets the scent of a case, she starts to smell it everywhere. Intuition, maybe? I don't know."

"Intuition? You really believe in that?"

Jack smiled. "How come women get a nice word like intuition and men are stuck with 'guts'? I feel a little cheated."

"Deal with it. Your guts, or let's go with 'instincts,' have served you well before. What's Sydney's gut telling her?"

Jack sipped his wine again to buy himself a few seconds. This conversation was quickly getting into the classified zone, and while he trusted his wife completely, it was just something that people in his line of work didn't do. The job stayed at the office; you never brought it home.

"The Shepherds have gone quiet."

"Gone quiet?" Debra asked. "I don't know the term."

"It's a submariner's term. It means they've

stopped everything and are waiting. Usually it's to avoid detection, but sometimes ..."

"What?"

"Sometimes it's to lie in wait. To stay invisible until it's time."

"Time for what?"

"That, we don't know. But Sydney thinks something is coming, and she doesn't want to be away when it does."

"I see."

They drank in silence for a long minute. Jack broke away to gaze through the tiny window of the oven. Debra watched until she couldn't wait any longer.

"What do *you* think?"

Jack straightened up and returned to the counter between them. He picked up his glass and drained it, before setting it down and pushing it away.

"I think she may be right."

* * *

OUTSIDE THE HOUSE, a lite snow was falling. It gathered on the head and shoulders of the still form of Harper as he stood among a group of pines, silently watching the couple in the kitchen not thirty meters away.

Would Jack be home? Harper didn't know. He'd been checking every night for the past few days, and Jack's schedule was chaotic at best. He'd almost planted a tracer on the Aston Martin the previous night but had held off when he'd learned that every vehicle entering the Hoover building was scanned automatically for such devices. His wife's car was not an issue, though. He'd tracked her around town and determined that she was a creature of habit. She visited her work and a few other places on a regular basis, and he'd checked on a few of them before ruling them out.

His best option was still right here. The Randall home was in an upper-class neighborhood. One populated by the rich and powerful. The movers and shakers of DC. It was better to have it happen here. The message it would send would be loud and delivered right into their midst. Like a slap in the face, the ones who thought they were in charge would have no choice but to feel it. It was a lesson he would deliver soon.

He examined the couple again as Jack pulled the pizza from the oven. They ate where they were, with her on the bar stool and him leaning on the counter opposite her. They looked like any other middle-aged couple. Perhaps one whose kids were out for the night and giving them a rare evening together alone.

All the better.

Jack's schedule was the only unknown. The simplest plan was to take care of Jack's wife first, and then merely wait for him to come home.

"See you soon, Jack," he whispered.

Keeping himself in the trees, he made his way back to the concrete of the street and jogged the five blocks to his car. Just another suburbanite out for some evening exercise.

29

"Revolution is the festival of the oppressed."

—Germaine Greer

"The Vice President? I ... Are you sure?" Anna said.

"He's been doing this since you were in high school," Dayton said. "He's become the operations leader for The Trust. They think they operate in secret, but the General and William have been following their actions for years now. William has been gathering information on every action they've taken. Which politicians they've compromised or placed in office. Which companies they've used to launder or conceal their activities. And whom they've killed to get what they want. They've taken out world leaders, staged terrorist actions to further their own goals. Even killed our own people. It took a long time, but William found the information. He has it all in a secure location, and we're ready to reveal it to the world."

"These protestors? They're all ... from us?"

"No. Not all of them. The protests started on their own when the Shepherds began showing the public what was going on. Our people are sprinkled among them now, but the protests were not our goal; they are a byproduct. One that we've taken as a sign that it's time to activate Rubicon."

Anna shook her head and tried to wrap her head around what it was he was telling her.

"So ... what is that you want me to do?"

"The Shepherds all have their assignments. They're all in place and ready to go when the time comes. We added a name last night, one that I'm handling myself. But it's in the lion's den. I could use some help."

She thought hard about what he was saying. Was this the time to join him, or was this the time to call Jack Randall and reveal herself to be the Shepherd that had contacted him?

"You mean Vice President Haney?"

"Yes."

She recalled the scars on his back and the stories she had heard from other soldiers about what had happened inside Fallujah that night. Several of her fellow soldiers had not survived the battle. Many more had come home scarred or permanently injured. Their faces paraded past in her mind.

"What do you need me to do?"

THEY TRICKLED in one at a time. Some of them driving off-road trucks and wearing jeans and T-shirts, while others arrived wearing suits and steering German sedans. The empty hangar served as a parking lot, and they wedged their cars in tight so as to have enough room. The cars would be hidden from any prying eyes until they returned. From now on, they would all stay under-cover and out of view of overhead cameras.

No matter what they arrived in, they all brought a variety of gear with them. After learning the environment and terrain they would be traveling to, they all picked through their respective piles, discarding the desert gear in favor of cold weather items. A few had tried to speculate on what the mission might be, but that was squashed by the man in charge. They would find out soon enough.

When the count reached forty, they were told to get ready. An hour later, an 18-wheeler pulled up to the hangar. It had the name of a well-known trucking company on the side and sported up-to-date plates and inspection stickers. The truck backed into the hangar far enough to keep the rear doors inside. The men frowned at their trans-portation, but it was not much different than the windowless aircraft they had all spent countless hours on while in the military.

"How long?" one of them asked.

"About thirty-four hours."

"Seriously?"

"Bring a book."

"Funny guy."

The men eyeballed the trailer's interior. It

wasn't the first time they had used it, but none of them wanted to get in until they had to. The narrow box was outfitted with three Port-a-Johns and a long row of bunks down one side. Chairs and footlockers filled the rest of the space, and bare overhead lights were strung down its center. It would be their home until they arrived at the target. The only bright spot was that it was quieter than a plane.

"Where's the King?"

"I'm sure he'll be along soon."

"Any idea where we're going?"

"Somewhere cold."

"Shit."

CHARLIE WAS WANDERING. It was something he'd been doing more of over the past few days. He had a restlessness that he couldn't label. A gnawing worry that he couldn't explain. Most new soldiers acquired it quickly, the fear of the unknown keeping them on edge and awake until the first shot rang out. At that point, the test was over: They would either overcome the fear and let training take over; or run, forever unable to take the test a second time. After the first encounter, they could

sleep again, many of them right up until the moment they crossed the line of departure and entered enemy ground.

He knew one soldier who had actually napped
while they were pinned down and awaiting air
support. After reviewing the action back at the
base, he had not faulted the man. There was
simply nothing else to do, so why not get some
needed rest? The mental picture of his battle
buddy sleeping while the bullets cracked overhead now brought a smile to his face, even if it was
short-lived.

But this was different. The Shepherds were
taking an action that America had not seen for
over a hundred years. And he was a part of it. It
would unfold over a thousand miles away while
they sat in this fortress of stone and wood. So why
was he awake and wandering the mansion's halls?
He didn't know.

His steps brought him back to his own room. It
was a far cry from his room in the DC slums. One
that he'd never felt he had earned. While its size
was large, it's features were Spartan. Charlie had
no use for decorations, and even if he did, he
lacked the talent to do so. The walls and desk held
a few photos of him and his fellow marines. A
couple of them included the General at the LAV

they had both occupied for months together. The desk held a variety of textbooks, and a few maps adorned the wall above it. The bed was covered in a Marine Corp blanket, the Globe and Anchor stretching across its width. It looked like what it was: The room of a former soldier who was now a student. The only difference was the stone walls and the hardwood floor.

Charlie entered and paced. It was late. He should really be in bed. He needed rest to be prepared for whatever the General required tomorrow. Was he ready?

Ready and Prepared. Two different words that most outside the military would say meant the same thing. Charlie knew better. Maybe that was it?

He opened his closet and found the footlocker under an extra blanket on the floor. It bore the scars and scrapes of travel and the name of its owner on the top. Charlie pulled a key from the chain around his neck and opened the lock.

Inside was a 9mm Berretta pistol. He had both loved and hated it for some time. Its high-capacity magazine and large ejection port had served him well while in the States, but once deployed to the desert, he had discovered that the feature served as a funnel for the desert sand. After the second feed jam, he had acquired a Glock and never looked back. But the Glock had been left behind in the burned-out carcass of the LAV, never to return. The Beretta had found its way back to him, and he'd kept it ready ever since.

He pulled the weapon from its nylon and checked the chamber. The shine of brass told him it was loaded and ready, just as he had left it. The holster was black now, and road low on his hip with a half-dozen magazines riding the belt above it. He strapped it on now and made a minor adjustment before sliding the pistol home.

Under the pistol was armor. A vest the General had ordered for him and the rest of the security people here. He donned it as well and shrugged his shoulders until it settled in place.

In the bottom of the trunk was a plastic case. He pulled it free and set it on the bed, before opening it to reveal his M-4. Dayton had offered him a wide assortment of weapons, but he had always gravitated back to the M-4. It was what he knew and trusted. It was familiar to his hands, and they would operate it under the worst conditions without required thought. He hefted the weapon, and its weight and shape melted into his grasp. His fingers found the forms and outlines of the rifle, and his mind labeled each as they checked its operation. Like the Berretta, it too was loaded and ready.

Charlie spun in place and dropped to one knee, the butt of the rifle found its way to his shoulder, and his cheek met its stock behind the scope. The sights lined up on the chest of the moving figure across the room, and his finger left the guard to find the trigger.

He held the position for a moment and then exhaled, watching himself in the mirror as he did so. Getting to his feet, he set the rifle on the floor and leaned it against the bed. The armor was stripped off and hung on the bedpost along with the holstered Beretta. He rotated it so it faced the pillow.

Keeping his shoes on, he lay in the bed. Now both ready and prepared.

A few seconds later, he was asleep.

THE MAN HIMSELF APPEARED, and they all gathered around for the briefing. A mountain terrain target. One that was isolated from the world. They would travel by road non-stop across the country and leave the truck behind at a remote roadside location outside of a small town. Then they would travel overland for several miles, through snow-covered mountain terrain, before making their assault. The arrival of so many men, all of them with a military air about them and well-armed, could not go unnoticed by the local population. Other travel options were deemed too dangerous.

A satellite picture of the target was thrown up on the screen, and they all examined it closely as the man pointed out its strong points and weaknesses. The attack would be from three directions. The first to cut off all outside communication and close any exits. The second to drive the occupants inside and keep them there. The third to annihilate them. A variety of vehicles would then be used to make their escape. The men grumbled as they asked questions and game-played contingency plans, but in the end, they agreed with the overall plan. Besides, they had thirty-four hours of travel time to go over and refine it. There would be little else to do.

With the usual bellyaching displayed by all soldiers, they climbed into the trailer and settled in.

ANNA WATCHED behind them as Dayton worked the lock. The facility was like any other and had become familiar to her over the last few months. The late hour and industrial neighborhood had made the cab driver pause, but some encouragement in the form of extra cash had worked to get them there. The man had the car moving before they had slammed the back door, and Dayton had moved them off the street and into the unit by use of a gate code. They now hoped their arrival had gone unnoticed; they didn't want to have to deal with any would-be thieves on their way out.

The lock succumbed to Dayton's attention, and he lifted the door only long enough for them both to enter. Using the light of his phone, he secured the lock and then located the light.

As expected, Anna saw a row of locked cabinets covering two walls, with a van under a cover occupying what space that was left. Dayton stripped off the coat he was wearing and fired up a space heater, before moving to the first cabinet.

"What should I do?"

"Check out the van; make sure it's ready. There's gloves on the bench."

Anna did as he asked and found a two-year-old panel van under the cover, its windows darkened and its interior spotless. The faint odor of bleach still hung inside. After checking to see if the keys were in it, she turned them enough to see it held a full tank of gas. The tires were new and showed little wear. Other than starting it, there was nothing else to do.

Sliding out of the van, she was shocked to see what Dayton had on the table.

Two grenade launchers. The exact same make and model of the one he had used in California when they had rescued Six. What shocked her even more was what covered the rest of the steel surface.

Dozens of rounds. Some, she knew; some, she didn't. All of them lined up by type and color. There seemed to be one that dominated the group though. She walked forward and picked one up to confirm her suspicion.

"Incendiary rounds? There has to be over a hundred here. What exactly do you have planned?"

"It's going to be the two of us against a small army, and while we have surprise working for us, it'll only get us so far. The best alternative is firepower."

She placed the round gently back where she had gotten it and watched him root around inside another cabinet. He produced two vests and held one out to her.

"Here. Adjust it so it fits."

She took the item and did so, counting the empty pockets adorning its front. She'd never worn one before, but she had seen them on several soldiers. It was a lot of weight to carry, and they seemed to go to the larger men.

"I load mine from the bottom up. Incendiary, then HE, and smoke and CS up top." He started loading his vest, and she followed his lead. There were no flares or other illumination rounds present —the mission was not one they wished to advertise.

"Why the smoke and CS?"

"In case the cavalry arrives before we can get out. It'll keep them at a distance and give us a chance to disengage."

Anna liked the sound of that. Attacking a target in DC would immediately bring the hammer down on their heads, she didn't wish to engage with any police or soldiers if they didn't have too. They were not the enemy.

"So, what's the plan?"

Dayton slammed the cabinet closed and spun around.

"There isn't one. I've had no time to recon the

target or consider any other options. We're left with the basics. It's a schoolyard fight."

"Meaning?"

"You never got in a fight when you were a kid?"

"I can't pull Haney's hair; he doesn't have any."

Dayton smiled at her answer before opening a second cabinet and pulling out weapons. He stacked them on the table, and Anna automatically began checking each one.

"It's the same advice every good dad gives their son. If you find yourself in a fight, remember one thing: hit first and hit hard."

He punctuated the statement with the addition of two submachine guns.

30

"The revolution has always been in the hands of the young. The young always inherit the revolution."

—*Huey Newton*

The truck was parked on an angle, and the doors were pulled open by the gravity as they were released. The men were lined up in two long columns, just as if they would be jumping out of a plane. They were all off the truck and on the cold asphalt of the road in under a minute, and the last of them had disappeared into the wood line a minute later. The two drivers paused only long enough to erase the men's tracks in the snow, before boarding the truck again and setting off up the mountain. They would pass through the next town without stopping, refuel in the valley below, and then head back to North Carolina. Their portion of the mission was over.

The forty men they had left behind however, were just getting started. They separated into two columns and stayed one-hundred yards apart for the first mile. When the terrain got steeper, they merged back together, leaving only one trail and no way to know their numbers if someone should happen across it. The hours of inactivity had made their muscles stiff, but the steady climb and thin air was soon overcome. They moved without speaking, their weapons cradled in their arms and aimed left and right. They paused only twice: once to let the point man get ahead after some particularly deep snow; and the second when the noise of a snowmobile had reached their leaders ears.

They made the ridge before dark and changed course, dropping down into the thickest trees they could find, before moving lower. Here, their pace slowed. They were on the target's land, now, and unaware of any detection devices he might have.

The slower pace let the cold take hold. Frost formed on eyebrows and deployment beards. Ears and noses grew numb, and feet became less sensitive to what they were treading on. Some men worked the actions of their weapons to assure they were not freezing up, while others blew snow from their scopes and sights. The temperature dropped with the sun, but they traveled on. They had eight more hours of darkness; they would have to make use of every minute if they were to be close enough to attack the target on time. Every minute spent getting there translated into a greater chance of discovery. The last thing they needed was a stray hunter or snowmobiler stumbling across them. On the way here they had decided that if that were to happen, it would not end well for the party that found them.

From across the valley, Carter watched them fade into the trees through his scope.

⁕

THE COMPUTER DINGED AGAIN, demanding his attention. William muttered a curse before clicking the icon and examining the file. It was another message from the mystery man, Haney's right hand. William had made the messages a priority, and now he tapped his finger impatiently as the message was decoded. His wait wasn't long, and he was soon speed-reading its contents. They took his breath away. He reached for the phone.

"Sir, we have an issue."

"What is it?" the General said.

"Haney's man. I've just decoded another message. They aim to launch a false-flag operation. Tomorrow."

"Tomorrow? Where?"

"In DC, sir. A government building, I believe it's the … Sir! He's targeting Jack Randall!"

"I see. And trying to pin it on us, no doubt. Shrewd. I think—"

"Sir, there's more."

"Yes?"

"He has information on us."

"Us? You mean the Shepherds?"

"No, sir. Us. You. It mentions your companies. How did he know?"

"I don't know, William. But we have to assume he's coming here."

"What are your orders, sir."

The General thought only for a moment; while

the threat was a real one, he could not let it distract from their mission.

"Send the files now."

"Now, sir?"

"Right now. Send the files and then warn the security forces."

"Sending the files will take hours, sir."

"I know."

THE GROUP NUMBERED FOURTEEN. They ranged from age twenty-two to fifty-eight and came from all walks of life. They had arrived at the house in twos and threes after being picked up at various rendezvous pints throughout the city. Introductions were brief and rather vague. A first name here, an accent noted there, but nothing was expanded upon. They had come together for a common cause, one that required a bit of anonymity, as much for their own safety as for that of the mission. There was no political social talk; they were all past that point now. The time for that would come after the mission, so that was what they focused on.

Their host had several photos for them, and they now studied them as they were passed around. They were mostly of vehicles. Some parked in motor pools, others in and around private residences. The group examined each one and assigned a method and a time for dealing with them. Most were quite simple and would require only seconds to execute. Others were complex and had dual reasons for their implementation.

Divide and concur. It was what they had been subjected to for some time, and now it would be their turn to utilize the tactic.

"How many strips do we have?"

"I have forty of the small ones. Ten of the large."

"Pliers?"

"Enough for all of us."

"What about the last driver we need? Is he coming?"

"He's trying. I rode all day yesterday and watched everything. I think I can handle it if he doesn't make it."

"Okay."

They both paused and looked around the room. An outsider would label it a neighborhood get-together. Even if the group was a bit on the diverse side. The accents were from all corners of the country. Some of them sported winter tans, while others the pale skin of northerners. In a city normally flooded with tourist, it was something they didn't worry about. Still, they were hardly what one would label as revolutionary.

"Look at us," he spoke. "A bunch of nobodies. You really think we can pull this off?"

"I have to believe it; the alternative is unacceptable."

"Yes, I agree. But ... "

"But what?"

"What if we're unsuccessful? Have you made any plans if that happens?"

The man turned to his host and smiled.

"No."

"No?"

"Nothing." The man gestured at the people in the room. "I may have just meet all these people, but they are *my* people. Whatever comes, I wish to face it with them. If I were to run ... that would be a white flag, a surrender. And who would I be if I did that?"

The man offered nothing but a slow nod of his head. They both sat back and watched their new friends converse and enjoy their time together.

Tomorrow, for just a few hours, they would all be very busy.

END

I welcome any comments, feedback, or questions at randall.wood@scribecount.

I also welcome any input pertaining to mistakes I may have missed, not necessarily typos or grammar, as they are self-explanatory, but mistakes about procedures or content. Mistakes of this nature tend to pull the reader out of the story and make it less enjoyable. If you should find such an error, please fire off an email in my direction. The beauty of e-books and print-on-demand books is that they can always be updated to fix such things.

I also welcome any and all reviews, with one small request. With the controversy over fake reviews garnering so much attention, it gives your review greater credibility if you do so in your real name and with the verified purchase icon. Doing so helps readers call honest attention to their favorite writers and keeps the integrity of the online review process intact.

Who knows? Your review may end up on the back of the next book.

You can find links to purchase all the Jack Randall Thrillers, including links to purchase directly from me at a discount, at http://randall woodauthor.com/universal-link.

What happens to Jack?

Jack and his crew venture on in the subsequent books in the series. The best place to find out more, and get those books at a discount, is by visiting my website at https://randallwoodauthor.com/books/. There you will find the complete library of my works, bonus content such as short stories and character bios, cool swag, books that are unavailable anywhere else, and an inside look at how I create these stories.

What happens to Danny?

Sign up for my email list at https://randallwoodauthor.com/newsletter/ and you'll get a free novel with Danny's latest adventure plus additional content, previews of coming books, discount offers, and a whole lot more.

Want the latest book the minute it's ready?

We can do that too. Just opt-in to the subscription option at https://randallwoodauthor.com/subscription/ and get the latest book automatically delivered to you the day it comes out, months before it hits the shelves anywhere else.

Want to know even more?

You can also learn about the places, organizations, government workings, weapons, gear, and law enforcement tactics used in the books, by visiting my Facebook page at Randall Wood Author.

Stay in touch!

Sign up for my email newsletter at https://randall woodauthor.com/newsletter/

Subscribe at https://randallwoodauthor.com/subscription/

Follow me on Facebook at Randall Wood Author.

I welcome any comments, feedback, or questions at randall.wood@scribecount.com.

Want a sneak peak at Jack's next adventure?

Read on!

A SNEAK PEEK AT BOOK 10: REBIRTH

"I loved the Shepherds & Jack Randall series; I read them all & couldn't put them down, except to take breaks to slow down

the adrenaline rush. A MUST READ!!! Randall Wood, you are an amazing writer!"
—*Ana Alicea*

re•birth
a period of new life or growth

REBIRTH: CHAPTER 1

"True patriotism hates injustice in its own land more than anywhere else."

—Clarence Darrow

Northern Virginia

Dayton drove, and Anna did her best to keep track of where they were. She was unfamiliar with the city and had only a short time to get herself familiar. The flight to Dulles International Airport had been uneventful, and they had been dropped off at the private terminal with their presence unacknowledged. An SUV was parked in the hangar, and Dayton punched in the code to open the doors, before retrieving the keys from under the seat. The items they had brought with them were quickly transferred over.

Now they were doing over eighty-miles-per-hour with the afternoon traffic on 267 as they moved east. Anna spent the time memorizing the map she had brought with her. They would be in suburbia for some time before they reached the city.

Or so she thought. Dayton surprised her by pulling off at the next exit. She read the signs before they turned north and then glanced behind them for any threats before asking.

"What's in Reston?"

"Monkeys."

"What?"

"Sorry. Local joke. I have a few things here that we'll need. What's that map telling you?"

"The place is a suburban maze, but at least it's

wooded. I'm a little worried about the jogging trails. I mean, they're both a blessing and a curse. We can use them to get close without drawing too much attention, but someone can just come jogging right into our plans, too. All we need is some suburban mom or some elderly dog walker seeing us, and the cops will be on their way."

"I thought of that, too. But we don't have much of a choice. We may have to do this in stages. Just keep working on the area with that map I gave you."

Anna exchanged the map in her hand for the one Dayton had given her. It was a military map, complete with gridlines and red terrain markers. Obviously, Dayton was sticking with what he knew best, even though it was an urban environment. Several locations were marked in his own personal code. Most of them were decoys in the event the map fell into the wrong hands, but she knew his codes enough to pick out what he had marked as important.

Their target was in South Kensington, next door to Chevy Chase. An upper-class neighborhood populated by the movers and shakers of Washington DC. The homes ran into the millions and were spread out on large well-wooded lots.

Narrow two-lane roads twisted their way through the trees, and Anna found that also an issue. It would provide them cover from passing cars, but they would have to rely on their ears to warn them of their approach.

A notation on the map made her pause. Was this coincidence? She planted a finger on the location and measured the distance. About a mile; a little more with the curving roads. Less, if one went straight through the woods. She held up the map, so he could see it.

"Is this what I think it is?"

He glanced at it and nodded before returning his gaze to the traffic.

"Jack Randall's residence. Hell of a coincidence, huh? I keep forgetting the man is worth millions himself. He's not what you picture when you think FBI agent."

"I'll say."

She returned the map to her lap. Washington DC was laid out like the spokes of a wheel, with the National mall in the center. She looked for the nearest spoke and saw that Connecticut provided a straight shot into town from where they would be. About five miles, give or take. It could be covered in minutes, with the right vehicle.

But they wouldn't be going that way.

"You have our exit planed?"

Dayton's face changed, as if the question were both amusing and troubling at the same time.

"For years," was his answer.

Anna decided not to pursue it and returned to her map. It was a discussion for another time.

A few miles later, they pulled into the driveway of a small home. Dayton guided the SUV around the back and up to a small detached garage, before checking the mirrors to make sure they were out of sight from the road. Anna examined the home through the glass and then followed Dayton when he got out.

The house had once been nice. A craftsman style bungalow with a wide front porch. She could see a few places where the owner had put in the time and effort to make it a home. There was a picket fence needing paint. Extensive landscaping needed attending. A downspout that had pulled away from the brick. But other than that, it looked like the average middle-class home you would find on the East Coast. Now, the leaves had mixed with the patches of snow and combined into drifts that clogged the door and path to the home's back door. It was obviously not a home that was occupied by its owner much. Dayton gave it all a cursory look, before moving to the detached garage.

"What's this?"

"This is ... This was my parents' house."

Her eyes widened at the information. His tone and the condition of the house told her they were no longer among the living, but the fact that he had brought her here was something on top of that. With the address, she could find out who had lived there. That information would lead to the real name of Dayton Knox, and he knew it. She turned and glanced at the street, and then at the map in her hand, before stuffing it away in her back pocket. It had all just come together.

"How far to the CIA from here?"

"About four minutes. Little more with traffic," was the quick reply.

It was a confession. Or an admission, take your pick. But now wasn't the time. They had things to do.

She followed him inside the garage to find a red muscle car inside. A lite coat of dust marred its paint only slightly. Dayton gestured to it as he walked past.

"A 1972 Oldsmobile Cutlass Supreme 442. Everything is original. My dad and I restored it when we were both home. Took us years. I forgot to put the cover on it. He'd be pissed."

"It's gorgeous."

"It is." He kept walking to a heavy door in the back of the garage. He bent down and reached under a workbench. She heard the beeps of a keypad sounding as he worked it without looking. The door clicked twice, and he pulled it open.

"Shut the door and come in."

Anna slid the inside lock home on the exterior door before following him inside. She found a storage room like any other you would find in the area. This one had a steel bench with a vice and few tools hanging on the wall. A set of cabinets stood side by side, and Dayton was working the lock of one. She had a sudden flashback of their day in the mountains in the stable.

He flung the doors open, and the contents revealed themselves.

Her mouth dropped open.

MONTANA

CARTER IGNORED the pain in his chest and forced himself to maintain the brutal pace he'd set. The snowshoes now impacted the soft ground as fast as he could keep his legs pumping, and he traded possible detection for speed as he made his way down the mountain. The trees were thick, and his face now bore the marks of tree branches he'd been unable to avoid, but he ignored the sting and let the cold numb them as he plodded on.

He'd watched the men advance through the scope, until the last of them disappeared into the wood line before launching himself into action.

The men had puzzled him at first. Were they the General's men? Out in the mountains for some winter combat training? He wasn't sure, but their number and their actions made him think the opposite. They were coming from the wrong direction, and they were making movements as if the operation were real.

The mansion was under attack.

Jolted by the revelation, Carter made a decision. And once it was made it required action. He'd counted forty men, all heavily armed. They were too many for him to handle with a hunting rifle and a knife. He had to balance the power. He had to warn the General.

But how?

The GPS had offered his only alternative. But could he get there first?

He now leaped from drift to drift with both feet as he worked his way down the steep slope, his lungs burning in the thin air. He was traveling slightly away from the route to the mansion that the attacking party was taking, so he felt it was safe to move fast without worrying about the trail he was leaving behind. Speed was his only savior. Until he had to loop back.

His legs were aching from the exertion, but he ignored them and moved on. The hours he'd spent in the gym were now paying off, and Carter called on his reserves of strength to keep him moving. The long underwear he had pilfered from the garage was now stuck to him by a layer of sweat, and the cold air would occasionally find its way into his coat to chill him. He ignored it all and rapidly sucked in the thin air to feed his muscles, slowing only when he got too dizzy to stay upright.

Eventually, he came to the valley floor and grabbed a tree to stop his forward progress. His breath clouded his view, and his head swam as he took in the view.

There. A mile away down the valley. The barn, and across the stream, the cabin. He fumbled with the binoculars to get a better view and was disappointed to see no signs of life. The chimney had no heat escaping, and the snow around the perimeter was undisturbed. Of course, there could still be someone there, as the snow had been coming down for hours. But he felt sure there would be lights on inside and some signs of the fireplace being in use, if there was someone. He'd find out soon enough.

He pushed himself off the tree and made his way to the edge of the tree line. Keeping just inside it, he passed the barn and went directly for the bridge and then the house. He'd hoped to find a vehicle of some kind on the other side, but nothing presented, making him think there really was nobody present. He shed the snowshoes before mounting the stairs to the deck. A quick look through the windows told him his suspicions were right: There was nobody there. He tried the door and then put a shoulder to it, before cursing its solid oak construction. But there was always another way. He leaned the rifle against the wall and moved around the side of the cabin to the woodpile. Under the tarp, he found the axe right where he remembered it being stowed and hefted its weight as he returned to the door.

The impacts were loud, but less than that of a gunshot. He put his weight and considerable strength behind them and got the job done quickly.

The warmth of the cabin welcomed him as he entered, and he checked the alarm pad only long enough to see that it was active. He searched every room and then checked the shelves and cabinets for any form of communication.

Nothing. No phone. Not even a charger. He needed to warn the mansion! But how?

He gazed up at the cameras. He'd noticed them the second day of his training, and like Dayton, had accepted them as something that he would be subject to while he was here. At the time, he had dismissed them; but now, maybe he could make them work for him? He ran for the stairs.

THE WHITE HOUSE

THE PRESIDENT HELD STILL and watched his wife as she retied his tie for him. Her face had adopted the pursed-lip and furrowed brow she unconsciously painted on it when she was concentrating. It was a quirk he found beautiful, and he smiled as she tugged and pulled, before finally slipping the knot up in place and folding his collar down around it. Only then did she notice his gaze.

"What? Is this the right tie?"

"I love you. You know that?"

"I do." She kissed his cheek and then held him at arm's length.

"Are you ready for this?"

He patted the inside pocket of his jacket. Inside was an envelope and a small device. It, and his own determination, were all that he needed once he left the room. She would arrive before he did and be seated on the balcony next to a few carefully selected guests. She would leave when he got started, and the Secret Service agents would safeguard her return back to the White House. After that, he was unsure what would happen.

"Henry has the copies?" he said.

"One for each network. He'll hand them out when the time is right. You called the kids?"

"Yes, they'll all be home by the time you get started. I didn't like lying to them, but I simply said we wanted them home tonight. Nick protested, but Mary read between the lines, I think. They'll be there."

"I can move armies with a simple command, but when it comes to my own children..."

"Yes, well ... they'll understand soon enough."

"Indeed."

He walked to the mirror and checked himself. He looked tired, he admitted, but then he had reason to be.

"It's time to go."

"I know." He made no move to leave, though. She joined him at the mirror and held his arm.

"Good looking couple," he remarked.

"Yeah, they cleanup okay," she went along.

Would they be able to look in the mirror after tonight? The question was on both of their minds. The other was if they would be able to face their children. They would have the answers to both questions soon enough.

A knock on the door cut through their moment of reflection.

"Yes?"

Henry stuck his head in.

"Sir, they need you downstairs."

"Very well."

The boy pulled his head back and shut the door, and they turned to face one another. She picked imaginary lint from his suit.

"I believe this is the most important thing you've ever done," she remarked.

"I think so, too."

"Try not to screw it up."

"Yes, dear."

Hand in hand, they departed the room. Outside, they were met by the Secret Service agents and a few staff members.

"Lead on, gentleman," the president spoke. "History awaits!"

The men smiled at the man's brevity. In an hour, he'd be speaking, live, in front of the entire world. The man was allowed a joke if he pleased.

They moved down the hall and descended the stairs, neither of them looking back.

REBIRTH: CHAPTER 2

"The patriot volunteer, fighting for country and his rights, makes the most reliable soldier on earth."

—Stonewall Jackson

THE J. EDGAR HOOVER BUILDING

Jack chose the stairs and took his time. He was still working out why he was here. It was a busy night in DC. One that he had always avoided in the past. Between the president's speech and the numerous parties thrown by the lobbying groups, the town would be packed with people. Add to that the growing number of protestors, and he'd had a hard time getting through the traffic.

The protestors had puzzled him. They now numbered more than he had ever seen at once. He'd read a report about an unprecedented turnout for several causes. Permits had been issued for most, but it was impossible to predict the number who would show up for each. The State of the Union address always drew several protests, this, augmented by the nationwide outrage induced by the actions and revelations of the Twelve Shepherds, had been pointed at by the press to explain the large numbers.

So far, there had been little fallout. Despite their numbers, the protestors were behaving themselves. The capitol police had reported only a few minor scuffles. Jack had almost called Danny to get his take on what was happening, but that would have resulted in a quid pro quo, and he wasn't ready to give up what little information he had on the Shepherds just yet.

Jack arrived at the top floor and pushed his way through the fire door. The hallway was occupied by a few agents, but nothing like its usual level of staffing. Deacon was in. Jack had seen the lights on in his office from the street. He'd check in and see how his boss was doing.

Margaret was at the desk with the TV on in the corner. On it, Jack could see the House chamber. Grey haired men and woman milled about on the floor as they waited for the President's arrival. Jack's skin crawled slightly as he took the sight in. A den of snakes. He couldn't imagine what it was that drew some into their ranks.

"Jack? Were you bored, too?"

"Hey, Margaret. Curious, I guess. Is there anything happening?"

"Not so far. I think they'll be back up in a minute."

"Who?"

"Sydney and Mark. You didn't know she was here?"

"No. She didn't tell me she was coming in," Jack confessed. Evidently Sydney had also found it hard to stay home.

"How's he handling the promotion?"

"Okay. Bit of a shock. He expected it to go to Nick in New York."

"Nick doesn't have the Shepherds case," Jack said.

"True."

Before they could say more, the door opened behind him. Deacon held it for Sydney as she carried in a plate of fries and a Mountain Dew. Deacon followed with a cup of coffee.

"Jack! Glad you could join us. We just went on a coffee run to stretch our legs."

"Evening, sir. You've been here a while?"

"Since this morning," he replied.

"You?" he asked Sydney.

"Since about noon, after I dropped Lenny at the airport." She shrugged, and Jack realized she didn't have an excuse to be here either. She went around him and set the plate of French fries down in front of Margaret, who immediately grabbed one and stabbed it in the ketchup.

"Oh, these are so good. Thanks, Sydney."

"No problem." They shared a smile before following Deacon into the office. Sydney took Larry's desk chair and Jack used the one in the corner. Deacon grabbed the remote and turned on the TV. It was more of what Jack had seen out in Margaret's office.

"Larry's on his way in from Reagan," she said.

"He find anything?"

"I guess not, or he'd still be out there."

Jack nodded and pointed at the TV.

"Anything new this time around, sir?"

"I haven't seen a copy, but from what I hear, no. Just more of the same."

Jack sat back and sighed.

"Any threats?"

"Outside of the usual? No. We're following a possible lone wolf up in Boston. Nothing really to go on, other than he started hanging with the wrong crowd online, wearing more traditional clothing, and missing a lot of work. His old girlfriend tipped us off. So far, he's just running his mouth. We haven't seen him shopping for weapons or bomb-making materials yet, but if he does, we'll pick him up."

Jack nodded at the news and said nothing simply because he had nothing to add. His focus had turned to the domestic side.

"Well, let's hope it's a quiet night."

KENSINGTON, MARYLAND

THE SUV WAS A CADILLAC. One with all the options, including tinted glass. As such, it blended into the neighborhood with ease, and they cruised its streets without drawing so much as a glance from those out and about. On the oft chance that they were stopped by a curious patrolman, they had kept the gear inside large gym bags and hidden under the cargo cover in the back. On the seat between them were a few printouts from a local real estate website. Any officer who stopped them would receive a barrage of questions about the neighborhood and a request for directions. From experience, Dayton knew that most would quickly lose their curiosity and then disengage as soon as possible.

Dayton slowed the SUV at the site of the jogging trail. It had paralleled the road for the last half mile, dipping in and out of the trees on their left. Now it crossed the road near the target and then the small stream on the other side. Dayton pulled off the road and then spread the map out on the steering wheel for the benefit of anyone passing by. He spoke to Anna without turning his head from it.

"See that little bridge over there? How much space you think is under it?"

She examined the bridge. It was only a foot or

so off the water and more decorative than needed. A few small shrubs had been planted on both sides to prevent erosion, and they created a shadow that only served to hide the space underneath.

"I think that would work. Big enough to hold what we brought, and there's some cover in those trees on the right."

He traced a line on the map. "The trail and the water lead to Rock Creek and then go under 495 toward DC. Plenty of places to stash the car and then jog back here. Plus, we've got this small curve here."

"I like it."

"Okay. Get ready while I do a lap."

She unbuckled and began crawling over the seats to the back, while he put the SUV back on the road. A half mile later, she was ready, and he did a U-turn.

"I'm at Old Spring. I'll give you a countdown."

"Okay." She was now in the backseat with both heavy bags on her lap. The items gave off metallic sounds when she moved as the objects inside knocked against each other.

"Road's clear, behind," she called out.

"Clear in front," he answered. "Five seconds."

Anna opened the door a crack, before she

grasped both bags firmly. The SUV braked hard and stopped in the road right next to the trail.

"Go."

A second later, Anna was out the door and running for the bridge. The door slammed itself shut as Dayton sped away. In twelve steps, she was at the bridge. She threw herself down on its cold wooden surface and stuffed the bags underneath. They were quickly swallowed up by the darkness. She rolled to the other side to see if they could be seen before throwing herself to her feet and jogging in the direction Dayton had gone. The process had taken her less than ten seconds.

She stayed on the trail and maintained a moderate pace. Just another suburban mom trying to stay in shape. A half mile later, she saw him approaching, and she checked behind her.

Nothing. The rush hour crowd had not left the city yet. She angled to the road just as he pulled up and was back in the passenger's seat a moment later.

"We're good. Heavy bastards. Plenty of room for them, though."

"Okay. What's next?"

"Escape routes. Let's shop for houses some more."

"Okay."

Dayton slowed at the next intersection and signaled a dog walker to cross with a polite wave. When they moved on, she noticed his smile.

"What?'

"I was just thinking about our effect on future home prices."

It was dark humor, but she understood its purpose. On top of that it was just plain funny, and they allowed themselves a short laugh before getting back on mission.

"How far to the next exit?"

"It's ... right here. Turn left."

<hr>

The National Mall

THE CROWDS of protestors stopped their rotation and slowly gathered at a few key buildings. All of them had cell phones, and they were checking them more often than usual. A few were watching the TV coverage of the Address, while others were conferring with other members of the group.

"Look at the cops on the end there."

Her husband turned his head slightly to do so. He saw a group of three officers, all listening to the radio one of them held in his hand. They seemed a bit agitated.

"Hold on," he told her, as he reached in his pocket and changed the frequency of the small radio. He had the police band pre-programed and now listened in to their dispatcher. His wife waited and hopped from foot to foot in an effort to keep warm. The wool mask on her face keeping the cold at bay, only allowing her eyes and mouth to be seen.

"What is it?" she prodded him.

"The cops are seeing the crowds moving in from the streets. Not sure if it's just a few nervous rookies, or if they are sounding the alarm. No incidences reported; just a big crowd moving in."

"Well, we've been getting them used to that sight for a few weeks now. Let's hope they don't get scared and do something stupid."

He nodded and then held up a finger to listen.

"They're getting ready to move the president to the Capitol building."

They both looked up and noticed a change in the crowd. No doubt they had gotten the same news.

"Time to take our positions."

RONALD REAGAN WASHINGTON NATIONAL AIRPORT

LARRY STRETCHED in the aisle of the aircraft, while he waited. The flight from Montana had been a long one, and the hours spent in the narrow chair had only added to the several he had spent in a car over the last few days. His frame was just not made for it, and it had taken its toll. Now, he ached all over. He vowed to ask—no, beg—Jack for his plane if this ever happened again.

And he had nothing to show for it. He and a crew of field agents had covered every train and rail yard between Denver and Canada with no luck. A few tramps had been held for questioning, but most had no idea what was even going on in the country. They didn't know who the Twelve Shepherds were or what they were doing. Their worlds consisted of the trains and the next meal or bottle they could acquire, and not much else. After a few days Larry had given up. The trail was cold again. Their guy could be in Canada drinking whiskey, or in Mexico doing shots of tequila. Until another lead came to them, they were back to square one. He'd put himself on plane for home.

The plane was on time for a change and Larry was surprised. In his experience the later the flight, the more likely the delay was to happen. But the weather had cooperated, and he had been lucky enough to sit next to a skinny bookworm this time. The woman had kept her nose glued to a Rosalind James novel the whole trip. He had glanced at the cover long enough to see what the story was about. Romance in New Zealand. He doubted there were any professional assassins in the plot.

Now he stood with the other "spring-butts," as he called them. The people who jumped to their feet the second the seat-belt sign went off. He never understood the action. They just had to wait until the door opened anyway, and then again until all the people in front of them left and made way. He'd rather sit while he waited, but the book-worm had asked him for her bag, so he had stood to retrieve it for her. His cramped legs had welcomed the activity, so he chose to stay upright.

He searched his memory while he waited. Had he driven here or taken a cab? There had been so many lately he had to think hard. Cab. Good, at least he didn't have to walk through the snow. Was there snow? He bent over to see out the window and orient himself. In the process, he noticed the look of fear on his seat mate's face.

"Ma'am? You all right?"

Her eyes traveled from him to the Colt Python

.357 revolver hanging in his shoulder rig. It had become exposed when he'd bent over.

"FBI. Over thirty years," he quietly told her.

"Oh ... I'm sorry. What you must think."

"It's okay. Happens all the time."

The woman offered another overly displayed smile by way of apology, and Larry waved her off, letting her stand and walk out ahead of him. This airport was close to several law enforcement, intelligence, and military facilities. There were probably a dozen guns on board every plane flying in or out, but he didn't think it was the time to tell her that.

He made his way off the plane and into the terminal and was surprised to see it low on foot traffic. Whatever the reason he took advantage of it and increased his pace. He found a line of cabs waiting outside and let himself be ushered into the first. Thankfully the man had the heat cranked up.

"Where to tonight?" the man asked.

"Hoover Building."

"You got it, G-man."

The young man dropped the cab in gear, and they were soon out of the airport and angling toward the highway. The lights of the capitol shining bright. But something else soon caught his attention.

People. Hundreds of them. All of them bundled up against the cold weather and crowding the sidewalks on both sides of the road.

The crowds got thicker the second he crossed the bridge into the district. He'd seen some footage while waiting for his flight in Montana, but it didn't match the reality. The crowds looked several times what he had seen, and they seemed to be lining the streets on all sides. He watched them after tapping out a message to Sydney at a red light. They were standing in place and looking past him at the bridge.

"What are you looking for?"

REBIRTH: CHAPTER 3

"A patriot must always be ready to defend his country against his government."

—*Edward Abbey*

THE MANSION

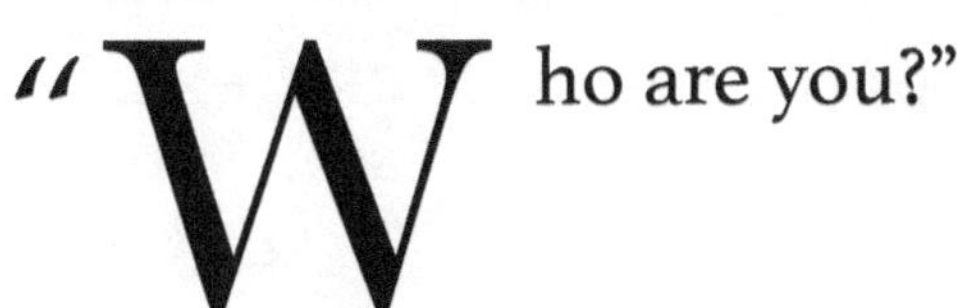

ho are you?"

William had been deep into a file from Haney's mystery soldier, when the computer had alerted him of an intrusion at the cabin. The bears in the area would occasionally try the door, in hopes of gaining entry, and once a bison had walked up the stairs to explore the deck. But the bears were all in hibernation now, and the bison herd was in the lower valley this time of year. He tapped keys and soon had a view inside the structure.

A large man. Decked out in civilian hunting gear. A thief? He didn't seem to be. William watched as he passed up the gun rack and the electronics, roaming the house. If he was a thief, he was an industrious one; it was no easy task venturing that far into the mountains just to rob a remote cabin. The man reappeared in the kitchen, with what looked like a bedsheet. He spread it out on the kitchen floor and then crawled across it, his right arm moving in all directions.

"What is he...?"

Suddenly the man stood and flung the sheet into the air. It landed draped across the long couch, directly under the camera. He pulled and tugged until the sheet was spread evenly, before stepping back and pulling off his hat and scarf. William leaned in close to the monitor and examined the intruder's face.

"Number Six?"

William's jaw dropped as he watched the man gesture to the sheet. He taped a key and froze the image, before blowing it up and reading it.

Attack coming. 40 men. Get ready!

"What the hell?"

Number Six stopped waving his arms and moved to the door. William saw him put his hat and scarf back on, before plunging out into the snow. He left the door open, and the snow blew in behind him.

William broke out of his shock and grabbed for the phone.

"Charlie! I need you here, now!"

"What's going on?"

"Just get here quickly!"

THE WHITE HOUSE

THE OFFICIAL SPEECH was in a leather binder, and he had two copies: one, he would hand to the vice president after taking the dais; and the other he would keep to refer to in the event that the teleprompter failed.

He now walked the hallways and office pits of

the West Wing, thanking each person he came across. Many of them were young, called to the West Wing by their inner drive to serve, forgoing pursuits which would benefit them much more than their time at the White House. The president kept a smile on his face as he shook hands, slapped backs, and posed for photos. They were all so driven, so dedicated to a job that paid them so little, yet it rewarded them in ways they could never count.

It was almost a shame to crush that, but he had no choice.

He completed the tour with a stop outside the office of his speechwriter. The few glowing words to praise the man and the document he had produced came off well, and the crowd cheered when the president was finished. The speechwriter got a genuine hug from the president. The speech was a work of art, but it was far from the speech the President had asked for several months ago. The final product had been twisted and tweaked into something that pleased everyone while actually saying very little. He'd found himself wondering if it contained any of his original thoughts.

At a signal from Henry, the president broke away and headed for the door. The young man fell into step next to him, and the President leaned in for one last order.

"Not until I start speaking."

"I understand, sir."

"I won't forget this."

The man's face broke for only a moment before he recovered.

"Yes, Mr. President. Is there anything else I can do for you?"

"I need you to go back to law school and graduate as soon as possible. They'll need you."

"Yes, sir. I will."

The President put his arm around the man and gave his shoulder a squeeze, before breaking away and leaving the building. A few steps later he was in the Beast, and the motorcade was pulling away.

"The first lady?" he asked his escort.

"Secure in the Senator's office, Mr. President."

"Very well. Let's get this show on the road."

"Yes, sir."

MONTANA

AFTER HE CLEARED the snow away, the barn door slid open with little effort, and he pulled it shut behind him. His tracks were being covered by the falling snow, but not fast enough. Either way, the screech it gave off would warn him if anyone else entered.

Ignoring the ATVs and Gator, he searched for a snowmobile. After finding nothing, he made his way to the armory. Knowing the walls were made of steel with a concrete core, he didn't bother trying to break them down, as it would take more time than he had. He'd have to finesse his way in. The keyboard was under a protective plastic cover, and when he raised it, the welcoming red light mocked him.

Unless Dayton had changed it, the first two numbers were eight-five. He'd managed to see them once and had made a mental note of them. Why, he didn't know. He'd never thought he would return here, but it was how his brain worked. There were two more and then the pound key. He just had to figure them out—and fast.

He moved to the stall with the heavy bag hanging inside and scooped up a handful of dust from the floor. He held it up to the keyboard and lightly blew it across, coating the number pad with a fine layer. The eight and five keys clouded quickly, along with the two and the six. He wondered how many chances the pad would give him. Standard was three before he'd be locked out. He shook his cold hand and flexed his fingers before carefully punching in a code.

8-5-2-6

The red light blinked three times and then returned to normal.

"C'mon."

8-5-6-2

Again, the red light blinked three times before denying him.

"C'mon baby, work with me here."

What could it be? Had Dayton changed the code but used the same numbers? Or was it something else. What if he—"

"Dumbass."

8-5-2-6-#

The light blinked three times and then turned green. Carter wasted no time yanking the door open. The seal parted with a pop, and he was inside.

He dumped the backpack on the floor and moved to the racks. What to take? Long gun? Shotgun? Both? He needed something for both outdoors at long range and indoors and close. He settled on what he knew best: a M2010 Enhanced

Sniper Rifle with a scope. He adjusted the sling before setting it on the table. Next, he selected an Benelli M4 Super 90. Ammo for reach was located under the table, and he soon had both weapons loaded with plenty of extra. A combat vest was found, and he loaded it with as many magazines as it would carry. A full bandolier of 12-gauge shells in double-ought went on the M-4, and several more filled his pockets. Another rack offered a variety of handguns, and he chose a pair of Glocks in 9mm. Both went into belt holsters, and he slid them around so they were just above his belt in the small of his back. Extra magazines went on the belt next to them.

What else?

Grenades. He found a box of frags in a locker and filled the vest with them. A pair of CS canisters were attached to the backpack, and a couple of Willy Pete joined them.

"What else? Think Carter!" he scolded himself.

Another locker revealed a variety of mines. Bouncing Bettys, Anti-tank mines. Cubes of C-4. Detonating cord.

He found what he wanted in the second locker. He loaded two of the concave devices into the backpack with the necessary hardware. It was getting heavy.

He looked at the two Barrett M82s on the top shelf but quickly dismissed them. As much as he could use their range and power, they would be like hauling boat anchors in the snow. He needed to stay as mobile as possible.

"That's it. Get out of here."

He loaded the pickup and was about to leave, when a thought struck him. Were the attackers coming here, first? It only took a second for the idea to form. He returned to the last locker and removed one more item, before closing the door behind him.

"You boys want to play? Let's play."

The Mansion

THE FLASHING LIGHTS of the district police motorcycles could not be missed. They moved away from the gate, and the first of the Secret Service's SUVs pulled out behind them. It was not an unusual sight in the nation's capital but tonight was different. Tonight, the President of the United States was addressing the country and the entire world. So, on this occasion there were dozens of cameras in attendance. The movement of the most powerful man in the world could not be missed.

And certainly not by the watchful eyes of William Ockham. As soon as the president had appeared in the doorway and waved to the reporters gathered outside, William had picked up the phone and called the General.

"Sir, he's moving."

"Very well. Send it."

"Yes, sir."

Despite the millions of dollars of hardware at his disposal, William reached for a phone on his desk. The two messages had been in the draft folder of the tiny device for over an hour now; all he had to do was push the button.

"Rubicon," he muttered. He wasn't sure whether it was curse or a prayer.

He pushed the button, and the first group-text went out to twelve people. A few buttons later, another message was sent. This one to thousands.

***

WANT to know what happens next?

Get your copy of *REBIRTH* direct from the author at https://randallwoodauthor.com/product/rebirth-a-jack-randall-thriller/!

REBIRTH is also available on all major online retailers; you'll find links at http://randallwoodauthor.com/universal-links.

(Did I mention the books are discounted if you buy directly from me?)

ABOUT THE AUTHOR

Randall Wood is the author of the bestselling Jack Randall series of thrillers and the Half a World Post-Apocalyptic series. He is also the founder and CEO of ScribeCount, a data aggregation company that provides sales dashboards, marketing analytics, and a variety of other services to the author community.

When he's not penning stories or crunching numbers, he and his wife divide their time between the beaches of south Florida and the mountains of western North Carolina. Whether they are hiking or swimming they are usually accompanied by Henry their giant of a Great Dane.

Randall welcomes readers to his website at www.randallwoodauthor.com and his fellow writers to ScribeCount at www.scribecount.com, where he tries hard to not refer to himself in the third person.

9 781938 825552